Brian:

Enjoy the journey

June Paul $2.00 od 12/01

THE
EMERALD
CLOAK

Dedication

I dedicate this story to the memory of those hardy
men and women who spent their entire lives
overcoming the obstacles facing the early settlers.
Without their tenacious spirits molding our history,
Canada would unlikely be the freedom-loving
country it is today.

June Packwood

The Emerald Cloak

by

June Packwood

Borealis Press
Ottawa, Canada
2001

Canadä

*We acknowledge the financial assistance of the Government
of Canada through the Book Publishing Program (BPIDP),
and of the Ontario Arts Council,
for our publishing activities.*

National Library of Canada Cataloguing in Publication Data

Packwood, June, 1941 –
The Emerald Cloak

ISBN-0-88887-259-3

I. Title

PS8581.A27E44 2001   C813'.6   C2001-902195-X
PR9199.4.P32E44 2001

Cover design by Bull's Eye Design, Ottawa, Canada

Printed and bound in Canada on acid free paper.

Contents

Book 1

Book 2

Book 1

Introduction

Cherry Creek, Upper Canada – 1868

She sits comfortably in her ancient rocker; her tired feet propped on the hearth, soaking in the warmth of the dancing flames. The hearthstone is polished to a soft sheen. Waves of heat from the fire permeate the clutches of herbs and dried flowers hanging from the rafters, releasing delicate scents of chamomile, mint, sage and heather. The warm, peaceful atmosphere within, helps to dull the rage of the relentless, driving winter storm ravaging the land she calls home. The harsh reality of another Canadian winter makes itself apparent as screaming, icy winds whip around the corners of the solid log dwelling. Drifts of blinding white snow creep up the sides of the house, wrapping the windows and doors in a protective coat against the bitter gales. The cozy warmth within is the result of endless days of preparation by Molly's family. Piles of dried maple wood frame the huge hearth of the fireplace, its sweet sap caressing the senses. Flour, pork, eggs, and other necessary food staples line the walls of the larder, built off the kitchen corner of the large common room. This same home has brought comfort and security not only to Molly and her family but also to many a weary traveller or sick neighbour crossing its threshold over the years.

As Molly enjoys the amenities of her home she recalls the roads often paved with pain and suffering that led her to this comfortable period of her life. From as far back as her memory allows, to the time she sat helplessly by the bed of her dying mother, she has dreamed of mastering the powers of healing. Her pursuit of medical knowledge over the years has brought her into contact with a broad spectrum of healers. Of the European-trained medical doctors, most were reputable, but there were those among them that blackened the name of the profession. The ancient Indian shaman, she found on the often disease-ravaged reservations, had taught her much about both life and death. She had not even totally dis-missed the side-show, snake oil hustlers who regularly made their way across the country, flogging their wares. She had stopped at nothing to accumulate what knowl-edge she could in this vast country almost devoid of regular and reliable medical attention.

Many years ago, as was befitting the times, she was expected to marry and produce a family of strong, healthy men and women. The country was still a frontier and only the hardy could hope to survive the many hardships. Now as her gaze sweeps the room, she reflects with pride on the results of her endeavours. She has fulfilled these obligations and she feels proud to be wife and mother to this family of diverse individuals. Liam, her husband of some twenty-seven years, is a powerfully built, gentle-natured man, with laughing eyes that have always endeared him to her. As her eyes rest on his massive frame, she reflects on the wealth of emo-tions he still evokes in her. A minute smile crosses her lips as she contemplates the strength this gentle giant emits. So rarely in their years together has she heard him so much as raise his voice. But God help anyone who should ever so much as utter a threatening word to his progeny. He is her life, the father of their children, and the essence of her being. His strength has brought them all through many setbacks, and periods of hardship over the years. Now that they have found security and peace, that same strength assures them it will some how last.

The pride she feels as she surveys her first born, fills her eyes with mist. Matthew, has always been of an independent nature and has never forgotten that the land is their provider. Over the years he has become a master of the woods and an ardent hunter, in order to ease the burdens on his father and his people, as they strive to make a decent living in the family-owned sawmill. Unlike the rest of her brood, Matthew was born in Ireland, the land of Liam's and her heritage. Memories of those times, the good and the bad, would often rush back as she thought of Matthew as a babe. He has experienced life at its fullest and is now a proud young man with a family of his own.

The twins, Erin and Sean, arrived some eight years later when the family lived in Québec City, some years following their perilous journey across the Atlantic Ocean. Molly sighs as she muses over the two most opposite personalities Liam and she have created. At the time of their birth, life had been very difficult for the whole family and they had all suffered many hardships. Sorrow swept their lives with sickness, terrorism, and even death. The birth of the twin boys had been a much-needed catharsis bringing hope and joy back into their lives. Being small at birth they had required much attention as infants but had grown into strong lads with equally strong wills. Erin wants nothing more than to work beside his older brother Matthew who he idolises but also continuously challenges. Sean, named for Molly's youngest brother, is gentle in nature. He finds solace in his administrations to the family's many domestic animals. Because of his interest in animal husbandry, the farm work falls mostly on his shoulders, which he accepts with relish. The farm is his domain. How could two lads born just minutes apart be an eternity apart in character? Molly chuckles to herself as she remembers moments past that weren't always so amiable as she was witnessing this evening in their parlour. If she had named them for their nature, she would have called them Wind and Fire, because one was often fuelling the other into hot debate until their father, in exasperation, would step in as referee. But Lord help the outsider who threatened to come between them.

The only child not present in this tranquil scene before her, is their only daughter Kathleen, a sloe-eyed beauty. Tears well up, coating the thick lashes on Molly's eyes, as she reflects on this gentle child tucked safely in her bed. Kathleen lies quietly in her room recuperating from this winter's onslaught of Influenza. Normally, every available hour not in school, or helping her mother with the daily chores, she spends buried in books. Her thirst for learning seems to consume her every waking hour. Many times Molly would shake her head in frustration when finding chores unfinished. But she had to admit, Kathleen was in so many ways, not unlike herself as a child. Molly's own mother, had she lived, would have felt these very same frustrations, mixed with undeniable pride, had she been able to watch her own daughter grow to womanhood.

Now, as Molly enjoys the warmth and comfort of their home and the love of her growing family, she reflects on the trials of the past forty years, which have strengthened the lives of the family she so dearly loves. Without their love and support she would never have been able to follow her dream. Without Liam's selfless devotion she would never have enjoyed the freedom to employ her special talent for healing others. Without her relentless drive and tireless care, many desperately ill people would have succumbed unnecessarily. Her care, even over the past weeks, has eased the suffering of many and undeniably saved the lives of a few. She is free now to relax, knowing this insidious disease which robbed so many of her friends and neighbours of their loved ones, is once again held at bay. Now she is able to return to the job of living and caring for the daily needs of her family. Once again she takes the time to thank her Maker for sparing her and those she loves.

Chapter 1

Northern Ireland, Creggan in County Tyrone – 1830

At the tender age of five, Molly was bewildered by her mother's behaviour. Mama was always the first one up in the mornings, preparing breakfast for the rest of the family, and seeing them all off to work or school. After the house was quiet, her mother would take her on her ample knee and tell her stories, cuddle and tickle her until she giggled helplessly. It was their time together and she cherished those moments. Why was mama staying in that stuffy bedroom, with the curtains continuously drawn closed, allowing neither fresh air nor sunshine to penetrate? For sometime now, Aunt Mary was staying with them day and night, preparing meals, cleaning and always whispering in her raspy voice, "you must be quiet lass, and not disturb your mother." Why did her mother not want to be disturbed? Why didn't she want to cuddle her and tell her stories? Why did Aunt Mary have to stay so long and always order everyone around? Aunt Mary was cold and bony. Her eyes were always red and watery and the skin hung in folds beneath them. She never smiled like mama and da. She didn't think Aunt Mary liked her very much. She didn't think Aunt Mary liked anyone very much.

The house on Cobble Hill Circle although a two up, two down row house was situated at the highest point of the circle enabling its family to look down on many of the crowded row houses below. Molly's da had always sworn he would never see his family living in the squalor and filth of Miner's Row. It was the dream of most of the miners and their families to be free of the filthy gutters and stinking middens they found themselves trapped within. Youngsters played in the garbage that littered the streets. Most were ill fed and poorly clothed, with vermin infested heads and scab-pocked limbs. Medical attention was unaffordable for most, which allowed the cycle to manifest itself.

The O'Connor family had never lived in these conditions. Hard work and determination enabled John O'Connor to provide decent accommodations for his family but it was not always possible to keep them safe from the rapid spread of influenza, typhoid and many other highly infectious diseases. The miners worked in cold, wet conditions, usually confined together in small pockets deep below the ground's surface. Infection and disease spread rapidly when carried into this environment. Now Bridget O'Connor lay dying after weeks of fighting off a seemingly minor chest ailment. Pneumonia was taking its toll in the village and had crept its surreptitious way up the Circle to the O'Connor household where it found a home in the tired, weakened form of Bridget O'Connor.

Whenever Molly got the chance, she crept quietly into her mother's room. While waiting for her mother to waken she would sit and trace her fingers over the flowers sewn on the goose-down coverlet of the bed. Finding her daughter sitting quietly at her bedside, Bridget would raise her hand to stroke the top of Molly's head only to drop it back on the coverlet as more strength was sapped from her already weakened body. Bridget's gentle eyes appeared sunken into her head with dark sooty smudges dusted around them. Her cloud of raven hair framed a pale, ghostly face against the crisp whiteness of the newly changed pillowslips. She had always been a beautiful woman, but now her beauty was almost ethereal as she appeared to lie so peacefully in her bed. Her voice was barely audible and she seemed at times to have trouble breathing. Some of her words would come in gasps and end with fits of coughing.

"Molly, be a good child now and help your Aunt Mary. She is going to need you here more than ever now. No running off when there's chores to be done. Your da needs you to be a big lass now."

Molly waited as Bridget caught her breath and fought for the strength to carry on. For some reason she didn't want to hear what her mother was saying. Something was wrong. Ma never talked to her this way.

"Ma, please don't talk any more. I'll get you some sweet tea. Please stop crying."

Molly ran from the room, with lips trembling and her eyes brimming with salty tears. She knew that sweet tea would make her mother happy. They only drank sweetened tea on special occasions or when someone felt poorly and needed comfort.

When her father and brothers arrived home from their shifts in the mine there was no longer the jovial teasing and laughter that normally always filled the house with gaiety. Everyone now spoke in hushed tones, and very often, as soon as the evening meal was finished, the boys would excuse themselves, leave the house and head for the local pub or sporting field. They usually stayed until they were ready to head for their beds. It was just too painful staying in the house, knowing their mother was lying so desperately ill in the next room. Molly missed their teasing and the scary stories her youngest brother Sean loved to tell her before she was tucked into her bed.

This night as John O'Connor entered the house, his eyes rested on his youngest child as she helped his sister Mary with the preparation of the evening meal. She was already very accomplished for her age and more than willing to take on any new task given her. That very morning before he had left for shift he had sat on the edge of the bed of his darling Bridget. He knew he was losing her and there was nothing within his power he could do that would keep her with him. The moments had been tender as he held her fevered hands within his and they talked in whispers of what must be done to prepare their family for her eventual death.

Now as John looked upon Molly he realized, she of all his brood, would naturally feel the effects of the loss of her mother the most. The rest would suffer the deep sorrow, but would manage to continue on with their lives with relative normalcy. She was little more than a bairn and her needs were instinctively maternal at this tender stage in her life. As tears began to sting his eyes, he thought, 'I can't delay a moment's longer telling the poor wee thing, her mother is dying.' He wondered if there was anything worse in his life he would have to relate to this child he most cherished. He could already feel her pain and despair, magnifying his own feelings of helplessness. Lifting her into his arms, the dreadful feeling that she would feel betrayal, filled his heart. Expecting to be swung high above his head, she would squeal with anticipation. Why did she have to grow up so soon? Why should she be burdened with the loss of her mother when she was barely more than a babe? But as he held her in his arms, he knew she was not expecting the usual playfulness and light-hearted fun. Her eyes portrayed apprehension as she held his gaze.

"Now my darlin," he started with hesitation, while fighting back the tears that welled up in his eyes, "come here and sit on your old da's knee."

Kissing her gently on the brow, he struggled to sound light-hearted. But how could he find a way to tell this child, hardly more than a babe, that she would very soon lose her mother?

"Very soon, mama will be leaving us to go with

Jesus to a better place, where she will be happy and no longer have to endure pain."

Molly's eyes grew huge as with a quivering voice she asked her father, "Can we all go with mama?"

"Not yet my darlin. But mama will always be waiting for us and one day we will all be together again, God willing. Right now your mama needs peace, and for all that she loves us and would rather we all be together, for now she must go alone."

Laying his huge hand on his heart and then on her tremulous chest, he whispered, "but we must remember, mama will always be here whenever we need her and she will be listening whenever we need to talk to her."

Confusion obscured the light that previously shone in Molly's eyes as she attempted to make sense of what her father was now telling her. She couldn't understand why her mother would want to leave if she loved them so much. She couldn't love her and still leave her with Aunt Mary. Horrible bony Aunt Mary.

"No ... da, I'll do my chores, I promise, I promise," she pleaded. "Just tell mama I'll be good and do all my chores. I'm sorry, I haven't been a good girl. Please da, tell mama I won't ever be bad again. I'll do everything I'm supposed to do. She won't ever have to tell me again. Just tell her she can't leave. I don't want her to be gone forever. Please da, tell her we don't want her to go."

Her sobs gradually choked out her pleas to her father as her tears stained the collar of his shirt. She clung to him so tightly he thought his heart would break.

'Dear God,' he thought, 'how can You do this to this babe?' His heart pounded in his massive chest as he crushed her too him, not wanting to expose her to the inevitable loss of her mother.

Chapter 2

Northern Ireland, Creggan in CountyTyrone – 1840

Her mass of bouncing, red curls shone in the sunlight as she raced home to where John, her da and brothers Sean and Colin would be arriving from their shift in the mine. They would be hungry as wolves and she had not yet begun to prepare their evening meal. Lately it seemed she was having less and less time to care for the daily needs of her family. Occasionally she would arrive home much later than da and the boys only to find they had already prepared the tea and were awaiting her return. She would inevitably feel twinges of guilt until her father would assure her there was no need for her to feel any remorse. They always knew where she would be. If Mrs. Murphy wasn't having a new addition to her brood, then one of the local youngsters may have taken a tumble and broken a bone. There was always someone needing her help.

Although, still just fifteen years of age Molly had spent the years since her own mother's untimely death, searching for reasons behind life's injustices and why someone like her mother could be snatched away so suddenly. There had to be some way to prevent so many diseases and deaths and she was determined to make the search a priority in her life.

With no resident doctor in Creggan and very few families able to afford reliable medical treatment, Molly's help was readily accepted by most. Dr. Leary, one of Tyrone's most reputable doctors, would make his circuit visit once a month and in emergency situations could generally be reached within a day. Recognizing Molly's increasing desire and ability to care for those in need of medical aid he was more than happy to have her assist him on his monthly visits.

In Molly's earlier years he would smile indulgently, but recognizing her desire to learn would always attempt to explain all he could, as far as she could comprehend. The more she listened, the more she learned and the happier she became. The older she became the more she realized that the practice of Medicine was her greatest desire, and being with Dr. Leary was her only way of creating the possibility of fulfilling the desire. As she rushed to prepare the evening meal she reflected on the day's events that kept her so long from home. A mile down the road, Mrs. Clancy was about to give birth to her eighth child and was experiencing many difficulties. Her poor body was worn out with year upon year of pregnancy and birth. It seemed that this time her will as well as her body was rebelling. Molly didn't have the heart to leave her alone for long, as the younger children were nothing but a burden and their demands did not take into consideration the trial their poor mother was going through. The family was too poor to afford the services of a doctor and the local midwife was busy with yet another birth some miles away. Mrs. Clancy's health was very poor as most of the food that was brought into the house fed her brood, leaving little nourishment for her. Molly had attempted to build her strength up the past week by preparing extra turnip and potato cakes for her da and brothers and taking the leftovers to Mrs. Clancy. Her efforts generally only satisfied the hungry pleading eyes of the younger children hanging on to their mother's skirts. Very little was consumed by the intended Mrs. Clancy, resulting in little improvement to her weak, undernourished state.

John knew of and admired his daughter's keen interest in the health and welfare of others around her. Since the death of her mother some ten years ago, Molly had helped countless neighbours and friends as well as family through many periods of sickness both mild and severe. She was not squeamish at the sight of blood or hesitant of mopping up after the sick. She never had to be asked twice and oftentimes just volunteered her time without forethought. With her father's encouragement she learned to read and write. The mental notes she carried she eventually converted to a written record of each and every person she treated. She kept a diary of symptoms, the treatments she administered, and the results of each case. Midwives were thankful for her help because they found she often knew more about their patients' past medical history than they did. She never hesitated and always listened to and followed instructions carefully. By the time Molly reached fifteen years, numerous children were born in County Tyrone with her assistance. Many new mothers were more than thankful to have her there to lend her support. It was easy for her to acquire an attachment for each new being she helped bring into the world and from there it was only natural she should be called upon to help when illness invaded the families.

As the majority of her friends and neighbours came from the poor working class there was often very little professional medical attention available, which they could afford. Ultimately most people relied on their own experience and knowledge, midwives, and the generosity and kindness of folks like Molly. From the elders she learned of ancient remedies for infection, burns, sprains and the like, which were passed on from generation to generation. By keeping her diaries she was able to note that sometimes, what was a good remedy for one person may not always help another. She would eventually have a relatively complete medical history on almost everyone she helped treat. This she had accomplished in a very few years and at a great demand on her time.

Da and the boys were a great priority in her life as she was wise enough to know that her tender love and care, combined with good nutrition and a clean healthy home, would keep them from acquiring many of the ailments of the locals. She had discovered over the years that the very poor, who often lived in filth and squalor and consumed a very meager diet, were generally the first to be afflicted and the slowest to heal. She had nursed her family through many outbreaks of influenza and chest ailments as well as the usual results of accidents in the mine. Such mishaps happened often and were generally unavoidable due to the cramped conditions and the lack of concern for safety by the mine owners.

On one such occasion, a mine tippling collapsed and crushed the legs of a young miner. Molly, unbenounced to her father and brothers, pleaded with the shift foreman to allow her to enter the mine to tend to the splinting of his legs.

"Mr. Burns," she pleaded, "if I am able to reach him soon enough and tend to the splinting myself the possibility of permanent damage could be lessened."

She also hoped to eleviate the horrific pain he would experience on the lift to the surface by administering a moderate dose of laudanum as soon as she was able to reach him.

The foreman knew his life would be worthless if so much as a hair was lost from this girl's head, but he also knew there was a boy's life hanging on bare threads down in the collapsed shaft. The boy was now being freed from the rotten, splintered timbers that pinned him to the shaft floor. Fortunately, a depression in the floor had cupped his spine preventing it from being severed, but his legs had taken the brunt and seemed hopelessly crushed. He realized there could be no time to waste and he had little alternative but to allow Molly into the mine if they were to save the lad's life.

"Careful, Molly girl, and take no unnecessary chances or I'll order you brought right back up. Do you understand girl?" he admonished. At her nod he said, "God speed then lass. Do what you can for the poor bugger."

The descent into the mineshaft was the single most horrifying experience of Molly's young life. As the cage went down the vertical shaft and they left the beams of daylight and freshness of the air far above, panic constricting her chest until she felt about to choke.

Somewhere off in the distance a miner was saying, "Molly, Molly, take deep breaths girl. You'll be all right lass. It happens to everybody their first few times down. Close your eyes girl and breathe deep."

The cage jolted to a halt with the screeching of metal rubbing metal and they made their way into the main artery of the mine. The farther they travelled into the shaft the worse she felt. The conditions in the mine horrified her as she waded through inches of cold stinking water and muck. Her soaked skirt clung to her legs as the cold crept up her limbs. Her knees ached as the cold became increasingly worse. The walls, shored with blackened timbers, ran with foul, slimy water. The stench was sickening. Molly shivered as fear caused her to sweat even in the icy dampness. The smell and dampness she found almost unbearable and she wondered how these men could face going down into the bowels of the earth day after day, yet so rarely complain. She had, on occasion, heard her family and neighbours voice their concern that just this sort of accident was waiting to happen.

It seemed an eternity of groping and slipping before her eyes adjusted to the cloying darkness. Even before they reached the injured miner she could hear moans from ahead. She thanked God for those moans, for that meant he was still with them and fighting for his life. The foreman had explained the situation to Molly so she was well aware of what she would be faced with on her arrival at the accident site. With the veteran miner who had encouraged her in the cage leading them on, Molly and the foreman made their way as quickly as possible to the injured boy. His fellow miners had shored the remaining tippling and were clearing away the debris that had showered down upon him following the collapse. When Molly and the foreman reached his side he was fully conscious. His eyes were wide with pain and terror. Molly had never seen such a look of pure animal fear in her life. As she reached out and touched him in a comforting gesture his eyes softened, relaxed and closed. It seemed he knew this was his guardian angel and he was prepared to accept his fate.

"Help me, God help me. The pain, oh God the pain." Tears streamed down his face forming rivulets in the coal dust as he clenched his teeth against the agonizing pain.

She recognized him immediately as Liam Dermitt, despite his coal-dust smeared face and pain-contorted features.

"Liam, it's Molly O'Connor. We'll get you out of here as soon as I give you something to dull the pain. Try to stay awake while I secure your legs to these boards. The laudanum will help to deaden the pain while we move you."

While Molly was splinting the legs of the young miner he eventually lost consciousness. She quickly ordered the other men to carefully remove him from the shaft. Maneuvering the crudely-made stretcher out of the mine was most difficult for the miners but they bore Liam's dead weight through the narrow shafts and along the slimy mine floor. They knew that the smoother their journey, the least likely the lad would regain consciousness. Thus they made their laboured way through the shaft to the cage, where he was carefully eased aboard and lifted to the surface of the mine.

Upon reaching the surface, Molly gulped in the air, filling her lungs as if she could never get enough. Taking only a minute to calm herself and adjust to the brightness of the outside world, she returned her attention to Liam. The rain was coming down steadily and the chill in the air soon became bone-numbing. Sweat stood out on Liam's brow as he started to shiver uncontrollably. Recognizing his state of shock, Molly ordered him transferred to a properly-equipped stretcher and immediately carried to her home.

Turning to the foreman who was now organizing a cleanup crew to relieve those already below, she quickly asked, "Please contact Liam's family and let them know where he is. Have my da come home as soon as he can and send a messenger for Dr. Leary. Let him know it may be a matter of life or death. He must get here immediately! Liam has lost so much blood I fear for him."

With that, she turned and ran to catch up with the men carrying Liam up the hill to her home. Her skirts, still sodden with the cold muck from the floor of the mine, slowed her somewhat, but lifting them to her knees, she soon caught up. After briefly checking Liam, she rushed ahead to prepare a bed. She knew she was going to face opposition from her father when he realized she wanted Liam to be cared for in their home. She just had to convince him that it was their only option if he was to survive. Dr. Leary would surely see there was no other way and would help convince da. She would handle the reaction of her father later but for now Liam Dermitt needed her or he would likely not make it through the night.

Chapter 3

Northern Ireland, Creggan in County Tyrone – 1840

The week of sleepless nights had passed. Molly was getting no more than four hours sleep in a day. It had taken much gentle persuasion to convince da to allow Liam to remain in their home in order to give him her constant care. The majority of the hours in each day she spent bathing and dressing Liam's badly mangled legs. He constantly slipped in and out of consciousness and every moan and cry caught Molly's attention. She grasped what sleep she could in the daylight hours and tended her patient constantly in the quiet of the night to make sure da and the boys would not have their sleep disturbed. A bed had been moved into the common room to allow Molly more freedom of movement while she cared for Liam. He lay in the bed, cradled in her feather mattress. A tent was constructed around his legs so that the heavy quilts, which were needed to keep him warm, would not bind his legs and cause him more pain.

John arranged for Dr. Leary to be temporarily housed with the local school teacher and spinster, Miss Jenny O'Hara. This way the good doctor would be more likely to be near at hand until he felt it was possible for Molly to take care of the lad on her own. Dr. Leary was the most reliable doctor in the county, was a fully quali-fied practitioner and not predisposed to the bottle—rare qualities in rural Ireland. For who in their right mind, would subject themselves to such gruelling, often thank-less work and like as not, receive a chicken or pork hock in payment? Molly had made it clear that she would remain with Liam until he was safe from death's door, and from there hopefully back on his feet. Dr. Leary had seen the results of this type of accident in the mines before and knew it was probably a losing battle and this once proud young man would likely lose both of his mutilated limbs to gangrene. His only hope would be Molly and the constant care she would provide. But it would be the fight of her life and he held little hope for success.

"He hasn't a hope in Hell John, without Molly. She knows exactly what must be done and she won't hold back when he screams with the pain. Pain is part of the healing process and she knows and accepts that. Liam will likely never walk again but his only chance is Molly. Think carefully on this John. Your lass there can make all the difference in the quality of this young man's life."

The most logical decision was to keep him with them in the O'Connor home where Molly could also be comfortable and be with her own family. Knowing Molly's reputation and her diligent, caring nature, the Dermitt family was happy to accept her services. They were not a terribly poor family and would be generous in their contribution of food and whatever else Liam needed for his recovery. His mother Colleen would help where she could but much of her time would be taken tending to the rest of her family. Seeing her youngest son in such pain merely immobilised her and set her to tearful laments. The doctor provided Molly with medications including plenty of laudanum to dull the pain, bandaging material to help keep infection away, and salves and ointments to treat and soothe the abrasions. If all went well his bones would set and his physical scars would near to vanish with time. What Dr. Leary felt most concern for was the boy's spirit. If he should survive, the months ahead were going to be a tremendous test of his spiritual strength.

He could instruct Molly how to treat the physical results of this accident but the rest would be up to her and the will of the young man she would care for. He secretly offered a prayer for the survival of the boy, both physically and emotionally. If anyone could bring about successful results in both areas, he knew Molly was just that person. This would definitely be the ultimate test of her ability and stamina at such a young age.

*   *   *

For many weeks Liam's legs and feet remained swollen to the point of splitting the shiny, purple skin. The knees and ankles showed no definite shape and were kept splinted and motionless. Molly cleaned and dressed the wounds and abrasions several times daily, each time subjecting Liam to excruciating pain.

At times he would cry in agonising frustration, "Dear God Molly, just leave me in peace. How much more can a man take? What good's it going to do anyway? Every time Dr. Leary comes I can see the look on his face, telling me I'll likely never walk again. I know what this has done to me. I might as well be dead for all the good I'll be."

Molly would smile sympathetically but only say, "I would have never thought you to be a quitter Liam Dermitt. Now grit your teeth and even swear at me if you must but remember who's got the upper hand here."

Knowing the hours Molly was spending washing and boiling bed clothes and dressings and coaxing down what nourishment she could every time Liam regained consciousness, her father and brothers did their part by helping her in the preparation of meals and attempting to keep the house clean and presentable. They knew how fastidious she was about cleanliness and did their best to save her time to nurse Liam. But with having to wash pit clothes daily for three men, cook, clean, and nurse her patient, the daily routine was beginning to take its toll. She often found herself drifting off at the strangest times, in the middle of some chore. If she allowed herself the luxury of sitting down, she would immediately float off into a troubled dream world, only to awake with a start if Liam should cry out in his delirium.

Upon arriving home from shift one cold, wet day, John and his sons found their Molly slumped over the table. The fire was dead and the house chilled and damp. Her body was limp and she barely responded to her father's pleas.

"Molly, lass, it's yer da. Yer freezin lass. What happened love?" Seeing Sean already building the fire up in the blackened hearth, he whispered, "Look in the larder for some barley soup. Put it on quickly lad. She's cold as a witch's heart throughout."

Having got the fire going, Sean poured rendered fat onto the flames to coax the heat back into the room while John cradled Molly, rubbing her arms and wrapping her in a down quilt to drain the numbness from her limbs and put some colour back into her cheeks.

Colin meanwhile checked Liam, to find he was relatively warm and comfortable wrapped in the feather mattress and heavy quilts. Still, though unable to move, he was often conscious now.

Looking up into Colin's frightened eye's he weakly pleaded. "Molly... help her Colin ... help ... can't move my legs ... can't help her." He had been unable to go to Molly's aid although he had realised that something was amiss. In his weakened state he had attempted to call out, but there was no one to hear his pleas. Finally, his attempts wore him out, and he became unconscious again.

Colin gently assured him, "It's all right lad, we're here now. She'll be fine. Rest yourself now and we'll get you some good hot tea. Lie back and rest, there's a lad."

"This can not continue," John said, "or the poor lass will be in worse shape than the lad here." Without deliberation, John made the decision to acquire immediate help for Molly. He knew Molly would not relent in her care for Liam until she felt he was well on his way to good health, so it was up to him to find her reliable help. "Colin, get you down to the Milligan house and see if young Kate can come up to stay with Molly through the day. Tell old man Milligan she'll be compensated or the old bugger might refuse. He's so tight he squeaks, that one does. Kate is a good girl and can be depended upon to help where she's needed. Our Molly likes the lass and she's clean and all. If this goes on for long, as I'm sure it will, she'll be working herself into an early grave."

This event would mark the turning point in Molly's future and her dedication to caring for the sick. Liam's need for constant tending would prove to be invaluable experience in the months to come. As he gradually regained complete consciousness and came to realise the extent of his injuries he often became despondent and at times tried to prevent Molly from applying the salves and bandages to his legs. Each administration was a long and arduous task as his legs were splinted in order to set broken bones. Some of the lacerations and wounds were laid open to the bone and constant care had to be taken to heal layer upon layer of flesh. The pain was often excruciating and tears would stream silently down Liam's cheeks, soaking the bedclothes as he turned his head away from Molly's sympathetic eyes.

The passing time saw Liam's crippled legs and spirit improve dramatically. It was difficult to remain despondent with the likes of John and his sons teasing and cajoling with him in the evenings.

"Ah, sure now, some boyos would do anything to get out of the pit rot", John would quip with a wink.

"Yes, da, and how else could he get the attention of the prettiest girl in the county, with an ugly mug like he sports?" Colin snickered.

Eventually, Liam always having been a fun loving, good-natured young fellow would have to grin broadly and respond with every bit as good an insult. "I suppose now, it just goes to show you, who has the brains around here."

At times they would go on until Molly's laughter would bring tears to her eyes and the tensions of the day would dissolve in merriment.

Periodically Dr. Leary would stop in to visit and take a cup of tea with Molly and Liam as he examined the boy's progress.

"You've done wonders lass. This is one of the finest sets of healing limbs I've ever set me eyes on. Ye'll be up doing a jig before the Spring is out, young laddo."

He was always amazed to see the extent of the progress the young man was making but Liam would always remind him of the impeccable care he was receiving and the loving home atmosphere he was fortunate to be in. With the aid of young Kate who came daily to give her what help she could, Molly was once more gaining her own failing health back. Kate would insist Molly sit and rest for a spell with a cup of mash, or even send her for a nap or a refreshing walk. Soon the roses were back in her cheeks and the dark, smudges gone from around her eyes.

She was even anxious to help out when she could

with a new birth or sick child. Dr. Leary soon recognised the desire in her relentless drive to learn all that she could. He never hesitated in sharing what knowledge he had acquired from his formal training and also all the new techniques he would learn about in his practice. She absorbed like a sponge whatever she would hear. At times in her readings on what medical information she could find, she would share with the good doctor and even debate points with him on the use of the old or new methods. Together they became an excellent team and wherever possible the doctor when busy with a patient, would send her to administer to another caller if he felt the problem was within her boundary of experience. The village folk soon came to trust and count on her, and often called on her before confering with Dr. Leary. She was always very careful not to go beyond her limits and would never administer a treatment of which she was not absolutely certain was needed.

Chapter 4

Northern Ireland, Creggan in County Tyrone – 1841

As the Spring of 1841 entered into full bloom, so did the progress of young Liam Dermitt. His once pitifully damaged legs, although still badly scarred, were slowly becoming functional again. The exercises Molly forced him to suffer through were often agonising but each day became easier. Colin helped by constructing crutches so that when it was time for him to actually get up from the bed, he was able to place some weight on legs that had not held his body upright for months. Naturally at first, the pain, which was now second nature to him was overwhelming but he realised the harder he tried, the faster he would be back on his feet and hopefully back to work. He realised his family was beginning to suffer now because of the loss of his income and it was time for him to be contributing to the coffers once again. When a miner was sick or injured, no matter for how long, the mining company did not offer assistance to his family. They were expected to live off the good will of friends and neighbours. At this time, it never entered his mind that he may never be able to work in the mines again. Dr. Leary and Molly had discussed this often, but had never approached Liam or his family with the dilemma. How do you tell a formerly able bodied young man that he will never again be able to do the only work he has ever known in his life?

One evening Molly asked da if he would go for a walk through the village with her as she felt the need for the comfort his words always brought to her. As they walked, they talked of Liam's recovery.

"I'm so proud of what you've done lass. Without you that young laddo would never have walked again, never mind return to work as he's been nattering on about lately." Stopping in her tracks, she took her father's arm.

"Da, I'm so worried about Liam. You know yourself he'll never be allowed down in the mine again. He's living a pipe dream thinking he will. He wants it so badly he refuses to see the truth. Da, they won't want him anymore, no matter how well he's healed." She felt his great hand cover her's on his arm.

"I know that lass. But Liam must learn the truth for himself. He's in for a clobbering when he marches back into that superintendent's office. But it's little use any of us telling him that. He has to find out for himself. He's a strong lad. He'll survive. And you my young lass best stop worrying about things you have no control over. I have something else I want to talk to you about now."

Wiping the tear from her eyes with her fingertips, she looked expectantly at her father.

"Doctor Leary tells me you're a natural working with the sick and he would be lost without your help. He's asked me, if yer willing, would you consider assisting him as he works around the county whenever possible? I told him, you must decide for yourself, but that I didn't want to see you allow your own health to fail again. This would mean that reasonable boundaries must be set and we must have regular help for you at home. I know yer love for healing and helping others, so you must think on this and do as yer heart leads you."

Tears filled her eyes as her da talked on, for she knew if she followed her heart's ambition it would bring a certain amount of hardship to their home and family. Help was always available, but it was hard to find someone who would care for her home and family in the manner she would herself.

"I can tell by that look in those beautiful green eyes, yer worried about yer old da and those spoiled brothers of yours. But let me tell you something lass, it's time you do for yourself. We're all strong healthy men and there's no reason on God's green earth you should not follow your dreams. We can well afford a housekeeper and someone to fix the tea when yer off helping to save lives m'darlin. So you just stop worrying that pretty little head of yours and tell that old Doc Leary you would like nothing better than to assist him in whatever way you can. An opportunity like this may only come along once in a lifetime to be sure."

Yes, to be sure, Molly knew her da was right. If she wished to persue her desire to become a healer, there was no way she could turn her back on an opportunity such as this. Dr. Leary was her key to the world of healing. He recognized her possibilities and was willing to take a chance on her.

The love Molly felt for her dad overflowed in her heart at this moment. He would sacrifice his own comfort and well being to allow her to follow her dreams.

"I'm so lucky to have you for my da. So many other girls, even so much younger than I, are right this minute rotting their lives away, hauling coal out of the mines. Many will die before they even reach womanhood. You've allowed me to become a woman, search out my own destiny and now you encourage me to follow my dreams. I'm the luckiest girl in Tyrone you know— possibly the luckiest girl in Ireland. I love you da."

John's great arm circled his daughter's slight shoulders as they silently walked home, each with their own thoughts.

Chapter 5

Northern Ireland, Creggan in County Tyrone – 1841

The Irish lace curtains covering Molly's bedroom window fluttered with the warm summer morning breeze. The wispy tendrils of down curls framing her face lifted gently causing her to smile peacefully as she slowly began to waken. Molly stretched leisurely and allowed herself the luxury of day dreaming. The previous evening da and the boys had told her she was not to prepare their morning meal or tend to anyone else's needs. This was to be her day. It was, after all her wedding day.

Letting her mind wander back to the day her life actually changed course, she remembered the cold dank mustiness of the mine pit. Hers was not the only life to change on that fateful day. Liam Dermitt's whole world would change drastically with the crushing of his strong young limbs. Now as she thought over the events of the weeks and months following the accident she recognised the changes that had come over her as she nursed the handsome young man back to good health. At first he was a patient only and her main concern was the saving and mending of his legs. But with week upon week of tending to all his needs, it was only natural they would become fast friends and confidants. Molly watched him evolve from a despondent, brooding, crippled youth, to a smiling, caring man with laughing eyes and a cheeky mouth. They spent hours talking and sharing dreams. When finally Liam was again walking, he was anxious to build the strength in his legs so he would soon be able to rejoin his family and return to his job in the mines. He could only think of his indebtedness to Molly and her family for the wonderful care he had received over the months. Until the day he had entered the mine superintendent's office, he had not dreamed he wouldn't be returning to his former job. But the superintendent had a much different perspective of Liam's condition.

"Once a cripple, always a cripple. You'll never produce as you once did Dermitt. Those legs will always be a burden to you. No man has ever re-entered the pits after experiencing an accident like yours. The cold and damp will stiffen them like boards and we'll be down dragging you out on a stretcher again. Sorry lad, but you're finished."

Liam's breath had caught in his chest and the next he could remember was standing with his arms hanging limply at his side, the knuckles on his large hands swollen and bloody where he had rammed them with frustration and despair against the door of the mine superintendent's office.

As tears streamed down his cheeks he whispered in a barely audible gasp "I'm done Molly, done."

Gently leading him into the house, she sat him down while she tended to his bruised hands. His heart was a different matter. How could she hope to obliterate the pain that threatened to squeeze the life from him now? He was so proud of his recovery and finally felt like a man again. In a few brief moments his exuberance had been dashed to the ground, threatening to destroy all the progress the past months of recovery had accomplished. Sadly, Liam would be the only one shocked at the outcome. It was common knowledge that the mine owners did not want damaged goods in their mines. The miners were in the pits to make money for the wealthy mine owners and the welfare of the miners and their families was of little concern to them. Over the years, many a family could be seen vacating their shanties, huddled together behind a cart filled with all their worldly possessions. Most only acquired the bare necessities of a meagre life. One change of clothes for Sunday besides their daily work garb, a few household utensils, half a dozen pieces of furniture, maybe a pig and a few hens and for very few, a prized family possession in the form of a trinket, picture or a family Bible. Many would have no idea where they were bound, only that they were desperate for work and shelter. As they closed their door to what they for so many years had called home there would immediately be another family to take their place.

This of course was not Liam's plight, but his self-esteem and worth was foremost in his thoughts at this moment. Molly's sympathy did not seem to help at this point and eventually he trudged off home with his head bent to his chest. Right at this time, life seemed to be playing a cruel joke on this young man. Fortunately, life's fortunes change, as does everything in time.

*   *   *

Three days had passed. The sky was dark and foreboding, threatening to dump it's wet contents on a depressingly grey earth below. On his way home from the pit da had stopped for well-earned ale at the local pub where he had learned that the sawmill owner, Mike O'Toole was looking for a strong lad to apprentice. His last apprentice had come down with pneumonia and had died two weeks prior. He was swamped with work and in desperate need of help. Da had suggested he talk to Liam and his family and see if the lad would do. Mike was sceptical because of the injuries Liam had acquired in the mine but he was willing to talk to him and give him a chance.

"You say he's a good lad, John? Ten hours a day, six days a week, I'll expect of him. I don't want no slacker and no whiner. You think he's got what it takes?"

John nodded, "Mike, I've watched this lad for months now suffer through terrible agonies while he's mended. Believe me, he has the drive and the backbone to boot. Determination, stamina and guts, yes sir. Hire him Mike!"

Molly had just served up piping hot plates of her famous Mulligan stew to her da and the boys after they had shed their soggy clothes and rubbed down soaking heads. The rain had come down with a vengeance as they had trudged home from work. The roaring fire and a wonderful aroma arising from the boiler on the stove had welcomed them. Just as the O'Connors were finishing tea, a loud knock had come to the door and before any one of them could get up to answer or even call out in welcome, Liam entered soaked to the skin and appearing like a drowned rat. The startled look on all their faces indicated they had been caught off guard until Liam's face broke out into a broad, cheeky grin.

"What in God's name are you doing, out on the devil of a night like this and startling the sweet Jesus out of us, you young fool?" John exclaimed.

Molly had rarely heard her father swear and she now smiled to herself as she remembered that dark but truly wonderful day.

Liam had thrown off his dripping great coat, rushed over to Molly and picking her up in his arms had swung her around until the blood rushed to her head and she cried, "Liam, leave go, leave go."

As he lowered her gently to the chair he had placed a firm kiss on her forehead. "What in heavens name has come over you Liam Dermitt? You're acting like the cat that's just caught a great fat mouse," she gasped breath-lessly.

Getting down on his knees before her and taking both of her trembling hands in his own he directed his question to Molly's father but never unlocked his gaze from Molly's eyes.

"Mr. O'Connor, I wish to ask you if I may take your Molly as my wife, provided she will have me?" Only then, taking his eyes from Molly's, he had faced her father. With the trace of a tear brimming on his long dark lashes he said, "Because of Molly I have my life, because of you I've been given another chance to prove I'm still a man and capable of a man's work. Today I've been given the occasion to prove that I am able to provide for your daughter whom I have loved from the moment I set eyes on her those long months ago when she brought me from the mines and nursed me back to health. Mike O'Toole has taken me on as his apprentice in his saw mill. He has given me three months to prove my worth and depending on my performance will decide from there. This means I can learn a new trade, and no longer be a burden to anyone. I can do it John. Molly means the world to me and I want to be able to take care of her for the rest of her life. After I've proved to Mr. O'Toole that I'll be the best man he's ever had on the job, I know he will want me to stay on. After that, Molly and I could plan for the future if you will only give your Blessing and Molly will only say 'yes'." Turning again to Molly, Liam had whispered, "I love you Molly girl, and God willing, I'll be giving you all the happiness in the world if you'll only have me."

To this point Colin and Sean had sat with their mouths hanging open until Colin blurted out "For God sake da, get the poor sod off his knees, tell him 'yes', I can't stand watching him suffer. Take him out of his misery." John had turned to Molly and for a full minute gazed upon the one soul that had brought sweetness to his life for the past eleven years since his wife had passed away. He knew this time would eventually come, but he couldn't help but dread the loss of her daily presence in their home. She made them laugh. She made life bearable in the worst of times. She brought a glow to their home. She was his main reason for living.

"Well lass, the final decision is yours, but I can definitely see the love in his eyes, and I must admit you could do a lot worse than this lad before you now. But if he doesn't get up off those knees before long, he'll likely never walk again. So you both have my blessing and I wish you a long and happy life."

He fought back the desire to say, 'I can't bear the thought of losing you. You're the joy of our lives and without you, enduring life's dreariness, has no purpose.' But the look of shear joy in her eyes held his thoughts at bay. He knew that her happiness was paramount and his own thoughts, selfish. She could not spend all of her days looking after himself and her brothers as he had often pointed out to her. As kind and loving a person as she was, she would no doubt learn to resent them if she was kept tied to them when she was ripe for a husband and family of her own to nurture and cherish. So he had said the only thing he could that would free her from the obligations she felt for her family.

"I be needing grandchildren to fill my days when I quit the mines and these brothers of yours aren't show-ing much sign of settling down. Hopefully when they don't have their baby sister here to tend to them and fill their hungry bellies every day they'll get busy and find themselves wives. You'll be doing me a favour now by getting on with your life and bringing me lots of grand-children to torment their old grand da."

Until that very moment Molly had no idea of the degree of love she felt for Liam. She had shivered as invisible fingers ran up her spine. Her eyes had misted over, her neck and face became warm with the rush of blood she felt coursing through her veins. All she could see was Liam's beseeching eyes as she took her hands from his and fell into his arms.

"I never doubted you would be given another chance. You're too good a man to be wasted." She cupped his rain-drenched face between her hands and gently whispered, "and yes, I will marry you. To spend the rest of my days as Mrs. Liam Dermitt." Standing up now she gently tugged up on his ears and with a laugh that broke the nervous silence around her she had said, "Now, get yourself up off those knobbly knees or I will be nursing you for the rest of me days."

"Yes, and I'm ready for some of that apple duff, our Molly. This is just getting too sticky sweet for this lad." Scoffed young Sean.

With that they had all laughed and Molly throwing a towel at Liam said, "Get yourself dried off before you catch your death. I'll dish up some duff and mash some fresh tea."

*   *   *

Over the next few months Liam had surely proven himself and even increased his hours of work. He had wanted there to be no question as to whether he could be a good provider for Molly and he definitely didn't want any delays for their wedding plans. It had seemed the whole town was donating to the festivities. Even the poorest of their neighbours insisted on bringing a special dessert, a few eggs or maybe even a piglet. It was going to be a bonny wedding and a lively soiree.

With a start, Molly realised she was dreaming the day away and sprang from her bed. She shivered with excitement as the events of the day began to formulate in her mind. This was her wedding day. It had come upon her unbelievably quickly after Liam had surprised her with his proposal. There didn't seem to be enough time for all the preparation needed, but her friends and neighbours had pitched in without hesitation. She walked over to the dress hanging on her bedroom door. Lovingly she ran her fingers over the intricate creamy lace of the bodice and arms. Dozens of satin covered buttons ran from the back of the high neckline to the mid-hip area. The standing collar and the long sleeves were trimmed with minute pearls. It had been her mother's wedding dress and her mothers before her. As Molly took on the physical characteristics of her mother at the same age, there was little to be altered. The dress was well cared for over the years and although beautifully traditional was still quite fashionable. The gossamer veil also edged with tiny pearls draped gently over her shoulders and down her slender back until it barely met the floor. From her trunk she took the light slippers she had covered in creamy satin and slipped them on her feet. After pulling her hair into a luxuriant pile onto the top of her head, she carefully took the dress from the door and holding it to her body danced in circles around her bed until she caught her image in the mirror above the chest of drawers. With a shock she stared back at the face of her mother. She could see her mother smiling at her, yet with tears in her eyes and saying to her 'Be happy my darling Molly. Remember I will always be at your side'. Placing the dress on the bed, she ran from the room to where the wedding picture of her mother and father hung on the wall.

Gently taking it down and caressing her mother's

image with her finger tips, she whispered, "Oh, momma, I so wish you could be here with me today. I know you would love Liam. He's a good man and I love him with all my heart. He's kind and gentle but strong and determined. We'll make a good life together. I am happy, momma, so rest well." Placing the picture back on the wall, she smiled, then put her fingers to her lips, kissed them and touched the image of her mother's face and again murmured, "rest well."

It was Sunday and the wedding ceremony would be held an hour after the morning service. Kate, who over the months had become a dear friend, had taken it upon herself to solicit the aid of John, Colin, and Sean to set up the reception in the Creggan Miner's Hall. Saturday was spent by most of the womenfolk cooking, baking and preparing for the festivities. Wild flowers of brilliant colours festooned the tables and colourful paper streamers danced in the summer breeze from the windows. August was the month of festivals and sports events in the county and this was to be the biggest and happiest event the town of Creggan and possibly the County of Tyrone would see this year. As Molly's friend, Kate was determined to make this possible.

Weddings were naturally planned to take place directly after the morning church service. This would assure that the men would not be too far into their pints before the ceremony took place. It was not uncommon for a donnybrook to break out in the middle of any event, so precautions must be taken on the women's part to forestall any raucous behaviour brought on by the generous flow of spirits at the festivities.

A hush finally descended on the wedding guests as they turned to watch Molly make her way down the aisle of the church on the arm of her very proud father. The sunlight through the open doors surrounded her in a halo effect making her appear ethereal. The occasional audible gasp was all that broke the silence as she made her way towards the altar and her beaming husband-to-be.

Tears shone in John's eyes as he escorted her the last few steps to Liam's side. "I trust you to care for and love this woman more than life itself, as I know she will you. Take care of one another," he said as he placed Molly's small hand in Liam's. He then brushed Molly's cheek with a kiss and whispered, "be happy lass," then stepped back and joined his remaining family.

The somber atmosphere surrounding the ceremony soon evaporated as the newly married couple made their way from the church to the miner's hall in a gaily decorated cart and pony.

Being a small town, the cart was used for many purposes including funerals. But for this event the school children had taken it upon themselves to decorate it from top to bottom. Bright flowers and streamers bounced jauntily as the cart and its occupants made their way down the road. The village children skipped and danced alongside, scooping up abandoned flowers and throwing them to the laughing couple. On this particular summer day everyone's trials and tribulations seemed to have vanished. It was a time to celebrate, to set aside their worries until tomorrow and enjoy the present.

Chapter 6

Northern Ireland, Creggan in County Tyrone – 1842

It was the summer of 1842. The day was hot and sultry and Molly felt the need to escape the heat, if only for a while. She laboriously made her way out from the village and onto the fringes of the bog where large shade trees cooled the ground beneath them. She eased her cumbersome body slowly down the trunk of the tree until her arms and legs spread on the cooling blades of grass. As she thankfully closed her eyes from the glare of the midday sun she felt the life within her also settle into a more comfortable position. The breeze kissed the leaves and their music lulled her into the sleep of the contented. Molly and Liam were married almost a year to the day and were expecting their firstborn at any time. She knew it was a boy for he tormented her day and night with continuous cartwheels and well-placed kicks. She wondered if he ever slept.

"My Lord, I hope he wears himself out now, and sleeps when he's in my arms," she had commented to Liam one especially active night.

Her pregnancy had gone well, but now she was exhausted with the heat and was anxious for it to be done with. Today her back was causing her great discomfort but she had estimated another week or two before the birth and figured the heat and constant activity of the child were taking their toll. Kat had thoughtfully come daily to help her with the chores and cooking but today had sent word that she wasn't feeling well and felt it best she stay away. Molly took the opportunity her freedom brought her to escape to the cool hills.

Having fallen into a light doze she was suddenly shocked awake by a sharp twinge beginning in her back and radiating around to the front of her distended belly. She smiled to herself, thinking 'you young imp, you think you'll get the best of me don't you? Well let me tell you my young lad, in another week or two, you'll be out in this....' "Ah ... my God, ah, no, my God, not yet." Rolling herself over onto her knees she struggled to pull herself up the trunk of the tree and onto her feet. Another pain immediately wracked her body, only this time enough to take her breath away. "It's not time ah ... you can't come yet. No ... I've got to get home. Please lad, let your poor mother get home. No more, no more, ah ... God help me. Get me home." Between each fresh stabbing jolt of pain Molly stumbled her way around the perimeter of the bog, carefully trying to pick her way over boulders and around sharp clawing bushes. It had taken her twenty minutes to walk from home to the top of the bog. Now it seemed like it was taking her hours to get back home again. Every few minutes she would fall to her knees after enduring another series of spasms. Her birthing water broke through its barrier in a rush, soaking her dress and causing her to slip in the sodden grass. Sweat poured from her body as she panted and groaned her way home. Her throat dried and closed with each laboured breath. Her lips cracked as she grimaced with each piercing stab of pain.

It was midday and with the menfolk either in the mine or sleeping, the women tending to daily chores and the older children in school, there was no one to hear her cries as she stumbled from the bog, willing herself safely home.

As she neared the fringe of the village she began to scream for help. "Help me. Get Mary Duggan, NOW.

Liam ... ah ... Liam. Get Liam." A small boy, gathering greens for his pet rabbit, heard her cries and ran to his mother for help. Mrs. Murphy, two doors down from their house on Cobble Hill Circle, sent the lad after the midwife and then to the sawmill to fetch Liam. As Molly virtually crawled to the settee in the common room, Mrs. Murphy hurried to her side making her as comfortable as possible. She had six children of her own but would always remember the terror she felt at the birth of her first child. Mrs. Murphy's presence was comforting to Molly but the fear did not begin to subside until the midwife appeared. Molly had been present for the birth of many local children over the past few years and she knew she was in good hands with Mary Duggan.

Liam arrived minutes before the birth of their sturdy little son. Mary chased him from the room with a flapping of hands, telling him in her gruff manner "tis no place for the likes of you, mister." Knowing it was useless to argue with the old harridan, he paced back and forth across the threshold until he heard the first lusty wails of their babe. By this time, nothing would hold him back. As he entered the room, Mary met him with his son wrapped cocoon-like in a clean linen towel.

"Take him now, he won't break. Just stay out of me way now while I tend to yer poor woman here." Liam looked back and forth from the red squalling face tucked in his arm, to the serene face of his wife, propped against the white pillow brought from their bed. Another agonized gasp escaped Molly as she passed the afterbirth with a groan. Within minutes she relaxed and beaconed for him to come closer so she could finally see their son.

"I'd like to call him Matthew, after God's Disciple. He's going to be a powerful man, with a kind, loving nature. He'll be respected and looked up to. I want him to have a strong name."

Liam smiled at his wife and then down at this small miracle, his son, and said, "Matthew sounds just fine to me. Matthew it is then." As he tucked their son into the crook of Molly's arm he whispered, "Now my son, go to sleep. Give your mother some peace." He brushed his lips to Molly's forehead saying, "You've given us a fine son, my beautiful girl. You should be proud. Sleep now my darlin." As he quietly walked from the house he stopped on the door stoop only long enough to take a deep breath and suppress a holler that would have likely been heard throughout the whole County. A grin crossed his bemused face that told the world, 'I'm a father. My Molly has given us a fine son.' As he headed off down Cobble Hill Circle, tears of joy and pride ran down his handsome face.

The good news traveled swiftly in the village and soon many well-wishers were appearing with pots of stew, breads, and cakes for the family. Napkins and nightshirts came for the baby with offers of help for the new mother. A beautiful cradle had been fashioned by one of the neighbours and by that very night Matthew's name was carved into the head and it was presented to the proud family. Music filled the Circle and it was reminiscent of the wedding festivities of the prior year.

In the early evening as friends were wending their way homeward, the night air was shattered by the shrill of the mine siren warning of a disaster. Young lads ran the length of the streets crying the news of the latest accident in the mine. The joy of the evening quickly turned to horror and despair as wives and mothers fled to the mine praying to meet with their loved ones. Some looked for a husband while others had near whole families down the pits. The evening shift was the least popular with most, so the younger and least experienced miners were the ones to be sent down.

Kate, who's family was all safely home, stayed with Molly and Matthew as Liam with John and his sons headed down into the village to see what assistance they could give to the injured and their families.

"Colin, head out and find if Dr. Leary has been sent for. If not, find him!" shouted John as they made their way down the hill. But by the time they reached the pit superintendent's office Dr. Leary was already shouting orders and preparing for the arrival of the injured. No one had been brought up from the shaft in question. The rest of the mine was being cleared of miners as quickly as they could be lifted out in the slow-moving cages. Once again, the shaft where Liam had been so badly injured two years earlier was the scene of the latest accident. Only this time, there would be a dozen young miners trapped and injured, possibly lives even lost.

Tears of frustration rolled down John's grief stricken face as he thought of the useless hours of meetings with the mine owners as they literally begged for safer conditions to work in. "The bastards don't care a damn. Why can't it be them down in that stinking pit? They wouldn't be so quick to send their own sons down. We're nothing but dogs to the money-hungry pigs!" John felt himself losing control as he watched the families waiting and praying to be reunited with their own. The sobbing and wailing of the women broke his heart as he helplessly saw their looks of despair.

For endless hours into the night, miner after miner risked his own life to help free his comrades trapped below. Lines of bucket brigades were formed as they feverishly took turns digging out the fallen earth deep within the shaft. Fresh new timbers and needed tools were passed from man to man down the line. Not a word was spoken for hours. Ne'er a word was needed. All knew the likelihood that someone they grew up with, worked side by side with, drank with, laughed with and cried with, could have the life snuffed from them this day. Their limbs ached with the strain but not one would give up until their comrades were reached, hopefully alive and little worse for the wear. Hope for a better future was what kept these men alive as hope for a successful rescue kept them going now.

Evening wore into the deep of night as the exhausted rescuers continued their vigilant efforts. All knew that a death sentence could be struck in an instance with the presence of the choking methane gas. The presence of this very deadly gas was monitored by taking canaries down into the shafts. A watchful eye was kept by the miners in the event one of these delicate little creatures should collapse, indicating the build up of the gas. The fact that the collapsed shaft had created a tomb with little or no air ventilation enhanced the chances of the build up of this highly explosive substance. No one knew this better than the rescuers as their picks and shovels threw sparks at all angles as they attempted to quickly reach their fellow workers. Constantly on the alert for any sound from behind the barrier of fallen rock, they were prepared to abandon all tools in favour of digging by hand. No one would put anyone's life in danger, including his own, in a foolhardy act. Caution was never thrown to the wind under any circumstances. Each one lived with daily danger and to tempt fate was considered a sin against one's mates. One foolish move could spell disaster.

Back up on the Circle, Molly, although tired from the evenings festivities following the birth of their son, was feeling the frustration of not being able to be with the miners and their families. She was being kept informed by her family and neighbours on the progress of the rescuers. This they would do, only if she promised to keep to her bed for as long as possible, for it was certain her help would be needed when the trapped miners were finally brought to the surface. Only the needs of her son kept her from dressing and hurrying down the hill. She was wise enough to know she must gain as much strength as she could muster in the next few hours.

The longer the recovery of the men took, the more chance there was for serious injury or even death. No one even wanted to mention the likelihood of the build-up of the deadly Methane gas. Molly dozed in and out of a troubled sleep until the break of dawn and the break-through to the trapped miners.

Matthew nuzzled at his mother's breast throughout the night and now slept peacefully as his father made his way home.

"Molly darlin, they're through. The lads have broken through." Liam whispered to his wife as he bent over Molly and their son. Molly searched her husband's eyes for the inevitable.

"Who, Liam? Who have we lost?" she breathed.

"Little Billy Martin and his mate Sean Kelly", he wept, unable to hold back the tears that had welled up in his eyes and threatened to splash down onto her now paled cheeks. "The lads figure the poor little buggers never knew what hit them, it came down with such a force. By the time we got through from our side, the boys had them dug out but they say, the poor lads could never have drawn a single breath once they were buried."

Liam's tears gathered the coal dust filming his grief-stricken face and mingled with Molly's as he held her close. Their son lay peacefully at her side.

"No son of ours will ever go down into those stink-ing holes, Molly. I don't care if we have to move to the ends of the earth. No son of ours will be a miner."

The determination in his face told her that this was to be a turning point in their lives. From now on life would not be the same. Creggan had been their whole world, from birth, through their childhood, their marriage, and finally the birth of their beautiful son Matthew. A door was finally closing behind them, but before completing this chapter in their lives, there were others that needed their help. Gently pushing on Liam's heaving chest, and releasing Matthew from the crook of her arm, Molly sat upright. Wiping the tears from his face she ran her fingers down his neck and onto his muscular shoulders kneading them as she spoke.

"Yes, my darling, you're quite right, no son of ours will ever be a miner. But right now there are a dozen sons that need our help. They also have mothers and fathers that fear for them and their lives. I must go to them now. I must help Dr. Leary. He can't be expected to do it all himself." She hesitated as Liam attempted to protest, but she quieted him by saying, "I'm well rested, and I won't do more than I must. You stay here and rest now and watch our son. He has just eaten and should sleep for a few hours quite contented. By that time I will have returned so I can rest again."

Knowing it was futile to argue with her, he hugged her to his chest in resignation, sighing, "Alright, m'darlin, I'll take you down now then while Kate is still here to watch Matthew. When John and the boys get back, I'll come with the cart to pick you up. That should be no more than a couple of hours which will give you enough time to whip them all in shape." This he said with a wry smile as he knew from past experience that his wife was the one to have everyone assigned a duty and all running smoothly, no matter how chaotic the situation. He kissed her warmly before she turned to splash her face at the basin. After instructions to Kate on Matthews care if he should wake while she was gone, she headed with Liam and the cart down the lane, past the homes of her life-long friends and neighbours, and on to Creggan Miner's Hall where an emergency treatment centre had been set up.

The look on Dr. Leary's face was not one of pleasure as he raised himself from tending one of the young miners. When he saw Molly approaching, his frown showed concern, not anger.

"What are you doing lass? Do you want to be joining these poor lads? You're not strong enough to be down here yet. Go back to your babe," he added gently. "I can manage once the worst are tended to."

As if on cue, Molly's response was exactly what he would have expected. "Dr. Leary, women have been giving birth since the beginning of time, and I'm no different. I'm healthy as an ox and you know it. Now, you tend to these lads and I'll just be here to do what I can to help. I'm quite able to fold more dressings and apply the ointments and salves. I assure you, I'll have everyone else running the errands and doing the lifting. I'm not a child. I know my limits. I have a capable mouth on me, as you know, and my hands aren't at all weary. You'll likely be far more worn out than I before the day is over. Now, no more resting on our laurels. What can I do first?" Shaking his head, and spreading his hands widely in a show of surrender he turned to carry on in the chaos of the moment.

Over the next couple of hours Dr. Leary worked feverishly setting broken bones, while Molly washed open wounds, applied bandages and administered lauda-num to those most in need. She organised a team of local women to prepare dressings and bandages, while others talked to and washed the oily coal dust from the faces of the injured miners to divert their attention while Dr.

Leary set their broken limbs. Dr. Leary insisted that the ten surviving miners remain together in the hall, in order for them to receive proper care. He did not want to have one more young man join Billy Martin and the Kelly lad in their fate. In twenty-four hours he would be assured of no internal bleeding and most would be able to head home in the care of their families.

By the time Colin and John arrived with the pony-cart to take their Molly home to her family, she had fully organised a team of village women to take shifts in keeping vigil over the injured men. She had, to her satisfaction and that of the doctor's, chosen the most reliable of the women to care for the bed-ridden miners. Dr. Leary remained at the hall but would take rest periods of an hour or two at a time. The fear of internal bleeding was paramount in his mind so he insisted that each patient be checked regularly for the signs of internal damage.

Upon arriving home the wails of young Matthew could be heard drifting down the hill. Liam had done his best to comfort the wee mite, but it was now time for his feeding and upon the arrival of his mother he grasped hungrily at her breast. Molly's eyes were closed as she sank into the feather ticking on their bed. Matthew ate greedily but was not able to keep his mother from falling into the contented, heavy sleep of the very weary. Watching his wife and child sleeping in such peace, Liam was hesitant to disturb them knowing Molly must be exhausted, no matter how much she protested to the contrary. He gently removed her boots and tucked a thick napkin around the baby. The summer heat had continued through the night in a most uncommon way, leaving the air in the house heavy and cloying. Liam pulled a muslin sheet up over his wife and child to protect them from the annoying summer insects and quietly left the room to join her father and brothers in the common room.

He sensed the tension as he entered the room. For years now Liam had heard and participated in discussions and arguments about the pros and cons of living in Ireland, remaining in Ireland and leaving Ireland. Once again neighbours and fellow workers had congregated in John's home to air their views and vent their frustrations. He now walked into such a discussion involving two of their neighbours who had joined John and his sons in an emotional debate. The mine was their lives and many homes only had one or two incomes, whereas the O'Connor household had four full incomes, three being from the mines, and Liam's from the lumber mill. This family was considered well-off by other townsfolk. Some even resented them despite the fact that they had worked hard to reach this point in their lives. But the majority of miners and their families had no other options in life. They could stay and likely face starvation or leave to encounter the unknown. It was as simple as that. The words Liam heard now, spoken by the guests in this house, stunned him.

"John, we've been good neighbours for some years now," came the indignant voice of Ryan Duggan. "How can you be considerin turnin yer back on Ireland, Sir? It's only a traitor would consider the likes of it. I always thought more of ya John." Duggan's chest puffed as he ranted.

"You've always spouted 'duty' and 'loyalty' to the rest of us. Now yer talkin desertion! I'll starve before I leave this God forsaken land," boasted Conin Reilly.

John's eyes blazed. "Then you starve Conin Reilly, but just remember, yer family starves with you. I have a brand new grandson lying in that room," John said, pointing to the room in which Molly and Michael now slept. "Be damned if I'll let anyone convince me Ireland is more important than my family. Be damned if I will!"

Liam's heart went out to John and his sons for he knew just how loyal and giving this whole family had always been. He was living proof of their steadfastness. "How can you doubt this family's loyalty? How can you two sit there and tell this family that they have a duty to the rest of you or that they would be traitors to leave this God forsaken place? How can anyone be envious of these people that have given so much of their time and lives to helping anyone of you in this stinking hole of a place? You envy them because they have the intestinal fortitude to stand up to those bastards that run this mine. They've slaved for years, scrimped and saved, but never denied their neighbours in any way. Who do you or any of your cronies come to, Ryan, when you need a helping hand or someone to speak up for you? Good old John O'Connor and his boys. Sure, they'll get it done boys." By this time Liam's eyes rested only inches from Ryan Duggan's blood red face. "Who the hell do you think you are? After all these years of relying on this family there's not one man jack of you has the right to question what the O'Connors do or why they do it. It's time you did for yourselves and quit depending on others to protect you. Why don't you get off your duffs, get together and demand some action?" All this, Liam had related in a calm, controlled manner, ever conscious of not overstepping his boundaries in his new family's home. But he also very clearly conveyed his feelings to those guests present so that they eventually lowered their gazes, nervously got up from the table and shuffled outside, muttering to themselves as they headed homeward down the hill.

Watching them leave, Liam closed his eyes and exhaling slowly between pursed lips, turned and apologised to John.

"Forgive me John for being so outspoken. It just tears my heart out to hear them maligning the character of this family. But I'm sorry. It wasn't my place to do it in your home."

John rose, clamping Liam on the shoulder said, "You forget lad, this is your home as much as ours. Don't worry yourself now. We're proud to have such an ally. I'll tell you a secret. I've often longed for someone to boot some of these mouthy buggers in the arse. Some of them spend their lives whining but always expecting others to do their dirty work."

*   *   *

As the weeks and months passed, this was to be only the first of many such confrontations as anger at the mine owners grew and festered. Fear of losing their jobs and the threat of starvation and homelessness stared into the faces of the miners of Tyrone and their families.

Chapter 7

Northern Ireland – Creggan and Belfast (1845-1846)

Rumours of diseased potato crops and tenant farmers being ousted from their homes crept in as migrant families filtered into the township pleading for work in the mines. Realising the growing tide of itinerant workers was increasing the mine's work pool, the owners were less inclined to address the needs of the miners and the continual deterioration of the working conditions in the pits. This, along with the rising unrest in the rest of Ireland led to more and more talk of possible emigration to other countries such as England, Canada, the USA, and even as far off as Australia. More and more discontent grew over the next few years as the potato famine attacked Ireland with a vengeance. Economic desparity became evident through all walks of life throughout the whole nation. Starving people left the only homes they had known for generations. Packing up their meagre possessions they let out in search of work, shelter and food, the bare necessities of life. It became a daily occurrence to see a cart being hauled into the village under human power, often filled with gaunt-looking children with distended bellies and sore pocked skin, evidence of progressive malnutrition and starvation. In the early years, the charity of the miners and their families took over as they offered the poor starving creatures shelter and food. But the longer this continued the more self-preservation took over and eventually the migrants were being run out of the village as hungry and as diseased as they entered. It was one thing to give what they could to the poor. It was another to jeopardise the lives of their own families.

Bitter arguments and fights continuously broke out among once fast-friends and neighbours. Life in the once-peaceful mining village was becoming more and more threatening. There was more talk of leaving. Those who had the means were looked down upon by the poorer and labelled deserters. But as the years rolled by even those less fortunate found the means to pull up stakes and leave. The threat of possible starvation led even the most patriotic Irishman to carefully consider the alternatives. Posters were pinned up in the villages with the quote from II Corinthians 4:7 which read "Weep sore for him that goeth away; for he shall return no more, nor see his native country." Most could not read but everyone knew the quote word for word.

"Is this bloody rain ever going to stop? I can't remember the last drop of sunshine I saw in this God forsaken place," Colin complained as he, Sean, and his father trudged up the hill after completing another dreary shift. The pits were flooding more day by day until soon they knew it would be impossible to work until the waters subsided. "Those bastards should shut things down until it's safer to go down there, but no, every cart full is another dollar in their lousy greedy pockets. How much more of this crap do we put up with?" Day by day, there was more growing discontent among the miners. Working conditions continually deteriorated and itinerant labour threatened the positions of the experienced miner. The inexperienced worked side by side with those who had generations of miners in their families. Tempers flared daily. Distrust and hate bred daily among those who felt those who had no business being there were threatening their livelihood. They were farmers. What were they doing in the mines? Surviving!

'Will peace ever return to this valley?' Molly wondered as she sat by the window watching the miners climb the hill heading for their homes. More and more often discussions arose as the miners wondered if they would ever be able to escape the strong arm of the mine owners. There was less laughter in the home and more argument. Everyone agreed on the problem. It was the solutions that had them looking in different directions. No one wanted to uproot their families and leave the only place they had ever known. It was the devil you know for the devil you don't. Fear of the unknown was in all their hearts.

"Get your wet clothes off now. The fire's hot so we'll have them dried in no time" Molly greeted them at the door. "I've mashed the tea and have some fresh baked scones as a treat."

"Thanks lass, hot tea will do wonders now. Where's that young rapscallion hidin himself Molly girl?"

"I'm here Uncle Colin," Matthew chirped as he poked his tousled head out from under the down quilt of the day bed. "Throw me up to the roof Uncle Colin. Throw me. Throw me." Matthew squealed in delight as he ran into his uncle's arms.

"Thank God your home, Colin. This child has been driving me to distraction the day. This rain be driving us all crazy soon, I'm sure." Molly laughed as Colin threw his young nephew up into the rafters.

"So, you're drivin your poor ma crazy, are ya now? You're just like your Uncle Colin. When yer ma and I were youngsters, I tried me best to drive her crazy, so I did, but yer ma was too smart for me. Always the sensible one was our Molly." Colin turned and gave his sister a big hug. "Always the sensible one to be sure."

John smiled at his family. It was always good to see them happy. There was too much unrest and arguing of late and he didn't like what it was doing to his family.

As their head he knew the time was upon them to make the biggest decision of their lives. There was no sign of improvement in the foreseeable future. Now was the time to tell them his plan.

When Liam arrived home from the sawmill and his family was all around him John announced, "there is something we must discuss as a family. The time has come to decide our future. I had hoped it would never come down to this, but I feel we have no choice. The life we have known for so many years is crumbling around us. The future of our youngsters is bleak. I'm not a young man anymore and whether I stay or go isn't of much importance one way or the other. But you have the majority of your lives ahead of you. Matthew, and those yet to come, God willing, have no hope of a future here. What is there for them to stay for? So, it is time to decide what we must do and when." Heads were hung, to the person.

The first to speak was Sean. "To begin with, if one of us goes, then we all go. It's bad enough we have to even consider leaving without even thinking of leaving anyone of us behind. Kathleen and I want to go to Canada. We want to marry and then go to Canada. We've talked about this for some time now. We just didn't want to bring it up until we felt it was the right time. We don't want our children being raised in this turmoil. Maybe Canada won't be all we hope for, but nothing is left for us here. We have to take that chance." Sean continued excitedly. "Kathleen has been sending for all the books she can find about Canada and we're convinced that it will be the place to raise our children."

"Well then," John said, raising his hands into the air, "I would say Kathleen should be in on our decision making if she is to be part of our family. What do you say we find out what she knows about Canada?" Each in turn, looking from one to the other nodded in agreement.

Molly finally broke her silence, "Da, if we are going to discuss this, I must tell you something. For the past three years I have been taking money from the house-hold expenses and put away some twenty-seven pounds. There's also extra shirts and trousers I've sewn from time to time that I put away just on the chance something might happen and we be needing extras. We also have an abundance of blankets, towels and linens." All eyes were on Molly as their mouths had dropped open. " My Lord, quit your gapping. Do you think I do nothing but sit on my laurels around here? I'll have it be known, I've been giving this a good deal of thought for some time now. I knew it was only a matter of time before we would all be talking of leaving and I wanted to be prepared."

Liam beamed at his wife. "Well now, and sure you're full of surprises my girl. You've always been the one to never talk of moving on when the topic arose."

"Well Colin," Sean quipped, "you may be sure she's our sister."

John broke his silence with a smile breaking his lips, "yes, and she's my daughter," he said, folding his arms around her. "And to think I've held back on bringing up this whole conversation because I thought it would dear-ly upset you. Your sainted mother would be proud of you my darlin girl."

*   *   *

From that day forth, the thoughts that had grown month by month in the minds of the whole family were finally out in the open. Liam's family were brought into the discussions, as Thomas, his elder brother, had talked for years of emigrating, but where he did not know. Liam's parents Patrick and Colleen also realised the futility of remaining when their children were married and gone. Thomas and Liam were all they had and it was their wish to have what family was left, close to them.

"We're getting old, like you John. Both our families have been hard workers. Now with Liam and Molly we're joined as one. We want to be part of the new life whether it be in Canada, Australia, or wherever, just count us in."

*   *   *

Finally, the time had arrived to formulate definite plans. The women got together daily making arrangements for sufficient clothing, cooking utensils, medical needs, foodstuffs and whatever else could be arranged in advance. After pouring over books and books of information brought home by Sean's wife to be, Kathleen, it was decided that Canada would be their future home. Being a school teacher, Kathleen had the greatest access to the most information and her time had been well spent over the past months collecting all she could lay her hands on. Now that the decision was out in the open, she could barely contain herself at what she had found, especially on her favourite subject, Canada. Her enthusiasm was contagious and now that a final decision had been made as to where they would emigrate, they all succumbed to the excitement.

As news filtered out to their neighbours and friends over the following weeks, most agreed with their decision but many turned away, treating them as if they had already gone from them. But as time grew near to their departure, many came to wish them well and God's speed, for in the end they all knew if they too didn't leave they would likely eventually starve as the mines shut down, one by one.

*   *   *

A few evenings before their departure, a soiree was held by their life-long friends and neighbours in honour of the O'Connors and the Dermitts,. Most would never forget that these two families had often held things together in times of trouble. They would be sorely missed.

The fiddles and melodeons shrilled, the liquor flowed and memories became more and more exaggerated. The menfolk reminisced over their feats in the mines, wild nights in Dooley's Pub and the few but memorable social events that dotted their lives. Who took out the most coal, who took down the most arms, who fathered the most babes, who could drink down the most in a night at Dooley's and leave under his own power. Laughter, arguments and the odd fight broke out. The women remembered the births, deaths, mine disasters when their men may have come out mangled or dead —the foundations of their lives in Creggan. Many shed tears they had held at bay for years. Life as they knew it was falling apart and it must never be forgotten.

Well into the night, John raised himself from his chair while he was still able. "My good friends. I speak for my family when I say, this night will be remembered fondly by us all when we be far away from you all and probably missing the whole damned lot of ya. Thanks to you all for making this a special time for us to remember when we're lonely and thinking of Ireland and our lifetime of friendships that will remain behind us. God love ya one and all, and keep ya safe. Until we meet again, fare thee well." Applause rang the rafters of the hall as John smiled down on them all. "Before I sit down now and get back to some serious drinking, I would like my daughter Molly to come forward." Molly looked around her in puzzlement as she made her way to the platform.

"Da," she whispered, "what are you doing? Do you want me to help you back to your seat? Come on da."

John reached down to take her hand as she hopped up onto the stage.

"Now, Molly darlin, bear with me for just a moment," he whispered loudly.

The whole crowd broke into a rhythmic clapping as they chanted, "Molly darlin', Molly darlin', Molly." John reached behind himself where there was a box beautifully wrapped in printed fabric.

"You were too young when your mama died, God rest her soul, to remember much of her, but she left something behind, especially for your. She asked me to give this too you when I thought the time was right. Now is that time. We're leaving Ireland, our home, our people and all our life's memories. The one thing I never want you to forget is your sainted mother. Every time you put this on you will be reminded of her and where you came from." Tears filled his eyes as he handed Molly the box.

Sitting down, she carefully removed the fabric from the package. The box inside had been beautifully crafted. As she opened the lid the scent that arose from the box immediately emitted memories of her mother, long laid to rest. A brilliant emerald green cloak rested within. Black and gold brocade braiding trimmed the hood and the outside edges. As Molly lifted it from it's home of fifteen years, she brought it up to her face smelling and feeling its beauty. Tears streamed down her face and blurred the features of her father. "Oh, da I love you. What more perfect gift could I have as we leave our home. I will always think of mama and Ireland when I wear it. Have no fear; I will never forget Ireland. Ireland runs in our blood, no matter where we be."

Cheers rose as hugs and kisses were mixed with tears and laughter as the party worked its way towards the small hours of the morning. It was to be the last big soiree to grace the Creggan's Miner's Hall for some time to come.

Chapter 8

Northern Ireland and Liverpool, England (1846)

The Belfast dockside teemed with humanity, the noises and smells exciting and terrifying at the same time. Molly's practical nature took over as she followed every movement of her excited family, not wanting to let anyone out of her sight. Other than John O'Connor, the family had never ventured far afield from their home in Creggan. The city of Belfast was new and exciting to them all. The smells of the dock were both fascinating and revolting. Rotting fish, the city's sewage, and un-washed bodies, melded with fresh salt sea air, roasting nuts, and potatoes. Sailors screamed orders from ship decks to workers below them on the docks. Men scurried from dock to ships like rats. Hockers sold their wares to curious passers by, each trying to outdo the other—"Get the best roasted tatties in Ireland. Maybe even better than yer sainted ma's."

Others were crying their farewells to family and loved ones as they prepared to board steamers to Eng-land.

The crew members of the *Princess* unceremoniously shoved and jabbed as they drove their quarry on board. The ship loomed above its soon-to-be passengers like a monster waiting to devour its victims. Fear showed in the eyes of some, excitement in others, but all seemed to portray the fear that they would never see Ireland again as they looked back at the city and the hills beyond.

Four year old Matthew hoisted on his father's shoul-ders, clapped and squealed with delight at the sights around him. Never in his young life had he witnessed such absolute gaiety and confusion.

He continually screamed, "Papa, mama see the big boat. Can we go on the boat? Papa please, can we. Please papa." Liam laughed at his son's exuberance. "Settle down lad or you'll be forgettin where ya be and pissin down me neck."

"Liam, shame on you. Hush with that talk now," Molly giggled. She found the festiveness infectious as they combed the docks enjoying the new experiences. The past days had been a mixture of exhilaration, sadness, uncertainty, fear of the unknown, and melancholy as they prepared for the first leg of their journey to Canada.

*   *   *

They had spent the last months in preparation for this very day. They argued, laughed, dreamed, worried and fretted their way to this first stop on their journey. Molly was the prime organiser and they had spent countless hours meeting and discussing the preparations. There was so much to consider. It was not just a few days jaunt to the countryside but a whole new chapter in their lives and every detail must be considered before their departure. In the beginning there were many disagreements and conflicting ideas, but eventually the details were all worked out to the satisfaction of both families. Of course they knew they were venturing into the unknown and many rumours and stories came to them from the families of those who had already made voyages to other countries. Such stories had to affect their thinking and many were cause for consideration when making their final decisions. Many told of relatives that had been held in quarantine in their ships off the coast of the Americas because of the dreaded cholera and typhus. Others said Canada was not the promised land they were hoping for as employment was difficult to find and the Irish were treated with disdain and considered intruders on the land. Even more elaborate and far-fetched tales were spouted by those who were not leaving their homeland. How much was to be believed and how much was sheer fantasy? It was decided their survival would be dependent on their numbers. Where one or two could not persist, larger groups would have a fighting chance.

Many of their friends and families still could not understand how they could bring themselves to leave their beloved Ireland. They were labelled traitors and heroes alike. Some envied them. Some reviled them. But all respected them for their courage and conviction.

They had left Creggan by horse and cart with one of John's lifelong friends and work mate escorting them on the first leg of their journey to Belfast. Settling them on the dockside with all the possessions they had deemed necessary to take with them, he had wept his farewell as he hugged each and every one of them.

"Molly, don't let any of these silly buggers run astray now. Yer the only level headed one of the bunch far as I can see. They're liable to go off half-cocked so keep them in line now, you hear."

"I will Uncle Paddy," Molly smiled, wiping the salty tears from his weather beaten face. "I shall remind them every day who is the boss. As soon as we arrive in Canada I'll be writing to you and Aunt Sarah with all the news."

"We'll be waitin child. God love ya all and protect ya," he whispered as he brushed her cheek with a kiss.

As the two brave families and their travelling companions stood now and looked up at the *Princess*, a steam packet readying to set out for the port of Liverpool, England, all the doubts and fears of the past months showed in their misted eyes. No one was speaking out loud but Matthew in his innocent glee, though myriads of thoughts were bursting in each of their heads. Tears pooled in their eyes and splashed down cheeks onto trembling chins, the men wiping them off hastily, the women letting them soak their bibs and collars.

It was finally time to board the ship much to the delight of Matthew who was now attempting to scramble down from his father's broad shoulders.

"Stay put lad. I don't want to be losing you before we ever start this journey. Hang on tightly while I get these bags aboard. Then you can run to you heart's content. But always with your ma or me, mind you. Do you hear me Matthew?"

Matthew squealed with delight, "Yes papa, yes papa —can we go now? Can we go on the big boat?"

As they ascended the steamer's gangplank which swayed precariously under the weight of it's passengers, Molly's eyes widened in horror.

"My God, Liam, the Saints preserve me, but I can't go up this thing." Shifting a valise to his already burdened left arm, Liam draped his free arm around Molly's waist and gently guided her aboard the ship.

"It's all right love, it's quite safe. Just hold onto me and put your other hand on the railing. Keep your eyes right ahead and don't look down. You'll be just fine my girl." As the gangplank swayed and vibrated, Molly silently wondered what else they would have to experience on the voyage ahead.

They all gathered on deck to wave farewell to Paddy, whom they knew they would likely never see again. The day was warm and seagulls circled overhead waiting for any morsel of food that may be thrown overboard or dropped on the ship's deck. Matthew's small booted feet pummelled his father's chest as he rode upon his shoulder, his small hands attempting to grab at the diving birds. Though he was a lively, happy little boy, Molly had never seen such unbridled excitement in her young son. His happiness was infectious to those around him as everyone attempted to capture the elusive scavengers. Once the steamer began to leave it's berth, it's passengers once again became subdued as they waved and called their good-byes to their loved one on shore. Liam lowered his son to the deck with Molly holding onto one small hand and himself the other.

As Matthew peered through the railings on the side of the deck he suddenly began to cry in fright "Mama, mama, Uncle Paddy's going away. Why is everyone moving away—he's getting smaller. I can't see him much. I want to go home mama. I want to go home."

Molly held her confused son to her as she sobbed "It's all right my darling, we're just going on a big ride in the boat. Uncle Paddy will be just fine. He has to go home to be with Aunt Sarah. See, he's still there waving to you. The boat is moving away from the dock so we can go to Canada."

Matthew stared at his mother, "But why is everyone crying mama? Even papa cries mama. Are we going far away?" Molly wiped the tears from her little son's round cheeks and kissed them.

"Yes darling, we are going very far away, but you'll always be with papa and me. And remember, papa John is with us, and Uncle Colin and Uncle Sean and Aunt Kathleen. Grandpa Patrick and Grandma Colleen will be staying with us now too and even Uncle Thomas. Our family will always be with us Matthew. So don't be frightened now love—we'll all be together."

With that he wriggled from his mother's arms and

scurried around the deck singing, "We're going on a big boat, we're going on a big boat." Molly laughed with relief at the fickle mood of her trusting young son.

As the last of Ireland faded into the horizon the two families gathered together to decide on arranging their sleeping and eating accommodations. The *Princess* was able to accommodate about 350 people, 150 of which could find cover from the night air, rain and wind. The passage to Liverpool cost ten shillings each for an approximate thirty-hour journey. No matter what the weather the emigrants were outside, especially if there were cattle or pigs on board, which took precedence over the human cargo. It was a well-known fact that the Liverpool Steam Packet Co. had little regard for the Irish, and once their fare was paid there was no concern as to their safety or comfort, whereas, the cattle and other livestock were paid for on delivery. Needless to say, the livestock received preferential treatment while on the voyage.

As the emigrants were told to travel light because they would have to carry their own baggage, very little of their possessions could be brought with them. Many were desperately poor and therefore had very little of value to carry with them, but the O'Connors and Dermitts having always been very resourceful people, were forced to leave behind what had taken them years to accumulate. The bare necessities were put down to food (which they must provide on the packet to Liverpool), cooking utensils, warm clothing, footwear and blankets. As few of them had ever left home before, and yet fewer had ever been to sea, this part of the voyage was to be a miserable lesson to most.

John and his sons scoured the deck looking for as comfortable a resting place as possible for the women and Matthew at least. If they must, the men would remain in the open to brave the elements. Storms could rise quickly on the Irish Sea and they knew their possessions must be tied down securely in order not to lose them overboard. At night they would tie themselves to one another just in case such a squall should overtake them while sleeping. Colin was the first to shout out when he spied a sheltered area amid a lifeboat and it's rigging. Two men had already crawled under to claim the shelter as theirs.

"Here now lads, there are three women and a small child be needing the protection of this dinghy. Come out with us lads and let the bairn be sheltered."

Two sets of black eyes glowered up at Colin and his brothers. "Get out of our space, laddie. First come, first served I say. There's plenty other room for yer women. Now push off or you'll be sorry ya every tangled with the Murphys."

Smiling calmly, Colin slowly raised himself to full height. "Sorry boys—just can't do that now." With lightening speed he kicked one large booted foot out to hook the first man around the ankles pulling his feet out onto the open deck. Sean O'Connor immediately grabbed the ingrate by his heels hauling him out from under the shelter while Thomas Dermitt, Liam's strapping brother, went in after the second man.

When both men were out and dragged to their feet Colin growled into the terrified face of the first while holding him by the collar of his ragged jacket. "Don't ever try to mix with an O'Connor or Dermitt again laddie, especially when it comes to our womenfolk. Understand?" "Now, I offer to you, once again, to join us on deck if you still be caring to." Colin wasn't particularly eager to have these two ruffians join them but he concluded it would be the easiest way to keep an eye on them in order to protect his sister and Matthew whom he adored. "Find yer sister Sean, and tell her that these two kindly gentlemen have graciously offered their shelter for the ladies."

As they settled the women into the sheltered area and draped shawls and blankets up to allow them further privacy, the steamer began to shudder more than usual as it crested the waves that became larger as they headed into the Irish Sea. The old steamer could only travel eight-nine knots per hour and the rolling waves seemed to want to devour her, making her shudder more violently with every attack. The moaning of the ship and the wailing of the passengers that were quickly succumbing to sea sickness permeated the air.

Molly busied herself with her mother-in-law Colleen, preparing a small meal for later on in the day. "I hope this infernal rolling and shuddering stops so we can all enjoy a wee bite soon. We have thirty hours at least ahead of us so we must try to down something."

Colleen was a quiet, rather mousy person who's large eyes were close to tears.

"It's all right love," Kathleen soothed, "I'm sure we'll be just dandy when the wind dies off."

"God help us when we're in the middle of the Atlantic Ocean, if this be any indication. God help us." Coleen whispered. With that they set to preparing the afternoon meal of beef tea, apples, and gingerbread.

The winds steadily increased as the ship's crew threw ropes to those passengers who were not prepared. The women and children were tied to the riggings with blankets and clothes while the men tethered themselves to each other with the ropes. The crew were cruel and either laughed at the suffering or completely ignored them. Their attitude, was that the Irish were ignorant, disorderly, and uncivilised. Their fare was paid and they were on their own. If they washed overboard, what odds? It was no great loss!

The hours passed into the night with the continued cacophony of crying and moaning of the wretchedly sea-sick passengers. Some swore they had never been so sick in all their miserable lives and there was no way out. They lamented leaving their homeland and were certain that the Hand of God was upon them for their treachery against their beloved Ireland.

The O'Connors and the Dermitts were less super-stitious but none-the-less ill. Molly had been prepared with peppermint-soaked sugar lumps to ease the queasiness. She had also brought ether drops which she could administer with water. At the moment, she was envisioning the Atlantic crossing and realising there was the possibility that it could be much worse than the Irish Sea for storms, she chose not to use the precious ether drops for now. Instead she convinced her family to eat dry crackers and tea in small amounts, in order to avoid the horrible dry retching the seasickness caused. It seemed a horrible waste of food and every last one protested but she convinced them it was the best alternative.

They remained huddled together as the ship rolled and pitched, their clothes covered with their own vomit, some losing control of their bladders for the fear of moving. Humiliation and fear welled up in them as even grown men wept and prayed as they had never prayed before. The storm stopped as suddenly as it had begun.

Crew members scoured the decks with sticks and ropes, prodding and cajoling the shaky tethered passengers to their feet. "Get on yer feet ya stinkin lot. Yer worse than the pigs below. Get the stink off ya before ya gets thrown overboard."

Somewhere in their shaky limbs Colin and Liam found the strength to scramble to their feet to light into the ignorant tar. Molly, immediately recognising their intent, screamed, "Colin, Liam no ... do you want us all overboard. We mean nothing to these animals. Leave it be. The only harm's to your pride. Leave it be."

The sailor leeringly looked at Molly, "right smart little lass you are now."

Colin held onto Liam's arms as his eyes blazed with anger. "She's right man, ignore the witless sod—he's only wanting to goad you."

With a deep breath Liam turned his attention back to his wife and son. "Sorry lass, you're right. I doubt this will be the last time we're faced with the likes of him. I best haul in me horns, now hadn't I?" His arm around her he managed a resigned smile.

Within an hour they were wiped down and cleaned up as well as possible. Sean had managed to fill a small bucket with sea water, enough to clean up the worst. Soon they would be coming into the Liverpool harbour where they would find accommodations in order to clean up properly and prepare for boarding a frigate to Canada. Right at this moment no one was looking forward to the next arm of their journey.

Thirty-three hours into the junket, cries came up from some in the crowd as England was spotted in the distance through a haze of yellow fog. Passengers rushed to deck side to see for themselves, the much-anticipated land. As they drew closer to land smaller boats came to greet the *Princess* and escort her up the Mersey and into Liverpool. The docks were lined with steam-packets and the larger sailing vessels they knew were awaiting departure for the USA, Canada and Australia. The past hours forgotten for the time being, they stared in wonder at the teeming port city of Liverpool as it loomed into view.

Albert Dock bustled with people hurrying about their business. Labelled containers of imported cotton, timber, cocoa, coffee, rice, molasses, oil, tobacco, crowned the dockside. Shore workers moved non-stop, clearing areas in preparation for the next cargo of goods to be delivered to Liverpool.

It was time to gather their things and get ready to disembark. Crew members prodded the unsuspecting passengers down the gangplanks and into the hands of swindling porters and runners. The weaker ones were pushed and shoved, often losing hold of their luggage that would immediately be swept up by some unscrupulous worker on the docks, never to be seen again. Witnessing these atrocities from the deck before their departure, gave warning to Molly and her family. Liam hoisted Matthew to his shoulders once again as they descended from the ship into the waiting melee.

"Hold together now as best you can. If we lose one another, we meet in front of the ale house over yonder called the 'Crow and Mast'," Colin cried into the din of noise. Finally on shore they jostled their way to the outskirts of the crowd. Porters and runners yelled into their faces offering accommodation, drink, food, and passage on the sailing ships to their destination of choice.

Matthew, frightened, began to cry. Not being able to see his mother following close behind, his panicked screams joined the rest of the fracas. Making his way out of the worst of the crowds, Liam finally put down his bags and began to take Matthew down from his shoulders. Within a second of his actions, a small being darted around him and picked up a valise.

Realising his mistake too late Liam bellowed at the top of his lungs, "stop that thieving scoundrel, he has my bag." Sean caught the action from the corner of his eye and dropping his load with Liam, took off after the guttersnipe. Within minutes he was back with the youngster in tow. Pulling smartly on the lad's exposed ear, Sean grinned at his brother-in-law as if to show off his trophy. An impudent face sneered up at Liam. His grimy clothes were too small and he wore badly-worn shoes tied to his legs with filthy rags to keep them from falling off as he would attempt to run off with his ill-gotten trophies.

Looking down at him Liam could not help but feel some pity for the lad, because he was just that, a lad. "Well lad, do you want yer ear back? My brother-in-law is partial to young lad's ears you know. Now, maybe we could rectify this situation if you were able to take us to a good, clean boarding house, with an honest landlady. Otherwise, I would imagine you will be visiting the port authorities with one less ear. So, what do you think lad?" Liam smiled beguilingly at the dirty youth.

"Awright, awright, lemme go, lemme go ya big lug. C'mon, I'll take youse to Miz. Flaherty's boarding house. Just lemme go!" Transferring his hold from the urchin's ear to his collar, Sean led the way to find their lodgings. It wasn't an easy feat to keep nine adults, one small child, and numerous satchels and boxes of belongings together, but soon enough they found Mother Flaherty's Boarding House. The urchin was released from Sean's grip and flipped a farthing for his efforts. Stuffing it in his rags he offered a cheeky grin and ran off into the streets, undoubtedly back to the docks before the best action of the day would be lost to him forever.

A rotund, jolly little creature, Mary Flaherty shook her head in dismay as she tried to figure out what she was going to do with ten extra people in her already near-to-cramped house.

"You look like such a bonny family, I can't be leavin you out in the elements now can I? Come in, come in. I'll call my Bridget and we'll make sure we get you all settled. How long you be stayin now?" Once learning they would be sailing to Canada as soon as passage could be arranged, Mary was determined to have them stay and be as comfortable as she could possibly make them for their remaining few days. She had heard the stories from the docks and she knew what lay ahead for this family of her countrymen.

"Thank you missus, we'll be little trouble to you. My family is very grateful for your hospitality." John said as he politely removed his cap. "We'll be leavin as soon as our passage can be arranged."

Mary beamed with approval of this handsome Irish gentleman. "Come then, if you don't mind the crowding, we'll get everyone settled in."

While the women packed away their belongings and prepared unused corners for beds, the men went out to scout and shop for food to prepare dinner.

"Stay out of trouble now, the lot of you. Especially you, our Sean. Kathleen doesn't want to leave for Canada a widow," teased Molly as she waved them out the door. She knew they were good, honest men but could often be hot-headed and impetuous. And this was strange and newly experienced territory to them.

Like a group of excited children they headed back to Albert Dock at the same time taking in the sights and smells of Liverpool. Being a port town it was alive night and day. Strangers continuously came and left. The streets were lined with pubs, their doors open to the streets to tempt the newcomers with the music and raucous laughter inside. Liverpool was the hub of commerce and it teemed with hockers, crimps and touts.

The narrow streets rang with laughter and cat calls "My, what fine handsome lookin lads. Come in loves, let Rosie show youse a bonnie time."

As Colin and Thomas called up flirtations to the scantily-clad ladies in the windows, John turned and playfully cuffed their ears. "On your way, my boyos.

Our Molly will have my head if I lose you now. On with ya now."

The friendly nature of the local 'entrepreneurs' turned to hostility at Goree Piazza where the twenty-two shipbrokers, emigration agents, and provision shops were located. It was strictly business here and outward dislike for the Irish was quite evident in the attitude of the attendants and clerks. The runners for the shipbrokers called 'crimps and touts' were everywhere doing their best to muster up business for their employers. The main occupation for most of them appeared to be pickpockets and thieves. While one talked and poked at a prospective customer, his partners stole what they could get their hands on which was more often than not, a great deal. After delivering the customer to the shipbroker, they vanished into the crowd, carrying with them the customer's intended passage money. Because so few of the emigrants stayed in England, unless they were rendered destitute after their foray with the local thieves, there was little chance of the culprits being caught.

The men spent the rest of the day finding their bearings and decided it was best to rise early the next morning and head for the shipbrokers. While making their rounds that afternoon, they made many inquiries about the shipbrokers, provision houses, and emigration agents. Many people warned them to be careful obtaining provisions as it was well known many houses often provided bad and rotting foods. They learned beyond a doubt that the Irish were hated and the more they could be swindled the better. In most cases they would be travelling to Canada on a sailing vessel with up to as many as 1,000 passengers in steerage. Their fare would cost slightly more than expected in the range of three-four pounds each, and it would take in the neighbourhood of four to seven weeks to cross the Atlantic, depending on the weather conditions.

They also learned of their good fortune in that their young urchin friend had taken them to the most honest woman in town, that of Mary Flaherty and her boarding house. Mary was also to be extremely helpful with her recommendations for their preparation. She liked this family very much and wanted to help them where she could.

Although they slept on cotton ticking, and some on blankets on the floors of Mary's Boarding House, they enjoyed their first night in Liverpool. They were all together and happy and could only talk of what they expected on their arrival in Canada and what they planned for their families when they arrived. They were hopeful and fully optimistic.

Chapter 9

The Atlantic Crossing — 1846

In three days all preparations were underway for the voyage. The men had combed the docks making careful inquiries about the ships available to sail within the next few days. Before setting sail, there was so much to arrange. The emigration agent informed them they must all undergo a medical examination before they would be allowed to leave England. They were then told of the provision shops where food, clothing and other necessities could be purchased for their voyage. Fortunately they had put together many of their needs before they left Ireland because they were soon to learn that these shops would sell poor quality food and drink at the very highest prices.

Mother Flaherty proved to be a generous friend with her suggestions on where to shop and what to provide for ten people over a six or seven week period. Molly and Colleen had already put together sufficient warm sensible clothing such as woollen stockings, cloaks, loose-sleeved shirts, cotton peignoirs, and sensible boots for all. To give them more space to carry food, drink and medical needs, Mrs. Flaherty suggested they all wear layers of clothing until they were settled aboard the ship. The food they prepared was basic and nourishing but of little variety. By law the ship owners were obliged to supply, weekly for each passenger, two and-a-half pounds bread or biscuit, one pound wheaten flour, five pounds oatmeal, two pounds rice, two ounces tea, one half pound sugar and one half pound molasses. Oranges, apples, gingercake and concentrated beef tea, might be provided but in minimal amounts. In metal tins they stored extra molasses, along with cheese, butter, bacon, salted pork, and vinegar. Apples and oranges they carried in sacks. Molly provided peppermint and arrowroot for seasickness but secreted laudanum and ether drops in a pouch attached to the waistband of her skirt.

Before their departure from Ireland Dr. Leary had presented Molly with a satchel filled with the basic needs of a country doctor. He knew they would be put to good and responsible use when Molly reached Canada. He had stocked it with a scalpel, gun-lancet, scissors, curved needles, midwifery forceps, and a trachea tube. He decided that in the future she would likely require an amputating knife and saw, tourniquet, silk for sutures and catheters. His selection of medicines included castor oil, Epsom salts, calomel, laudanum, and Friar's Balsam. The wealth of this wonderful gift from her lifelong friend and mentor convinced her to keep the satchel and its contents well hidden from her fellow travellers outside of her family members. She carried it in a securely locked but common-looking satchel. Other than the peppermint, ether drops and laudanum, which she secured in her belt, she hoped she would have little need for any of the other supplies while on board ship.

The medical examination they were all forced to undergo by the terms of the New Passenger Act, was both humiliating and useless. They were prodded and poked like cattle, by an emigration office appointed doctor, who was either drunk or totally incompetent. Molly suspected both was the case. There was no attempt at cleanliness as person after person subjected themselves to filthy hands jabbing into their mouths after checking heads for lice and other infestations.

As they approached Matthew, Molly drew him back

saying, "I'll open his mouth thank you! And not one of us has a louse or flea to his name, but if you keep up this nonsense, we'll all be dead before we reach Canada. Do you not know the meaning of cleanliness? If one of those people ahead of my family has a contagious disease, we might all have it before the day is out. Your procedures are disgusting and I don't want you touching my family."

The drunken doctor looked at her incredulously. "Shut up ya Irish slut. Who do ya think yer talking to? I'm the doctor here and without my approval you or your family won't get aboard a ship for anywhere *but* Ireland. I'll send ya all back grovelin where ya came from. Now get back in that line where ya belong and shut up until I'm done with ya all."

Laying a calming hand on Liam's raised fist Molly realized her mistake in usurping this man's authority. Without this excuse of an examination they could be refused their passage. Stepping back, she quietly bid her family to carry on while never taking her eyes from those of the doctor's.

"We'll do as the good doctor says, but once he's done we'll all be swilling our mouths out with salts," she said between clenched teeth. The remainder of the examination Molly suffered in seething silence. They were to learn later that the 'doctor' was paid one pound Sterling for every hundred persons inspected. Little wonder they were being herded through like cattle!

Their passage tickets had finally been stamped and they were prepared to board the *Looshtank* when she was ready to set sail. Because there was ten members of this family, funds had been raised and shared equally. The price per fare was four pounds Sterling for the men, three pounds ten shillings for the women, and Matthew to travel steerage. This they agreed upon after great haggling with the passage brokers as they found the prices ranged from three pounds ten shillings to as high as five pounds per person. Steerage, they all agreed, was their only option in order to save sufficient money for their arrival in Canada.

Twenty-four hours before the *Looshtank* was to leave Liverpool harbour, all passengers had the option of going aboard to secure their quarters. The *Looshtank* could accommodate some 450 passengers. Originally built as a cargo vessel to sail the seas of the Orient, she had undergone a transformation to become an emigrant ship. Loose boards were simply laid over the bilge to create temporary flooring. The walls of the ship were lined with roughly-constructed berths about six feet by six feet and layered about two-foot above one another. Each berth was expected to accommodate four people. The centre area was free to hold luggage, bags, trunks, and boxes. There was no security and absolutely no privacy. There was no attempt to segregate single, married, young or old. Ramshackle privies were constructed on the foredeck scuppers, and a cooking area was also designated on deck. By law a seafaring-cook must be provided on ships that held more than 100 people, thus the *Looshtank* provided its own meagre cooking arrangements.

The flood of humanity trying to jostle for their share of area continued to increase as the O'Connors and Dermitts fought their way up the gangplank and down into the hold of the ship. Molly stared in horror as they descended into the dark bowels of the frigate. To keep their family together as much as possible they were forced even farther down and away from the light from the hatches. Deep into steerage they secured a corner where they took possession of three berths.

"Little air we'll be getting in this cave but at least

we'll all be together," John mused as his eyes searched the rafters for a safe place to secure the two lanterns he was packing. Two berths were situated one above the other and the third on the corner. They were later to invite a fragile looking little girl from a large family to share a berth. The family of thirteen was crammed into three shelves, one holding seven children. Liam, Molly, Matthew, and the waif child the family called 'Baby' shared the single berth. Patrick Dermitt, and his wife Colleen agreed to share a berth with Sean and his pregnant wife Kathleen. Colleen wanted to be close to Kathleen, as since their departure she had come to fussing over her and making sure no harm came to her. Kathleen was due to deliver her baby shortly after their scheduled arrival in Canada, but as it was their first child, there was no guarantee when it might arrive. John, Colin, and Thomas shared the shelf above them.

As the women prepared the berths to make them as comfortable as possible, the men arranged the luggage securely in preparation for a possible rough journey ahead. The shelves were already covered with loose straw, and bales of rather musty smelling straw fenced off the centre from the sleeping arrangements.

"It smells worse than an old midden in here," Colleen retorted, wrinkling her nose in disgust.

"I guarantee we aren't the first to pass this way, my love," Patrick said smiling at his wife's fretfulness.

Kerosene lanterns hung from supporting beams casting eerie shadows on the blackened ceiling and the berths around them. The smoke-blackened timbers reminded them that countless thousands of emigrant travelers had already spent weeks being cooped up like animals in this dungeon. Their smells permeated the wooden shelves and floorboards, never to be eradicated.

As more people packed in and claimed their berths

the air was already becoming fetid and stagnant. Unwashed bodies, urine-soaked toddlers, cigar smoke and stale liquor penetrated the air. But the air was also filled with the sound of merriment as fiddles, flutes, and pipes emerged from sacks and trunks. Very little sign of grief was being displayed as the playing, singing, and dancing rose to a feverish pitch. The gaiety was infectious as children squealed, laughed, and danced around the bales of straw. Some of the men and women, who had already imbibed of excessive spirits on shore, were singing raucous songs of farewell to Ireland and England alike.

> Farewell, England! Blessings on thee-
> Stern and niggard as thou art.
> Harshly, mother, thou hast used me,
> And my bread thou hast refused me:
> But tis agony to part

As the great majority had not been treated fairly in their motherland, there was little regret shown on their impending departure. Whatever waited for them in their new land couldn't possibly be as bad as what they were being forced to leave. So it was time to celebrate, sing, be happy, and look to the future.

* * *

Finally, the time had come to depart. Though Molly and her family had no one on the docks to wave farewell to, they were still eager to get one last look at England and their final link to Ireland. Most were already on deck as scarves and hats waved in the salty breeze. Tears now flowed liberally as the emigrants called their farewells. Molly and Liam held onto Matthew who waved to no one in particular but somehow knew this was a very important moment in his young life. Tears filled Molly's eyes as she watched so many friends and loved ones of her fellow shipmates crying their good-byes. "God, be with you." "God's speed." "Write as soon as you land." "Blessings on thee." "Don't be forgettin us now." Greeting after greeting washed over her until the words were one constant blur. Her emotions were so tangled now, all she wanted to do was be away. Get this day of her life over with as quickly as possible.

After what seemed like hours, the *Looshtank* was finally underway, as small steam tug boats attached themselves to her and began to tow her down the Mersey and out into the St. George's Channel. Matthew clapped with glee at the little boats as they bounced alongside the bigger ship.

While traversing the Mersey a roll call and verification of the passenger list was to be performed. But first and foremost a search for stowaways must be conducted. All passengers were assembled on the Quarter Deck while a search was executed throughout the ship. The crew proceeded below deck with poles, hammers and chisels, in the event they should need to break open any suspicious looking chests or barrels. It was not unknown for stowaways to be secreted in barrels of grain or very small children hidden in boxes with holes drilled for air, to hide them away until well out to sea. Any manner of attempts could be made, in order not to have to pay the extra fare.

After stowaways were boarded onto the small tugboats to take them back to shore, the second ceremony, the roll call of the passengers would proceed. A clerk of the passenger-broker, accompanied by the ship's surgeon called for the tickets, assuring all those remaining on board had paid for their passage. As they came forward with their ticket a brief medical inspection was performed on behalf of the captain. This inspection although brief was non-the-less humiliating. Molly was relieved to see the doctor was clean. He seemed competent and was definitely not drunk. These ceremonies would take the time of the ten mile trip down the Mersey. If any stowaways or sick where to be found on board they would be placed on the tugs, freeing the ship to be on her way. Free to sail the St. George's Channel and out into the Atlantic Ocean on its way to delivering its passengers to a new land, a new home.

As it was the month of August, the air was fresh and warm. Many passengers stood at the railings watching as they distanced themselves from the land. Most wanted to put off the descent into the hole that would be their home for the next six weeks or so. Not as long as they could see land were they prepared to budge. The breeze whipped through Molly's glistening red hair as the sun warmed her skin and caused the freckles to pop out across the bridge of her nose.

"You look a picture, Molly. No wonder I love ya so much." Liam slipped his arm around his wife and enjoyed the moment of relative privacy as the ship crested the waves out towards the wide Atlantic. Matthew, seemingly unaffected by the departure, chased around the deck playing 'hide and seek' with his newfound friends.

As if giving the travelers a false sense of well being, the Atlantic behaved relatively well on the first leg of the voyage. The ship rolled and crested the waves with ease. The weather remained sunny and inviting so that most of the daylight hours could be spent on deck. It also enabled the passengers to air bedding and clothing, scrub and disinfect beds and living space. At Molly's insistence and the family's chagrin, they were to wash down daily, on deck, with seawater. Molly was following her belief that the cleaner they kept, the less likely they would be to contact disease. They also walked and exercised daily until nightfall when they were forced below to their berths. Evenings were spent under kerosene lanterns swaying gently from the rafters and support posts. There was always plenty of entertainment, whether it be from dancers as young as four and as old as seventy, or maybe a grand storyteller.

The men often sat smoking, swapping stories or gambling. The occasional argument would break out, but generally nothing serious would come of it. Nerves had not yet become frayed. So far they weren't tired of one another despite the cramped quarters and hours of boredom. All that was yet to come.

*   *   *

When the storm came, it hit with vengeance. They were awakened by one of the crewmembers screaming "storm coming, storm coming. Look lively now. Tie everything down. Take down the lanterns. Step lively now or make this black stinkin hole yer grave."

Groggily everyone arose from their beds. Soon the ship began to roll hard and it was difficult to maintain a footing. Hurriedly they tied down what they could but soon had to abandon their efforts and crawl back to their berths.

As the wind outside howled and the waves crashed against the prow of the ship, many in steerage took to wailing and crying. The hatches had been closed tightly against the elements and the air was becoming even thicker with the smell of spilled chamber pots and vomiting travellers. Clean-up was impossible until the storm subsided and those not yet physically ill huddled in their bunks in fear.

Sean's very pregnant wife Kathleen suffered the constant rolling more so than the rest of her family. Constant retching caused her terrible distress. Molly retrieved dry biscuits and cold tea that Kathleen forced down to control the retching. Colleen held her close, cradling her like a baby. Twinges of pain speared her back as the storm raged on above them.

"Molly, it's too early for her girl. What's going to happen? It's as black as a witch's heart in this hole. She can't be having the babe now. She's too weak from the retching. And what about the babe? It's too soon." Sean's concern lined his handsome face. Molly had already reflected on these very same thoughts.

"Just stay calm Sean. It may very well be false labour because of the stress of retching. If we can keep her as calm as possible it may pass. If not we do the best we can. Either way, don't show her such concern. She has enough to contend with and she needs your strength —now more than ever."

The storm raged through the night. The blackness below deck engulfed them adding to their fear of the storm. They were in the middle of a violent sea and about as secure as a bobbing bottle cork. Momentary lulls in the storm brought some peace until a crashing wave shuddered the hulk of the boat, sending its passengers into fits of crying and screaming once again. Many were certain they were doomed to a watery cold grave and attempted to prepare themselves to meet their Maker.

*   *   *

As the dawn broke, as if by a miracle, so did the storm. The crewmembers threw open the hatches and yelled down at the passengers to get up on deck for head count and to prepare for cleaning up. If there was any sympathy for the condition of the paid passengers, it failed to show in the demeanor of the deck hands. They were blatantly cruel as they scoffed and laughed at the condition of their human cargo. They had seen it too many times to waste their feelings on the likes of these pathetic creatures, Irish and English alike.

They had survived the first of many storms to come over the next few weeks. Their time was spent cleaning and scouring their living area, washing bedding and clothes. As with everything, experience helped in planning for the next event. But nothing could help prepare them for the terrible seasickness that would befall almost every last passenger when these terrible storms hit. Some lasted hours, others lasted for days. It was human misery at its worst when day upon day they were forced to lie in their own waste and vomit. Often many were too weak to clean up after themselves and their families, but the stronger ones did their best to pitch in and help. Some had been injured by flying boxes and barrels. Broken bones were set by the ship's surgeon. Molly and others helped where they could after tending to themselves and their own families first. The doctor's tools Molly had in her satchel were already being put to good use.

Each fine day Molly had her family sluice down with salt water on deck. The fresh water provided for each passenger by the shipping company did not provide for washing clothing so they scrubbed their clothing in sea water as best they could and used the reserved washing water to help rinse the salt from their skin and clothes. Molly knew the salt water was medicinal and would help ward off infection or disease. Many of the other passengers followed their lead. If nothing else, it helped to take their minds off their misery.

It was awe-inspiring to stand on the deck with the

sun beating down on them, looking out over the vast horizon to see nothing but mile upon mile of rolling sea.

"Somewhere out there is Canada, Molly darlin. Somewhere out there is our new home." Liam's voice was soft as if he feared by speaking too loudly they would be doomed to remain on this vast and unpredictable ocean.

Twenty-three days into the voyage, Molly awoke one morning to Matthew quietly sobbing and moaning by her side. Cuddling him into her body, she murmured to him as he irritably rubbed his legs and abdomen. He had been suffering from bouts of vomiting and diahrrea for the last couple of days and was becoming more and more lethargic. This morning he was disoriented and seemed to be suffering from pain he was trying to rub away.

"Liam, wake up, wake up. I'm worried about Matthew. He seems to be getting worse. I think it's more than stomach upset. Get the doctor. I want him to look at Matthew now." Not wanting to alarm Liam unduly she hesitated to tell him her suspicions—but she had seen it all before. She feared it was Cholera. Many around them had been experiencing similar symptoms as Matthew for days now. Now the pain he exhibited in his arms and legs seemed to confirm her worst fears.

Liam arrived with the ship's surgeon in short time and within minutes he confirmed Molly's misgivings.

"All right, young lady, you have your hands full now. First prepare a mustard poultice and keep it over the lad's stomach and liver. Keep him as warm as possible, regardless of his protests. We'll give him laudanum now to curtail the diarrhoea. As he settles down give him a mixture of powdered rhubarb, peppermint, and carbonate of potassa," the doctor instructed brusquely. Then adding quietly, "your son has cholera."

"I have most of these things with me doctor, but for

the carbonate of potassa."

The doctor stared at her in disbelief.

"I nurse, and the doctor from my home provided me with a good supply of medications" she explained.

"Then I hope you might find the time to help me, as I would say your young son is not the only cholera victim aboard. We have a lot of work on our hands. There's near to 450 passengers on board and I don't want to see our floating home turn into a coffin ship. Now, let's not alarm the others, but I will insist on an inspection of each and every passenger. Tend to your young lad while I make the arrangements for the inspection. If your good husband would care to come with me I will give him a supply of carbonate of potassa." With that, he turned on his heel and hurried from the airless dungeon.

The young child called 'Baby' who shared the berth of the O'Connors had been showing the same symptoms as Matthew. In fact many of the children were showing its signs. Molly explained to 'Baby's' family as calmly as possible what was occurring and they agreed that 'Baby' should be left with the O'Connors to be cared for by Molly and her family. Apart from her concern for Matthew, her next greatest concern was for Kathleen and her unborn child. She must be isolated from them wherever possible.

*   *   *

Over the following weeks, Molly shared her time between her family and helping the doctor with other passengers. She explained to families the importance of cleanliness and keeping chamber pots empty and as clean as possible.

"Those of you who can, must use the privies at all

times." Those that would listen followed her orders to clean off daily with seawater and to wash and change bedding as often as possible and immediately if it became soiled. When the weather allowed, hundreds of people were seen daily, sluicing themselves down with cold ocean water. The decks shone from the continuous scrubbing of soiled bedding and clothes. The privies had continuous line ups and many were to be seen with heads hanging over the deck rails whenever the winds were calm and the rains subsided.

Still more became ill with the cholera. Some of the older and weaker died but more survived than the ship's surgeon would have ever dared to hope for. He was amazed at the strength of this young woman who spent hours by his side. When he felt himself on the brink of exhaustion, Molly just seemed to be thriving. After several years on emigrant ships he found himself calloused to the lives and deaths of his charges. After all, they were nothing but ignorant emigrants. They'd given up on one life. How could they expect to succeed at another? At least until now that's how he felt. Now he saw how one person could put hope into the lives of others. Most were glad to follow orders once they knew what to do. Death was not their choice. They just needed to know how to fight it. And fight it they did!

Chapter 10

Miramishi, New Brunswick, Canada (1846)

By the time the *Looshtank* was three days from sailing into Miramishi, New Brunswick, Canada, sixteen lives had been lost to the cholera and forty-one patients were still recovering. No new cases had appeared in well over a week and the worst was considered over. Sixteen lives had been lost and one life was about to be brought into the world. On this third night from shore, Sean and Kathleen's new bairn was to announce his arrival into the world with the lustiest of tones. When Doctor Findlay was notified of the impending birth, he hastened to visit the captain and ask for special permission to bring the mother-to-be to his private quarters.

"After all Molly Dermitt and her family have done to bring this ship through the cholera epidemic, I find it only fitting that we should offer comfortable accommodation for her sister-in-law through her birthing."

"Quite right, quite right Findlay," Captain Morgan agreed. Over the years he had become jaded in his dealings with his migrant passengers, but he also knew the cholera situation probably would have been much worse if Molly and her family had not been aboard. "Have her brought up immediately. Anything Mrs. O'Connor may need will be provided."

Kathleen, although terribly exhausted and weakened from the long journey, was a hardy lass and fared well with the labour and birth. The change of scenery appeared to lift her spirits and give her the extra strength she needed to withstand the twenty hours of labour before Michael Colin John O'Connor was born. They had left Ireland as ten and would arrive in Canada eleven.

The arrival of baby Michael helped to ease the pain of many who had lost loved ones over the past weeks as his hearty cries travelled the breadth of the ship. He was lavished with gifts from many on board including Captain Morgan and the doctor. He was the shining light of hope after the past weeks of misery. The emigrant families saw him as a positive omen for what was to come in this new land.

*   *   *

Excitement had been growing over the past few days as it was announced they were close to their destination. They began to count down the hours and although all were weak and tired, the sound of music began to rise once again from the depths of the ship in the evenings. People began to smile again and complaining subsided as they anticipated the sight of land, the smell of grass, the feel of warm sod in newly planted gardens. Their dreams are what kept most of them going through the difficult times and now those dreams were to be realized.

"Land ahead. Land off starboard." The cry pierced the ship like a knife sending a wave of humanity scrambling to the deck above. Tears flowed unabashedly as they looked upon the foggy banks of New Found Land. Enormous craggy rocks topped with stunted jack pine and birch trees jutted out from the fog-blanketed shore greeting the weary travellers after their long arduous journey. As bleak and untouchable as this land appeared it evoked cheers of joy from the ship's crew and passengers alike. New Found Land was an English colony that lay within view of the shores of Canada. Very soon off the port side most would be resting their eyes for the first time on the country of their dreams.

Many remained on deck through the long chilly nights as they made their way through the eastern doorway of this vast country, into the Cabot Strait and up into the Gulf of St. Lawrence. Once they set their eyes on land, many were loath to chance missing their first glimpse of Canada. As they left the rocky shores of New Found Land behind, the cliffs of Nova Scotia loomed into sight off the port side and the Magdalen Islands to the starboard. The fog was a constant companion, often blanketing over the land they so wished to see. The miles of sandy beaches of Prince Edward Island looked like a paradise. The forests of New Brunswick appeared wild and uninviting. Finally they made their way into Miramishi Bay and began to spot signs of habitation. They envisioned, within hours, setting foot on the solid ground of their new homeland, Canada.

The approach into Miramichi was at first exciting as the passengers waved and shouted at other deep-sea vessels they passed in the bay. But the response from each was a deathly silence. Figuring the ships were empty and waiting off shore to load various cargo the emigrants looked ahead for the signs of people on the shores. As they eagerly watched, a steam tug coming towards the prow of the ship, signalled to the ship's captain to weigh anchor. Those on deck cheered the seaman on as he climbed aboard. To their amazement, as he reached the deck, he levelled a pistol at them, and warned them to back away from him. In astonishment they watched as he approached Captain Morgan. After a few brief words, the captain showed him into his cabin where they presumably continued their conversation. Confused and disappointed the people began to speculate on this unexpected behaviour from what they considered was a port official. All warily watched and waited for the captain's door to open.

"What do you think of that, lad?" John asked of Liam. "I never expected we'd be greeted with firearms. What do you make of it?"

Frowning in reply Liam mused, "can't say as I know. Can't say as I like it either. We've come thousands of miles to be treated like criminals."

All eyes were on the captain's cabin door. Few words were spoken in the stunned silence. Within minutes the door opened as the captain ushered the port official past the hundreds of eyes looking on in disbelief. When they finally found their voices, a cacophony of questions battered the captain.

Putting up his hands in an attempt to silence them, he ordered, "in ten minutes have everyone on deck. I have an important announcement to make." Taking a deep breath, he turned and walked back into his cabin, calling his first mate and the ship's surgeon behind him.

Speculations ran rampid until fifteen minutes later the doctor and captain met them on the deck. Moistening his lips he surveyed his charges. "The news I have for you today is not good, but we must also look upon ourselves as fortunate under the circumstances. The ships you see in the bay are quarantine ships. They are filled with typhus, which as you well know, is a very contagious disease. We have been ordered by the port authorities of New Brunswick to remain on board until the ship and all our passengers and crew are inspected. Dr. Findlay has explained to the gentleman who was just on board that we have no typhus cases on board, but naturally the authorities want to make perfectly sure we are not a threat to the citizens of New Brunswick. Because of the problem at hand, we may be forced to wait for some days before the inspection can be made to their satisfaction."

Cries rose from the disappointed faces looking on.

"I understand your disappointment. Believe me, I want to be off this ship as much as the rest of you, but we are forced to stay a while longer and we must make the best of it."

These last words brought a hue and cry from the assembled passengers. They had battled for six weeks to reach Canada, and now they were forbidden to go ashore. Sympathy showed in the eyes of Dr. Findlay. He had come to like many of these souls looking up at him from the deck. He had even found himself hoping they would find happiness and prosperity in their newly found home. "Please, please, bear with us. It won't be for long. A few more days and your new life will begin. We have no typhus on our ship and those of you who are still recuperating from the cholera are no longer contagious. Once the port authorities are convinced of this we will be free to go ashore," Captain Morgan iterated. "Now, we must spend our remaining time scrubbing and cleaning this ship until she shines. Let them find no possible excuse to quarantine us. I know you want to be off this ship as soon as possible. So, can we do everything possible to assure this happens?"

Although anger and disappointment was still boiling up in the crowd, most of the heads nodded in agreement as they shared comments with their neighbours. Most realised they had little choice and must make the best of a bad situation.

As the throng of passengers disassembled to make their way back to carry on with the daily routine, Molly heard her name being called.

"Molly Dermitt, ma'am, the captain requests the company of you and your man. Please join Captain

Morgan and Dr. Findlay in the captain's quarters as soon as possible." With that the first mate turned on his heel and left.

In bewilderment Molly turned Matthew over to Colleen and gesturing to Liam, led the way to the captain's cabin. After a brusque greeting at the cabin door, they were invited in to confer with Captain Morgan, Dr. Findlay, and the first mate.

"Thank you both for coming," welcomed the captain, as he offered them both a seat. "As you are undoubtedly aware, we could be looking at a very explosive situation here. You and your travelling mates have endured much on this voyage and I fear if the situation is not handled properly we could be facing a mutiny. It is rather inhumane of us to expect everyone here to accept what has been thrown at them so suddenly. It could be virtually weeks before we are allowed to set foot on land. We could attempt to make for another port, but I would be willing to hazard a guess, we would not be allowed entry anywhere on the Canadian coast." Captain Morgan paused, giving them both time to digest what he was saying.

"You're saying we are to remain on this ship until further notice from the port authorities?" Liam asked incredulously. "But there's many a hothead below that would jump ship at the slightest opportunity. How are you going to handle the likes of them?"

"I was hoping I could count on you and your good wife, to help me convince these people, that what we are being forced to do is in their best interest," the captain said as he massaged his aching temples. "If anyone was to jump ship they would be taking their lives in their hands. The port is guarding these ships night and day. They have been instructed to shoot first and ask questions later if anyone should be found in the waters between ship and land. They are not willing to take chances of disease infiltrating their communities. I honestly can't say as I blame them, can you?"

"What do you want of us captain?" Molly interjected. "What do you suppose we can do that you can not?"

"Over these past weeks, the people on this ship have looked up to you with respect as you've helped them through what is likely one of the worst nightmares many of them have ever experienced. Being sick on land is one thing. But sickness on the sea when you're battling storms as well is a living hell, as you can attest to. These people have come through the storms and the cholera much better than most I've been privy to see. By helping them, you have given them courage to go on. Well, now they must demonstrate that courage once again. We must keep them busy. Give them activities to keep their minds off the delay for as long as possible. The men will be the most difficult as the women always have the needs of their families to take up their time. We will have to recognise the troublemakers quickly and squelch them. That's where you and your family can be the most helpful Mr. Dermitt. You have lived in close proximity with all these people for six weeks now. You know them better than any of us. Can we organize activities to keep these men busy? Make them feel they are being useful. Keep them from rabble rousing. We will also order extra rations and I will do my best to have a variety of fresh foods and beverages brought on board regularly. If anyone can think of anything else I can do, speak up. I will do what is in my power to make this wait as painless as possible. Now, what do you say to these plans? Can we do it?" the captain scanned the faces in his office as he rested his chin on his clasped fists.

"We don't exactly have a choice now do we?" Liam

frowned.

"No sir, we don't," whispered the captain.

"Then let's get on with it." Liam said, as taking Molly's arm he turned to leave.

Chapter 11

Miramishi, New Brunswick, Canada (1846)

The days following the visit from the port official, proved to be as trying in some respects as the battle of the cholera. Now there was a boat full of relatively healthy but very weary, bored and frustrated people within sight of the new land they wanted to call home. Emotions ran high. Arguments and fights broke out for the slightest cause. The first day, every man, woman and child was kept busy disinfecting, scrubbing, and polishing every inch of the ship. With instruction from the captain, the crew was given the supervisory duties and ordered to instruct the passengers with patience and respect. Conflict between the crew and the passengers would be definitely detrimental while emotions were running so high.

Each day a port official came aboard to report to the captain and receive any requests he may have. Within two days, Captain Morgan was successful in having fresh fruit, vegetables and meat brought on board. Oranges and other fruits were a luxury now and helped momentarily to calm the frayed nerves of those aboard. Beautiful meaty stews were prepared by the women and the constant aromas blanketed the ship.

By the fourth day, port medical officers were brought on board to perform thorough medical examinations and peruse the medical records of each traveller. For the over 400 passengers, the process was slow and frustrating. Many complained bitterly, especially those who had not contracted the cholera. A few tried to refuse, possibly attempting to hide other concealed ailments. But in the end, each and every passenger and crew member was thoroughly probed and inspected to the satisfaction of the medical officers. There was no typhus found, only some lingering effects of the cholera, the beginnings of some scabies and other more minor skin ailments common to passengers on long voyages. Malnutrition was always a concern to many of the immigrants but not being a threat to their new countrymen, tended to be overlooked.

Within days, a report of the medical officer's findings was presented to the captain. At the same time, he was informed it would be a few more days before they would be prepared to accept these immigrants into their port. He was to find out that they would be put into quarantine camps on land where they would again undergo more medical examinations and tests.

Again Captain Morgan and the ship surgeon called on Molly and Liam to inform them of the latest decisions of the Canadian officials. "Personally, I don't believe the quarantining should be mentioned to the other passengers as of yet. I don't want them unduly alarmed. They will need to know before their departure, which will hopefully be soon. But as for now, we should concentrate on making sure we keep everyone as calm as possible. I plan on telling them the results of the medical examinations and explaining to them the delay while the port prepares to receive them through Immigration. We could give a farewell soiree for the final evening. Give them something to plan for. What do you say?" the captain ended as he motioned for them to speak.

Molly and Liam were still stunned by the news of the extended quarantine on land. Both attempted to mumble a reply but seemed at a loss for words.

Sympathetically the captain continued. "I know this

must come as a shock to you both, but it is common routine, especially at this time when so many diseased emigrants are attempting to enter the country. The Canadian authorities must be most careful. As you know typhus can run rampid and eventually kill thousands. So they must ascertain the good health of each and every one before allowing them entrance to the community. You do understand? You of all people Molly, must see the wisdom behind their laws. It is for the emigrants protection as well as every one else.

"Of course captain. We're just very disappointed I suppose. It has been so long since we have felt the welcome earth beneath our feet. We are just anxious to be a part of this country." Molly wiped the trace of a tear from her saddened eyes. "We'll continue to do what we can, captain. But the longer this carries on, the harder it will be to keep my countrymen content." Liam admitted. "Their patience has been tried for weeks now and they just want to get on with their lives."

In the cool of the evening, Molly and Liam took what little time they could find for themselves to stroll the deck arm in arm. "We've made it this far my darlin'. We have to believe the best is ahead of us. As uninviting as it seems right now, this *will* be our new home. We will find our dreams, for ourselves and our family. You will become a healer to be reckoned with. I will be the biggest sawmill owner in the country and our children will be strong and healthy and happy." Liam's chest puffed with pride as he anticipated their children to come. "Nothing will stand in our way, my beautiful Irish colleen." As he wrapped her in the emerald cloak, she felt the warmth penetrate her weary body, giving her both strength and hope for the future. No matter what obstacles they may encounter, the future was theirs to claim.

Gathering the cloak tightly around Molly he enfolded her in his solid arms and together they silently watched the winking lights on the shore beacon to them in the quiet evening. One day, light would shine from their own home somewhere in this vast country to welcome and offer solace to all that entered.

Just the beginning.

Book Two

Chapter 1

Miramichi, New Brunswick, Canada – 1846

The wall of fog lifted like the veil of a virgin bride, exposing the beauty of the land and taking with it the dull, heavy feeling of the morning. Each day hundreds of anxious travellers had waited on the open deck of the *Looshtank* in hopes that someone would come to free them from their floating prison. The weather remained pleasant as the first signs of autumn changed the landscape. Among the rich green colours on the shore, golds and reds fought their way to the surface of the Great Painter's masterpiece. Each morning the canvas changed before their eyes.

Passengers and crew remained in relatively good spirits despite their confinement. They ate well of the fresh produce brought daily from shore and the lingering affects of the cholera was dwindling as those affected gained back their strength. They prayed for release to freedom before more disagreeable weather was upon them.

The children flourished with healthy glows as they continuously flooded the deck with their singsong games, squeals of glee when catching an adversary at the games of tag or hide and seek. The odd child was found fast asleep in the most unbelievable places while hiding from his playmates. The ship's musicians met to reminisce and draw forth their more pleasant memories of Ireland as they played the lively tunes and encouraged their friends to dance and sing. The music came from deep within, the very heart of their Irish souls. The eerie quiet of the ships moored around them was unsettling to the travellers. They were not told if these ships were emptied of their passengers or to what degree they were diseased. The comings and goings of port officials led all to believe that life still existed on these floating homes, but to what degree they did not care to speculate. Just knowing the *Looshtank* was now healthy gave them hope, but for how long?

As they longed to just set their feet on dry land and smell the soil so close at hand, the tenth day of their forced confinement brought a much-needed reprieve. As a small craft neared their ship it was noticed there were four passengers instead of the usual two who normally transported the fresh food and water on board. Immediate speculations arose among the passengers and crew. A change in routine signaled the possibility of changes to come. After boarding the ship and being led off to the Captain's quarters, Molly and Liam were also summoned.

"Well you can be sure two of them are doctors by the paraphernalia they carry. I suppose we'll be requested to prepare everyone for yet another examination," lamented Liam.

As they made their way up the deck, their fellow countrymen plied them with pleas to get them released from their forced imprisonment. Some uttered empty threats extolling Canada as a cruel prison master, while knowing their fate was not due to Canada's actions. At this point, frustration beat down common sense.

As Molly and Liam approached the captain's cramped quarters the new visitors hugged the walls to allow them entry.

"Gentlemen, I would like to introduce you to the two people on this ship who are the main reason we are now in such a healthy situation. Molly and Liam Dermitt, of

County Tyrone. Molly is a healer and has been the primary reason for our success to which our good doctor has attested."

Doctor Findlay nodded heartily and smiled towards Molly and Liam. "Quite right, captain. If not for this fine lady and her patient husband, this ship would likely have been condemned to the deep." Continuing, the captain explained, "Molly's techniques have decidedly eased those who fell ill with the cholera and prevented an alarming spread of the infection. Liam's gentle but commanding nature, convinced the great majority to follow Molly's path and to keep the peace as much as possible. That, gentlemen, is no mean feat among four-hundred confined people with the threat of a deadly disease hanging over their heads.

"My name is Dr. Ian Langley, Mrs. Dermitt, Mr. Dermitt," the tallest offered as he shook their hands. "The other ships you see on our shores, did not fare so well as the *Looshtank*. Without the benefit of sensible care, they have become death ships. Doctor Cormack, here," introducing his portly, gentlemanly looking companion, "has been in charge of these ships; visiting them daily. None of them are yet disease-free. He is doing the very best he can, but without help his task is most daunting."

"As quickly as we can," Dr. Cormack added, "we transport the least sick to our quarantine stations, where Dr. Langley and his staff continue their care. Many, never set foot on land, never see their new home."

"We are continuously erecting new stations, but it isn't always easy to convince the Government of Canada to release more and more funds for such structures and of course enough qualified medical people are always hard to come by. To exacerbate the situation, the American government is diverting the ships carrying cholera and typhoid from their intended ports of entry in the United States, on to Canadian ports. New Brunswick, Nova Scotia, and Québec already have all quarantine stations filled to overflowing."

Seeing the frustration rising in his colleague, Dr. Langley continued. "Captain Morgan and Dr. Findlay have nothing but the highest regard for you and your family. I understand this may not be what you had in mind upon your arrival in Canada, but we are in desperate need of your services. We offer suitable accommodation for you and your family for as long as you can stay. You will be well paid. It may just allow you to establish yourself in our country. Will you consider our offer?"

"Your offer?" Molly asked incredulously. "I don't quite understand. You're offering us work with your quarantine station? Just what would we be doing? You know very little about my husband and me. As far as my medical experience is concerned, how would you be knowing just what I'm capable of doing?"

"Mrs. Dermitt, I again admit to you, we are in a desperate situation here. But, rest assured, I would never consider hiring you, but for the recommendation of Dr. Findlay. He and the captain have witnessed your expertise and sensibility for many weeks now. What better environment to prove your ability and worth? I trust these honourable men, enough to place my patients' care in your capable hands. It's as simple as that. The proof is in the pudding, so to speak. That said, what do you say to our proposal?"

"I'm very flattered by your offer Dr. Langley, but I must admit my past experience doesn't include many epidemics." Thinking for a moment, Molly continued. "Then again, I can think of no better way to gain such valuable experience."

"Wonderful lass, wonderful," Dr. Langley smiled. "You'll prove your worth ten times over, I'm sure. And the experience you'll gain will benefit you and your whole family."

"I'm sure you're right Dr. Langley, but this must first be discussed with our families before we make such a decision. I agree, working with the doctors in the quarantine stations will be more than I could have hoped for on our arrival, but you also must see the risk we are taking exposing our families to these highly contagious diseases every day. The standards and procedures we apply aboard this ship must continue to be practised where I work. I will accept the position only on your agreement Dr. Langley that these standards will be upheld and my family will be housed well away from the quarantine area."

Reaching for Molly's hand, both Dr. Langley and Dr. Cormack nodded their approval. "Good luck then. I'm sure your family will see how important this will be to the Canadian community and in the end how beneficial it will prove to be for your whole family."

In little more than two hours the decision had been made by Molly and Liam's family to accept the offer of the Canadian port authorities and doctors of Miramichi. Explanations and farewells were made with haste but no less feelings of some regret and sadness to be leaving so many friends behind. Molly hastily explained where they would be going and what they would be doing. They bid tearful farewells and promised to do what they could to speed the release of the others from the *Looshtank.*

*   *   *

Following the tearful farewell to their many comrades of nearly seven weeks the Dermitts and O'Connells congregated on deck with their well-wishers surrounding them. Matthew bounced once again on his father's shoulders as the family lowered themselves into the awaiting boat to take them into the town of Cornwall in Miramichi Bay. They were finally making their way off the ship and onto the long awaited shore. This was not what they had dreamed of for months but at least they were finally making a move in the right direction. The blessing of it was, they were all together with yet one more added to their numbers. Michael was wrapped close to his mother Kathleen's breast as the boat gently rocked its way to their new home.

The sea rose in strong and sparkling waves before them. Sewage didn't litter the approaching waterway as it had in Liverpool. The water sparkled, reflecting the clouds and trees on the shoreline.

"Oh, Liam, will you look at that." Molly's eyes widened at the scene before them. "It's so incredibly beautiful here. The leaves on the trees are changing to so many lovely colours. They're so close to the shore you can see the colours in the water. And the smell, oh Lord the sweet smell."

As the boat propelled its way toward the shore, its prow slapped against the briny water, the gentle sound lulling young Matthew to sleep in his father's arms. "I hope life will always be this peaceful for you, my little lad," Liam whispered into his son's shock of auburn hair. His free arm draped around Molly, pulling her closer. He felt at peace, knowing his family was safe around him. "Let us pray life will be less harsh than that we've left behind Molly darlin'."

The dockside of Chatham was a hubbub of activity. Although a small township compared to Belfast or Liverpool, everyone seemed to be doing something. Running here and there, shouting, greeting, laughing, arguing, swearing, the men looked hardened and healthy for the most part. The women appeared sun-drenched and hardy as they greeted the passengers while they disembarked from their small rocking boat. Matthew awoke as he was handed up to a strong set of arms waiting on the dock. In his bewilderment he began to cry looking back over his shoulder in fear his mother and father wouldn't be behind him. "There, there, young lad" a voice attached to the enfolding arms soothed him, "mama and papa are right behind you. Let's you and I help mama out of the boat now." Matthew began to laugh as the fragile boat rocked and his mother stumbled on all fours to reach the steadier surface of the dock. Liam grabbed his almost hysterical wife by the oxters and was attempting to lift her up as the boat was threatening to dump its whole cargo into the black, salty water so near at hand. Matthew squealed with glee, Kathleen resorted to tears as she squeezed Michael to her breast, John, Colin, and Liam balanced precariously as the craft rolled and shuddered under their amateurish attempts to remove their families and themselves from the boat.

Finally a commanding voice bellowed, "for God's sake, sit you down, before you have us all turned into fish food." The red-faced port official talked on until calm prevailed. "Now, let's proceed properly and with caution. My wife is waiting at home for me, with a wonderfully prepared meal, and I surely don't want to disappoint her."

Eventually, the wharf filled with the passengers and their belongings. John escorted the women and children to dry land, while Colin, Liam, and Sean gathered their possessions and lumbered along behind them. Throwing what little dignity they had left aside, they all proceeded to stretch out on the first patch of sweet-smelling grass they could find and dissolved into fits of laughter. Tears of sheer joy ran down their faces as they realized they had finally reached their dreamed of destination. A new and exciting era was about to begin for the O'Connells and the Dermitts.

Chapter 2

Chatham, Miramichi, NewBrunswick, Canada—1846

"Until your new home is comfortable and ready for you all, we will have you stay at the Chatham Inn," Dr. Langley offered, as he hefted valises and boxes up the uncobbled street and onto the board walk surrounding the Chatham Inn. "Few homes here are what you would call luxurious but I'm sure with the female touch yours can be made very accommodating. I have instructed Mrs. Kerry, the innkeeper to supply you with as much hot water as you find necessary. She can be a stingy one that, but she really carries her heart in her pocket. If she likes you, she'll give you the world if she can."

Pushing his way through the rough-hewn doorway to the inn, he turned to greet Mrs. Kerry as she bustled towards them, her grey muslin dress sweeping the floor. Her brisk step belied her huge girth. Ample breasts and hips bounced as she made her way along the entrance hall towards her guests. "Lord love me, you didn't warn me I'd be entertaining half of Ireland now did you Robert?" she grinned up at Dr. Langley in the most flirtatious way.

"Ah, come now Cora, it'll bring out the mother hen in you for sure. You'll love every minute of it, I'm sure of that." With that he unburdened Michael from the protective hold of his mother and promptly handed him over to Mrs. Kerry who proceeded to coo and sing to the wee lad as he emitted the first smile of his young life. Any remaining concern and tension was released as she led her brood into the parlour and at the same time instructed a young lad of about fourteen to remove the luggage to the rooms she had designated for her guests. "Put the belongings in the rooms on the second floor, Kevin, but not near Mr. Grady's room, mind you. If he comes out and asks what's going on, tell him I said it's none of his business. He'll find out soon enough." "Nosy old beggar he is," she said as she rocked Michael on her bosom, "but a good tenant. He won't be bothering you. I'll see to that."

"Now lad, what's your name?" she asked, turning to Matthew as she handed Michael back to his mother. Matthew buried his face in his mother's skirts. "You can call me Aunt Cora if you like. And Aunt Cora always has fresh spice biscuits in her kitchen for little boys that might like some."

With one eye exposed from the folds of his mother's skirt, a small voiced whispered, "Michael John Dermitt is my name," and the eye immediately vanished again.

"Well, Michael John Dermitt, you and your mother come with Aunt Cora and we'll see what we can find for a fine little boy such as yourself." With that, she made her way down the hall to the kitchen where delicious aromas wafted through the entranceway. Mother and son followed in her wake, expectant smiles upon both their faces.

After a palate pleasing meal of Irish stew and steaming hot homemade bread, for which the good Mrs. Kerry was famous, the family made its way upstairs to settle themselves and soak in much needed baths. Kevin was kept busy toting hot water for what seemed like hours as the family scrubbed one another until their skin tingled and shone pink. When the men finished, they helped Kevin refill the bath time after time, until all were done and they sank into their mattressed beds with clean white linen supplied by the good Mrs. Kerry. Blessed silence prevailed until dawn broke and Michael heralded the

new day with gusty wails from his makeshift dresser-
drawer bed. It was the first night since his birth some
weeks ago that he had not slept at his mother's breast
through the night. He had slept peacefully, swaddled in
fresh warm wrappings until morning broke. Kathleen
hurried to his side and offered him her breast as she
removed his wet coverings, but by the time she settled
him down everyone was awake and anxious to face their
first full day in their new homeland.

By the time they made their way downstairs to enjoy
the tempting smells of the breakfast Mrs. Kelly had prepared, the good Doctor Langley was seated, devouring
his own huge plate of ham, eggs, fried bread, and potatoes. "I'm usually long gone to the hospital by now but
I wanted to let you rest as long as you could, your first
morning." It was barely 7:00 a.m. but Dr. Langley was
usually on the job by 6:00 a.m. and rarely finished by
midnight most days. Most nights, in fact, he spent at the
station, as exhaustion would overtake him.

While they relished their second meal prepared by
the obviously capable Mrs. Kerry, Dr. Cormack came to
join them and Dr. Langley. They proceeded to describe
the conditions at the quarantine station and their frustrations with the lack of capable help the government
sent them. "It is difficult to admonish the government
that has been forced into a very serious situation. With
the American government refusing to permit diseased
ships to dock in their harbours, where else can they go?
They know if they send them up to Canada we can not
refuse and turn them out to sea. Many, many immigrants
are dying because of the lack of proper care but at least
we are able to save the stronger ones. The conditions of
most stations are horrendous because of crowding and
lack of proper sanitation, but what can we do? If we
don't quarantine, the sick will wander out into the coun-

try and die. But before they die, they spread the cholera and typhoid throughout the land. Are we prepared to let this happen? Most people have no idea how desperate we are here in New Brunswick and now up into Québec. There are stations on islands throughout the St. Lawrence Seaway, one of the largest being Grosse Isle, operated by a very capable and compassionate doctor by the name of George Douglas. The hospitals are little more than shacks with little or no sanitation. Most caregivers are unqualified but willing. Doctors, nurses, nuns, and priests work until they are bone weary and generally fall to the illness themselves and die. I'm compelled to tell you all this because it would not be fair of me to expect your help and you not know what you're facing. I sincerely hope you won't be scared off, but if you decide not to stay with us I will understand, believe me." Dr. Langley finished with a weak smile, then rose to leave. "I'll leave you to settle yourself in and discuss your future. When I return this evening we will take you to your new home if you decide to remain and help at the station." He bowed to each of them and left them to their thoughts.

A deafening silence descended over the little group as they looked to one another for an answer to their dilemma. Finally Liam's father Patrick spoke up. "Molly, lass, you and Liam are basically responsible for us all arriving on these shores, safe and sound. You are the one that will be most at risk, along with those among us who wish to work in the quarantine station. For that reason, you must decide for yourself what you want to do. I for one will respect your decision. These are our countrymen you will be helping and that be a hard one to turn your back on."

"I agree lass," Colleen added. "We'll be behind you all the way."

With that, everyone started to talk at once. All agreed, with the precautions Molly and Liam would take when returning to their homes and families. Molly outlined the safeguards they must all adhere to, in order to keep the families safe and healthy. Their future was being set out around Cora Kelly's breakfast table.

*   *   *

The men spent the rest of the day scouting the town and outlying areas in prospects of finding work. The lumber industry was still flourishing in parts of the province, dock workers were always needed, and other local jobs would crop up as current residents would pack up and head out in search of other work, or new land to settle and farm. People were always on the go, and with the influx of diseased immigrant ships showing up in their ports, some became very apprehensive about living in such close proximity to these coffin ships.

Molly, Kathleen and Colleen spent their first day sorting and cleaning their belongings as they waited for Dr. Langley to return and take them to their new home. Mrs. Kelly bustled over the children as if they were her own. She was in her element and it showed. Colleen helped her prepare the evening meal and they giggled together like long-separated sisters.

The stories of their homes in Ireland flowed like honey with their bittersweet memories. "Ah, sure, I haven't laughed like this in a thousand years girl." Cora gasped as Colleen related another yarn. "You almost make this old woman home sick, you do."

The men arrived famished for their evening meal. They had covered every inch of the townsite and Liam's brother Thomas had already secured a job on the docks. "It'll do me for now lads. Keep the wolf away from the door at least until something better turns up. We should really look into the lumber mills soon. Fall is coming and I understand many shut down over the winter months when the snow comes. But the money's there now, so it might be worth while, if only for a few months."

Liam greeted Molly with a kiss as Matthew ran into his arms offering a mangle of biscuit in his grimy little fist. Liam laughed, "sure you've been a busy little lad by the looks of things."

Matthew beamed at his father. "Aunt Cora helped me make these biscuits. They're for you, and Uncle Colin, and Uncle Thomas, and Grandpa Pat, and papa John. She says you need them to take to work in your dinner bucket. Are you going back to work at the sawmill da? Can you take me with you sometime da, like you did before we went on the boat?" In Matthew's young mind they were settled once again at home having had a brief adventure on a boat, but now they were back to normal life and events.

"Hold on there youngster. We've only been here for a day. Give your da a chance to settle in." John swept his grandson up into his powerful arms and spun him around the room. "We'll all have new jobs to go to very soon but first we have to find our bearings in this new land of ours. Tomorrow papa will take you out to see the sights. There may even be a surprise or two in store for a good little lad." Matthew hugged his papa John as they all left to prepare for the evening meal.

*   *   *

On the outskirts of town lay a plot of land shrouded with maple, apple, and various other fruit bearing trees. Immediately after dinner, Dr. Langley arrived to escort his new charges to what would hopefully become their new home. Tucked in a glen away from the sea and wind it was warm and peaceful with the sun beating down on the fruit-laden trees. Birds flitted from tree to tree and sang out bursts of warning as the newcomers arrived. Bees hummed near the ground, covered with fallen fruit. A clapboard house of moderate size sat dead centre of the glen. The roof appeared to be strips of layered birch bark, the windows small and grimy. A huge verandah surrounded the whole house with chairs and swing seats set in strategic places. It had the aura of being lived in, as if many children had passed through the doors, run down the battered wooden steps and off down the lane to whatever destination. The women could already envision clean windows with curtains fluttering at them and everyone sitting on this porch enjoying the evening breeze. The men inspected the broken steps, the slightly slanted chimney, the greying bare clapboard and envisioned a work party to make it suitable for the family to live in through the winter months so near at hand.

"If the inside is as good as the out, we could have a fine home here in no time. A little elbow grease and some white wash will perk this right up," John exclaimed, rubbing his hands together. "Let's see what we have on the inside."

Carefully, working their way up the crumbling stairs, Dr. Langley led the way through the resisting door as it groaned on rusted hinges. As they entered the common room the musty smell hit them. But what met their eyes, charmed the musty neglect out the door. A huge stone fireplace commanded one wall with a door on either side leading to rooms behind. One end of the huge room was a well-planned kitchen area with an iron cook-stove, cupboards, shelves, and an actual sink with sideboard. A pump was mounted above the sink allowing indoor plumbing. Only a few steps from the stove was a partitioned area the women immediately inspected. Squeals of delight came from the corner as they discovered a claw-foot, copper tub, large enough for a man's body to sink into. "Saints preserve us," Colleen whispered. "Tis the most wonderful sight these old eyes have rested on in a long, long time."

Matthew was already exploring and climbing a set of open stairs that ascended into the ceiling. Above their heads were two large loft rooms with small windows facing the front of the yard. Behind the common room, to the right of the fireplace, was another large bedroom, with a window to the rear of the house. The door on the left of the fireplace let to a larder equipped with walls of shelves and a door leading to the porch at the back of the house. A path, grown over with a season of uncut grass, led off into the trees behind, where a small outhouse could be found.

As Matthew stood on the back porch, a head poked up out of the grass. Large black eyes surveyed him and tall pointed ears flickered in the sunlight. His observer sauntered off into the treed surroundings and flicked a brilliant white tale in farewell. Matthew had seen his first Canadian deer. When Molly joined her small son on the verandah, she witnessed his huge eyes and gaping mouth. "Why, Matthew, are you catching flies now?"

"Mama, I just saw the most beautiful animal with big eyes, huge ears and a very white tail. What was it mama?"

Dr. Langley had joined them on the porch and explained to Matthew what he had seen. "That was called a deer, Matthew and you'll see very many deer as well as rabbits and mice. When you grow a nice garden you will be chasing them away before they eat up all you work so hard to grow."

"Oh, no I won't. I'll have them for my pets. Papa can help me catch them." They all laughed at his guileless naivete. But Matthew was happy and that was the main thing.

"I'm so relieved you have decided to stay with us. Tomorrow we will make a brief visit to the station. The conditions we work under are simply appalling. We lack so many of those things necessary to make our patients lives bearable. We are so desperately short-staffed we barely have time to tend to even the very worst off. People are dying for lack of attention."

"I hope you're not exaggerating my abilities Dr. Langley. You know I've very little experience with cholera and typhus. I feel like a babe in the woods and the more you tell me, the less confident I feel." Molly sunk into a chair as she spoke, her fingers massaging her temples as she wondered at the enormity of the task before her.

"Molly, you have far more expertise than the majority of people we have working at the station right now. Most are just simple labours and domestic women, but for the most part, they are dedicated hard workers. They'll listen to your advice as those on the *Looshtank* did." Dr. Langley attempted to soften Molly's feelings of inadequacy. He knew it was going to be difficult enough without her second-guessing her own ability.

The family had thoroughly inspected the house and had now moved out into the surrounding yard and out-buildings. Never before had they seen so much land allowed to one family. In their minds, the women already had the garden planted and harvested. The men had the roof repaired, a new midden erected and a corral prepared for an unspecified variety of farm animals. They couldn't believe their good fortune and they all planned to make the best of it, and as quickly as possible.

Very early the following morning, Drs. Langley and Cormack arrived to collect Molly and Liam to take them off to one of many quarantine stations in New Brunswick. Miramichi Bay was riddled with islands, now being utilized to quarantine the diseased immigrants, including those meant for America but arriving in Canadian ports, filling the quarantine stations with thousands more desperately sick and dying people.

"Our main filtering station is only a couple of miles away on the mainland. After we inspect and classify each immigrant, those quarantined will be transported to one of the islands" Dr. Cormack explained their procedures as they headed towards the filtering station. "Those who have been exposed but show no signs of disease are detained for a period of time here on the mainland to assure a clean bill of health before they are released. "The majority of your fellow passengers from the *Looshtank* will most likely remain here for a brief time, so you will be seeing them all again very soon."

"What about those who had the cholera but have survived it and are now regaining their health?" Molly inquired. "Won't bringing them here only expose them to further problems, especially in their weakened state?"

"Very good point, Molly," Dr. Langley agreed. "That is why we need people like you to assure the area they inhabit will be properly prepared and sanitized. Those affected with the cholera and typhoid must not be integrated with those who are recuperating. To most of our workers, they are all just sick people and some just need more attention than others. Our workers must be segregated as much as our patients to prevent the carrying of infestation from one patient to another. It is impossibly frustrating work, trying to convince everyone how important good sanitation is in order to prevent the spread of disease."

The journey onward by horse and cart led them through forested areas of pine and spruce along the shore of the Miramichi River. The wide-open landscape of Ireland was gone forever. The blackness of the forest surrounded them, in some areas barely allowing the bright sunlight to penetrate. But it was beautiful, mysterious and wild and filled their hearts with excitement. Emerging from the sweet smelling forest into a clearing the size of a small village, Molly's heart sank at the scene before them. Graying, paint-deprived buildings lined the length of the clearing. Built off on the edge of the clearing appeared to be numerous one-room cabins. A single larger cabin with smoke arising from its chimney, sat by itself, separating the two rows of the main buildings. Linens and blankets were piled high on its covered verandah. Women with red sweating faces and dry chapped hands, piled mounds of the linens into the cabin, barely hesitating to witness the newcomers in the cart. One waved and greeted the doctors in a thick Irish brogue. "'Tis goin ta be a perishin' hot one today doctor. Lord dancin', me feet are like two cooked doughboys already, sure."

"Top of the mornin' Bertie. I've brought someone new to meet you and the girls. This is Liam and Molly Dermitt just out from County Tyrone. I am hoping they will be joining our staff, so you ladies behave yourselves now and don't be scaring them off with your wild stories."

"Who'd be wantin' to scare the likes of this one off now? Sure he's the spittin' image of me poor Connor when he was a young charmer." Bertie winked at Liam.

"Down girl, get back to your laundry duty," laughed Dr. Cormack, his ample belly bouncing with mirth as the cart carried on to the dispensary. "She's a corker that one. One of the hardest working lasses we have at the station. You'd be well placed to befriend her. She has a great deal of influence over the rest of the women here."

The dispensary was bare but adequate and reasonably clean and tidy with the exception of the good doctor's desk and record area. Molly wondered how he knew where anything was. "I try my best to keep records of everyone who goes through this station, but I am so terribly far behind, I fear I'll never catch up with it all," Dr. Langley apologized as he fumbled to find sitting room for Molly and Liam.

"You need someone to take care of the paper work for you doctor," Liam stated sympathetically. "You surely can't handle all of this work yourself.

"I've been through two clerks already, but they don't seem to want to stay with me. They tell me that my records are impossible to understand and transcribe. I really don't understand why?" Dr. Langley scrambled to sort the piles of records causing Molly to smile as she remembered the eccentric ramblings of her friend and mentor Dr. Leary back in County Tyrone.

"I'm sure we can arrange something to help you out of this mess. If you would allow these records to be taken off the station, I may just be able to persuade my sister-in-law Kathleen O'Connell, who was a teacher in County Tyrone, to help us out. As you know she has a newborn son, but she loves a challenge and she would definitely have one with this jumble!"

"Well, now that you hopefully have this problem solved, let's move on to the next, shall we?" With a formal sweep of his arm Dr. Langley ushered them out the door.

As they entered the first building, next to the infirmary, a nauseous smell of stale body sweat, filthy clothing caked with vomit and permeated with weeks of lamp and cooking smoke, assaulted them. "These people haven't washed in weeks. Why are they here being processed?" Molly exclaimed incredulously.

Apologetically, Dr. Langley explained the procedure for processing the incoming immigrants at the station. "Unfortunately, we herd them through here like cattle. We lack the time and help to organize a more sensible approach. We need to separate the weak and starving from the sick and diseased as quickly as possible."

Molly's mind was turning cartwheels as they went from building to building inspecting the poorly equipped and dangerously unsanitary conditions of the station. Dr. Langley introduced her as his assistant. Some stared lethargically while others greeted her with warmth and exuberance when they heard her Irish name.

As they neared the end of their tour of the buildings, Molly's eyes fell on a young woman, crouched in a corner with a tattered bundle clutched to her breast. As Molly approached and knelt beside the woman, who seemed to be not much older than a child, her clouded eyes filled with terror as she concealed the ragged treasure in the circle of her body. Molly smiled reassuringly. "Can I see what you have in your bundle?" Something had told her to approach cautiously. Something in the woman's eyes had alerted her.

The woman whimpered, her mouth and chin trembling. Her eyes spoke of the misery she was enduring. Tears welled in her eyes and seeped over her reddened lids causing rivets to smear the grim on her cheeks. Molly reached out to her, stroking her hair back from her eyes. "It's alright lass. No one's going to hurt you. What's your name now?"

Her mouth worked but nothing escaped it. She seemed to shrink into herself as she clasped the bundle more tightly to her. Molly reached for the ragged treasure and a banshee shriek came forth that no human could possibly emanate. Molly was thrown back from where she had crouched before the woman as Liam deftly protected her from toppling backwards onto the floor. Never taking her eyes from the demented form before her, she whispered, "Doctor, please help me take the child from its mother. I'm sure the baby is dead, and has probably been for quite some time."

Incredulously, Dr. Langley starred at the woman on the floor. "How could you know she has a child in that rag? It's barely large enough to be a rag doll."

Within minutes the child was taken and the mother sedated with laudanum. Her only connection to happiness was gone forever. She lay upon a cot, starring blankly at her hands folded across her breast where she had held her child since its birth only days earlier. Molly noted her youth and prayed this woman-child would garner the strength to carry on.

After completing the tour they returned to the infirmary to have tea and discuss what they had seen of the station and its inmates. "You certainly didn't exaggerate the situation here Dr. Langley. If anything you managed to play it down quite nicely." Liam offered as silence fell upon the little group.

"Yes, I played it down," Dr. Langley gazed into his teacup. "I was concerned you wouldn't want to even set foot out here if you knew the complete sordid truth."

"You underestimate my wife then. Knowing her as I do, you would have realized she will be even more determined to turn this place upside down."

"Yes, and the sooner the better, I should think," Molly stood, splashing her tea to the floor. Her face was grim and condemning. "I'm sorry Dr. Langley, I know it's not your fault and you are doing the very best you can, but you obviously need more, much more. You need many assistants, not just one. It's time you were left to administer to the sick as your title implies and leave the rest to others. You and Dr. Cormack can not be expected to do it all alone."

With hardly a breath between, Molly continued. "Now, my husband and I must talk to our families and I would like to have some time to come up with some ideas on how we could improve on the terrible situation you have here. Would you come to dinner tonight? By that time we should have some ideas to discuss. Also I would like to arrange a proper Christian burial for that poor wee mite back there." Her mind whirred, as words blurred one into the other.

Liam raised his hands to the heavens in submission, smiling at the doctors knowingly. "I hope you're prepared for Hurricane Molly, gentlemen?"

Chapter 3

Miramichi, New Brunswick, Canada — 1846-47

Days rolled into weeks as the hot summer weather turned into crisper cooler evenings and longer nights. Forewarned of the Canadian winters the whole family had dived into preparations. Having missed the growing season, Colleen and Kathleen stored what fruit was available and stocked up on other provisions for the winter ahead. In their time away from the station the men had fashioned a sleigh, repaired the roof, and built a new midden in the trees beyond the back of the house.

Dr. Langley was delighted with Molly's efforts and her suggested changes at the Station. Within weeks, a wash house for incoming immigrants was erected. With Liam's expertise in the lumber trade and Colin's willingness, a crew of volunteers was quickly assembled and the building completed in short order. Kathleen had eagerly agreed to make an attempt at sorting the medical records of the patients and also spent hours transcribing letters of Dr. Langley's begging the government for more money to improve the facilities and pay his new employees. They all knew that for the present, their income would be little but with Thomas's dock work and Patrick taking up odd jobs, the family could survive quite nicely. Colleen spent her time with the children, much to her and their joy. Matthew thrived and became very responsible in his care of the chickens, goats and rabbits they had acquired over the weeks. Michael, although colicky became fat and rosy and healthy. Kathleen was happy to work at home and be able to give care to her infant son as well.

The routine changed at the station. Not all of Molly's suggestions were possible to fulfil, so change was gradual. The wash house was deemed a most important major change and Molly insisted that routine be adhered to most rigidly. As soon as a new group of immigrants arrived on the station, they were immediately stripped of their clothing, ordered to bathe with carbolic soap and scrub everything they possessed that was salvageable. Many protested they were being treated cruelly, but upon finding they would be shipped immediately to a quarantine island if they did not comply, they were quick to obey. Others were so sick and weak their efforts were painful. But she insisted that all should be scrubbed clean to help stop the spread of the diseases. So many still believed that cleaning their bodies was just exposing themselves to further infection. It was if the layers of dirt were protecting them from outside attack.

No longer was more than one person allowed in each bed, other than small children with their mothers. More wooden slat beds were constructed and equipped with sweet-smelling mattresses of spruce bows. Conditions were hopelessly crowded but definitely cleaner and safer.

Proper pits were dug and night soils were removed regularly. Soiled clothes and bedding were being washed constantly. Bandaging was changed on a routine basis and wounds not allowed to fester.

* * *

Eventually money and other aids began to trickle in from the government. Molly was paid as a full-time assistant, Liam and Colin paid on contract basis for their services, and two more full time cleaners and caregivers were enlisted and trained by Molly. Logically, it would be assumed that Irish employees would be better equipped to work with the immigrants, but that wasn't always so. Many of the settlers in the area had arrived long before the famine. They were most often Northern Ireland Protestants and had come to Canada to improve their lives. Resentment frequently arose towards the diseased immigrants, the majority being Irish Catholics. Flare-ups would occur, even among those who had travelled together over many weeks. Many were too ill to care, but there was always the feisty hanger-on who would fight to the bitter end. Molly's smile and gentle admonishment would usually calm the situation between combatants, but persistent troublemakers were quickly assigned to night soil bucket duty. Nothing sobered an agitator like a full bucket of human waste. Molly would smile and say, "You can't tell, when it's all mixed together, whether it be Protestant or Catholic, now can you?"

Liam and Colin found work in the lumber trade. The boom was not on now but lumber was still being exported from New Brunswick ports. When not at the mill or the docks, they found time to help at the station. John and Patrick stocked their home with fuel to take them through the winter and assured all repairs to the house were completed.

With winter setting in, fewer ships were arriving, resulting in fewer immigrants being processed and sent on to quarantine islands. It was time to prepare for local flu epidemics and other winter maladies.

In his infirmary, Dr. Langley poured over the records so neatly assembled and documented by Kathleen. Molly joined him to replenish bandages, clean instruments, and remove the soiled linens and dressings. "Kathleen has done a magnificent job with these records. I'm sure each and every patient is accounted for. You realise this is our most important weapon when we approach the government again. So many were lost in the shuffle before, but now all our work is documented and there will be no argument at least, in so far as the number of people we process here is concerned. Our mortality rate has declined significantly with the changes we've made." Looking up at Molly as she bustled her way around the infirmary, he said, "none of this would have been possible without you and your family, you know."

"Go away with you doctor. Sure, you knew what had to be done all along. You just needed a little shove by a red-head wielding a shillelagh." She laughed. "Now, I'm getting off home before you reduce me to tears. Good evening, doctor."

Liam and Matthew waited for her in the cart as she finished for the day. As Liam helped her up onto the seat, Matthew scrambled to her lap. "Papa John told me to give you this mama." Matthew said, "He said, you must wear it because the evenings are getting colder and we don't want you to get sick." Smiling, in his exuberance he freed the emerald cloak from the box it lay in since before their departure from Ireland.

The sight of it evoked emotions and memories she had not had time to think of in months. Recollections of her mother flooded back. For the first time in many years the memory of her mother's face was clear. She once again saw the black raven hair, fanned out on the pillow of her death-bed, the gentle, apologising eyes that begged forgiveness for leaving her little daughter. Tears welled in Molly's eyes as she pressed the cloak to her face and breathed in the essence of her mother.

"Mama. What's wrong mama? Why are you crying?" A confused Matthew whispered.

"It's all right lad," Liam patted his son's knee. "Mama is just remembering her own mama. Let her be now." Pulling her to him with his free arm, he reined the horse on and they headed home.

* * *

Winter attacked with a vengeance. It was well into the month of November. The nights grew cold and the mornings were white with frost. The leaves were gone from the trees and the evergreens stood out starkly on the landscape. As was often the case, Matthew arose first to check his chickens and rabbits. Since they had been invaded by a pesky fox some weeks earlier, Matthew worried about the safety of his helpless charges. After donning his boots and warm coat he quietly headed for the back entrance, through the pantry and cold room. A shriek that would raise the dead flooded in through the house, rousting everyone from their beds. "Papa, papa, come and see. Quick, papa." Liam fled from his bed, only to find himself standing knee deep in snow that had drifted onto the covered verandah through the night. By the time he realised what had happened the rest of the family behind him were dissolved in gales of laughter as they watched this giant of a man moored in snow up to his knees, with only the long underwear in which he slept, protecting his dignity.

"My, but you're a sight for sore eyes, so you are." Molly giggled.

Liam, regaining his composure, let out an indignant, "Humph, the young snip scared the bejesus out of me." And stomped off back into the house.

The snow had fallen quietly through the night, unknown to the sleeping family within. Matthew waded through it now, to his heart's content. It still came down heavily in huge soft flakes. Layer upon layer rested on the evergreens, forcing the tips of their boughs to bend to the earth in mock supplication. It was a wonderland, so soft and beautiful and perfect.

"Thank goodness I was able to get the woollen socks and mittens finished. I best get busy with the hats or you'll be freezin your poor wee ears off lad." Colleen rubbed warmth back into Matthews's fingers and ears as he stripped from his snow-sodden clothes before the huge fire.

"But grandma, what about the chickens? They must be so cold out there. They don't have any fur on their feet." Matthew worried.

"What are you suggestin lad?" Maybe that I should make mittens for the chickens? We could skin a rabbit or two and make some booties for the poor things." Colleen teased.

But Matthews's eyes opened wide in horror at her suggestion. Big squishy tears rose as he choked back the desire to cry.

"Oh, there lad, grandma is only teasin' you, sure. The chickens will be just fine. God, made chickens very hardy indeed."

It was Sunday, and Molly had already arranged to take the day to be with her family. Her days at the station often lasted well into the night and Matthew was missing his mother. Today she donned leggings and boots and headed off into the snow, much to the delight of her young son. They tended the chickens, rabbits and two little goats, Matthew proudly showing his mother the routine. "Pick up all the eggs son, before they freeze. In the spring we can let momma hen keep her eggs to sit on, so they will hatch, and we'll have little chicks running all over the place." Matthew beamed at his mother as they continued on with their chores.

*　　*　　*

Immigration trickled down to nothing as the winter wore on. The bay was blocked with solid ice, stopping traffic of any sort into the harbour. The quarantine stations were cleared out and prepared for the next immigrant ships to appear in the spring of 1847. News from home was bleak and it was expected there would be more sick and starving arriving from the shores of Ireland. The famine was still in its early stages. People were starving by the thousands. The worst was yet to come.

Winter in the glen was spectacular. Enough fuel and provisions had been stockpiled to last through the months of snow and bitter cold. Christmas was upon them and while visiting Aunt Cora at the inn, Matthew was to see a beautiful tree decked in coloured paper, baubles and strings of popped corn. "Papa John, can we go and get our very own tree for our house." He pleaded most convincingly and on that very same day, John and his eager young grandson ventured out to find the perfect first Christmas tree. The freezing weather only accentuated the joy in the clapboard house in the glen, as the two families gathered around, to decorate the shimmering spruce tree, supplied by John and Matthew. A beautiful star tilted precariously at the top.

"Well Bridget, darlin', what do you think of your little family now?" John mused as he looked up at the star so carefully crafted by the grandson Bridget would never see.

"Who's Bridget, granddad?" Matthew queried.

"She's your grandma, lad. And sure you're the spittin' image of her. You've the same black flashing eyes. She passed on when your ma was a wee thing like you." John cuddled his grandson closer.

"Then why do you talk to her granddad?"

"Because it keeps her here in my heart lad. Your grandma meant the world to me and I'll remember her always," He smiled down at his young grandson.

"I wish she was here with us now, granddad, so she could see our Christmas tree."

"She is lad. Just look up at the star." John pointed to the star at the top of the tree.

In wonder the little boy looked up to the star to see the faded likeness of a beautiful young woman with thick black hair and soft, gentle black eyes, looking down at him. "I think she's with us more this Christmas than since she left us. I know your grandma approves of what we've done, coming to Canada. I can feel her smiling at us now. She knows we're happy, and that's all she ever wanted of her family. I'm sure she's at peace now." John smiled at Bridget's memory.

Christmas came with the fury of winter. Icicles hung like fountains of glass from the eaves. The cold winter sun, unable to penetrate the icy appendages, shot prisms of light from their surfaces and through the small windows of the house. Light danced on the walls and ceiling adding to the merriment within.

As the weeks rolled on, the cold persisted. Wild animals became bolder as they crept towards the inhabited areas in hopes of finding food. Foraging was next to impossible as the snow deepened and hung like blankets on the trees. Matthew gloried in his task of filling a trough with hay and watching a giant moose and his mate saunter in and quietly feed, occasionally looking up at the clapboard house and the boy perched on the verandah railing. The big animal gently snorted his thanks and flicking white tails in farewell they both trod off into the woods beyond.

Matthew was growing accustomed to seeing these magnificent beasts and strangely enough, never felt a moment of fear while in their company. Yet he knew instinctively they must be respected and he must keep his distance. He was growing up fast in this new land, and loved every minute of it.

The black bear and slinking wolves were different

again. If they hung around, the moose would not appear. He learned that the bear, up to its time for winter hibernation, would forage for anything, while the wolf would attack their chickens, rabbits and even the goats. John purchased some geese, which they found made a huge commotion when the wolves arrived. They acted as a wonderful alarm system. Their honking and hissing was to save more than a few lives in that little barn yard that first winter.

Liam and Colin set out on their first hunting expedition, much to Matthew's dismay. Leaving the teary-eyed little boy behind with visions of dead moose and bears covering the back verandah, the women were left to explain the necessities of a supply of fresh meat and that nothing would be killed that was not essential.

The huge black bear that eventually found it's way by sled to the back porch allowed no room in the little boy's heart for understanding. His non-acceptance of the killing of the bear would never have endorsed the vision that Matthew would eventually become the families most accomplished hunter in years to come.

Life at the station became routine for Molly as she headed her way each day by horse and sled to join Dr. Langley in caring for those who had succumbed to the winter maladies of influenza, pneumonia, and most other chest related ailments. There was time to properly care for the ill and injured and but for the occasional difficult storm, life at the station became very relaxed.

The one very dark period that entered their lives as they flourished at Miramichi, was the very unexpected death of Liam's mother Colleen. Shortly before the end of the brutal winter, she succumbed to pneumonia and passed away. She told Patrick her dream had been fulfilled now that her family was safely away from Ireland. She could die in peace. They placed her in the rocker before a cheerful fire where she smiled and closed her eyes forever.

*   *   *

Of course the peacefulness was not meant to last, for in March 1847 word would arrive that many vessels would be arriving from Ireland and England with their cargo of desperate immigrants aboard. 1847 would prove to be the pinnacle of immigration in those years. The Irish famine would heighten to encompass millions of islanders with many of those millions starving to death. So many of those who escaped the famine in their country would often die enroute to their new homes in Australia, United States of America, or Canada. Those who survived to reach the shores of their chosen country were often turned away or were left in quarantine stations until they died or were cured of whatever disease was carried on the coffin ships.

As the ice melted in Miramichi Bay preparations were being made at the station in Chatham. Molly was determined they would be ready for the onslaught. The government had complied, the best they could. Improvements were being made at the quarantine stations at Middle and Partridge Islands. New staff was being trained and qualified. They were forewarned that this would be the worst of years but now they were prepared. They didn't want to see the same problems happening as did in the previous years, where the sick and dying were held on the ships for weeks on end. Their chance of complete recovery would be much improved this time around.

As the spring of '47 came, floods of immigrants began to arrive. The state of their health was appalling; on many ships they were starving as the rations had been used up and many of the ship lines were only providing what they considered the basic essentials to their passengers. Shipboard rats and weevils had eaten into many provisions and the remaining water was green and brackish, carrying disease. The passengers were treated worse than animals. The Atlantic was littered with those who failed to survive. Many were so beaten down upon their arrival, there was little will to live. So many sat starring vacantly off into space. They uttered not a word, but their silent prayers for death could still be heard. The diseased mind was becoming more of a challenge than the cholera and typhoid. Molly wondered, if they were fortunate enough to survive how they would face the harshness of the Canadian winter, not so many months away. Many had only the clothes on their backs that for the most part were filthy and ragged. There were women alone, having lost their men and children. Men who had lost their wives struggled with pathetically starved children. Some where completely alone and wanted no part of this new land. So the greatest challenge for those at the station, was dealing with the mental collapse of those in their charge.

Molly would arrive home in the evenings in shear exhaustion that came from the feeling of hopelessness surrounding her at the station. Hard, gruelling work had never held her back but the absolute despair enveloping her daily seemed to be taking it's toll as the season progressed.

On a particularly blistering hot day as the relentless sun beat down on the sheds housing the immigrants, Dr. Langley sent a runner to bring Liam to the station. He was concerned with Molly as she moved lethargically from patient to patient, attending to their needs. She spoke little and seemed to periodically labour for her breath. He knew she was drained both mentally and physically. Without rest she would likely become his next patient.

"Liam, I want you to take her home, and she is not to come back for at least three days or until you feel she is fully rested. Take no argument from her. The season is only half over and if she continues on at this pace, she'll end up as one of our casualties." Dr. Langley made himself most clear.

After some argument but relatively little resistance from Molly, Liam assisted her into the cart and they made their way home to the glen. Kathleen, happy to have her sister-in-law home, fussed about her. She missed Colleen desperately and was often lonely when everyone but the children were gone from home. Molly succumbed to the pampering and often spent hours in the coolness of the verandah, reading and relaxing until her husband arrived home. She was thrilled to turn the tables and cater to him when he arrived, tired and hot from working under the blistering sun. Matthew enjoyed the days with his mother, showing her his latest batch of baby chicks and giant sun flowers he had nurtured to reach over seven feet tall, their heads the size of a dinner plate.

Within days the roses were back in Molly's cheeks and the sparkle in her eyes. Dr. Langley had convinced her on one of his visits, that she was to consider taking time for herself every few weeks and to plan accordingly. "Yes, doctor, whatever you say now." She smiled at him impishly. But she did come to realise in the days following that she was much more efficient and useful to him when she was rested and healthy.

They were to learn that many more of the ill had been transported to Grosse Isle, a quarantine station in the St. Lawrence River, slightly downstream from Québec City. Grosse Isle had functioned as a quarantine station since the early 1830s when virulent cholera epidemics were crossing Europe and England, killing people by the thousands and forcing others to flee their homelands and migrate to America and Canada. Many of these immigrants were Irish. In 1847 when the potato famine was hitting its peak, hundreds of diseased-filled ships were entering the St. Lawrence Seaway and being inspected at Grosse Isle and Québec City. Some were being quarantined for a week while others remained well over three weeks. Three times the number of immigrants were coming through these ports as in the previous year. The quarantine station at Grosse Isle had been enlarged but was still not equipped to handle the sea of sick and dying immigrants landing on its shores. The demands on the staff were enormous and many became ill and succumbed to the typhoid themselves. Dr. Langley reported that the death toll at sea was being reported in the thousands and at least that many had been buried at Grosse Isle, only one of many Canadian ports affected.

The Canadian government apparently had no control over the colonial authorities who managed the British emigration. Because of this, they were not prepared for the onslaught of dying people arriving daily from the shores of Great Britain. The island's facilities were poorly equipped to house so many desperately ill people after having lived in the unsanitary, crowded conditions of the ships crossing the Atlantic.

"Dr. Cormack has made the decision to sail on to Québec and offer his support where it's most needed. We're going to miss him, and our workload will again be increased until someone comes to replace him. But, we are well equipped and our people are quite capable of handling the challenge. You understand, I will be spending more time at the other stations and I would like you to oversee the operation here? I don't want you carrying out the night soil buckets, changing linens and feeding the patients. You are to administer the processing of the patients as they enter the station and have them ready for me to diagnose on my return each day. Attempt to inspect the wards daily and give what treatment you find necessary, if such should be lacking. Report any changes to me and I will handle it in the evenings. If you leave the basic care and the work to the others, you will not overextend yourself. I need you healthy, now more than ever." He smiled at her pleadingly.

"I've learned what my limits are, doctor. Thank you for having such faith in me. I do hope we find a replacement for Dr. Cormack very soon though."

*   *   *

Summer wore on into fall and the days became cooler and more bearable at the station. The knowledge Molly gained while supervising the daily routine of the hospital would prove to be most beneficial to her future. More horrifying news arrived weekly reporting hundreds upon hundreds of sailing ships arriving daily across the Atlantic and north from American ports. By the end of the season, over 100,000 had landed in Canadian ports alone, bringing with them as many problems.

As the season of immigration began to draw to a close and work of most kind was growing sparse, conversations at home began to include plans of moving on. They had spent over a year in Miramichi, worked at various jobs, lost Colleen and for the most part were anxious to move towards their ultimate plans of homesteading in Upper Canada. Although they were happy in their house in the glen and were settled in quite nicely, there were dreams yet to unfold. The forest industry was dwindling in New Brunswick as most of the reachable area had been logged off in past years. The dream of having their own successful, family-run lumber mill in this area was minimal. They all knew that they must eventually head up into Upper Canada to realise that dream. They also knew there would likely be many stops along the way before they were able to finally homestead. It seemed senseless to spend another winter in New Brunswick or waste good travelling time before the worst weather settled in and the St. Lawrence River would be frozen solid and impassable. By October they were prepared to move on. Molly bid a sad farewell to Dr. Langley and his new assistant, a young fledgling doctor from Ireland.

"I knew this day would come Molly, but not so soon. You've made my work here at the station most bearable. We'll miss you and I'll have no one to put me in my place when I need it. I hope you and your family find that dream very soon. Please keep in touch with me from time to time. I'm sure Cora would want to hear from you all, now and then." Pulling her to him, he brushed her forehead with a kiss, turned and left.

Chapter 4

Québec City/Grosse Isle, P.Q., Canada – 1847

Molly sat reading the letter of introduction, Dr. Langley had suggested she may need on her journey. He had written directly to Dr. George Douglas, the administrator at the Grosse Isle quarantine station. Dr. Douglas was known to be very knowledgeable in the treatment of epidemic diseases such as typhoid and cholera. He was also a very humane and caring individual. If Molly and her family should decide to waylay their journey to Upper Canada and remain in the Québec area, Dr. Langley felt she could use his recommendation to Dr. Douglas. Lord knows they certainly could use her there.

After careful consideration on their mode of travel, it was agreed upon to take the land route across northern New Brunswick, on into Québec and follow the south shores of the St. Lawrence until they reached Québec City situated on the north shore of the river. By making this choice it allowed them to carry many more of their possessions than if they had decided to take a steamer around the Gaspe Peninsula and up the St. Lawrence.

"When God made time, he made lots of it. And we definitely have more time than money at this point." John offered. "It would be much to our advantage to take all we can manage to carry and going by wagon is the only way we can do that."

"It looks like we have about 400 to 500 miles to travel depending on which route we take. I personally think we should stick to the most inhabited route in case of problems." Liam suggested, pointing to settlements on a map of New Brunswick and Québec. "We should lay out a tentative route and plan accordingly."

"That way we can be sure to find new provisions when we need them, and not be left for miles in the wilderness without," agreed Thomas excitedly.

The feeling of adventure had returned once again as they all gathered around the map. Only Patrick, who had wandered off into the back garden, was silent. Matthew, sensing his grandfather's pain, followed, took him by his gnarled old hand, and asked, "what's the matter granddad? Are you sad?"

"I'll be missing this place, Matthew. It's so peaceful, and my Colleen will be staying here forever, without me. I hate to leave her behind as I'll likely never pass this way again," he said, squeezing Matthew hand and the tears from the corners of his eyes.

"But granddad, you said that grandma will always be in our hearts, so how can she stay here too? She'll be with us, and you can talk to her too, just like mama told me."

Patrick smiled down on his young, but so wise, grandson. "How did such a little fellow get so smart as you, now tell me that?"

*   *   *

Next morning, the sun shone blessedly down on them as they packed and repacked their belongings. John and Colin had fashioned crates in which to carry some of the chickens and rabbits. The goats would be tethered behind the wagon where they could follow along. They had also purchased another horse to ease the burden on their ageing mare. The two stood grazing in the yard, periodically nibbling on each others ears and snorting greetings to one another, their tails flicking at the black flies that attacked their sweaty hides. The wagon was loaded and ready. Seats had been constructed on the sides and rear to accommodate the whole family. The men would each take his turn driving and navigating.

Turning to bid farewell to their first home in this new country, there was some regret at leaving it, but that was greatly overpowered by the anticipation they were all experiencing as they prepared to begin a new adventure.

Many neighbours and friends of the past year had gathered at the dockside to bid them farewell as they loaded the wagon and animals on the barge that would take them across the Miramichi River to Newcastle and the beginning of their journey. Cora Kerry and her servant from the inn, were loaded down with food and provisions to see them on their way. Emotions ran high as Cora enfolded Molly and Matthew in her arms. The O'Connors and the Dermitts were well liked and respected in the area and folks were sorry to see them go.

The trip up river was slow and tedious, but the weather was favourable, resulting in calm waters that lapped playfully at the side of the barge as it lumbered on. The day was still relatively young as they arrived in Newcastle, so they decided to carry on until closer to sunset when they would make camp and settle in for the night. The weather remained clear and dry on this first leg of their journey, allowing them to make good time travelling through the northern forests of New Brunswick and on towards the southern shore of the St. Lawrence River and the Province of Québec. They estimated approximately one months travel, taking into account the possibility of inclement weather, possible breakdowns or family sickness, all which could slow down their progress.

While the weather remained good and everyone's energy and enthusiasm was at its peak they travelled from early morning until dusk. The surroundings enthralled everyone including Matthew, who continually watched for any appearance of the animals and birds of the wilderness. Setting up camp in the good weather was a playful experience for all. Fishing was good in the creeks, berries still available for picking and in some instances, bog plants such as watercress and wild onions could be found, adding flavour and interest to a bland diet. Creek beds, still low in water from the dry summer months, proved to be good camp areas where they could easily build cooking fires and have access to fresh water for drinking and cooking.

When the rain came, so did the change in mood and spirit. It was impossible to keep dry and a continuous battle to dry bedding and clothes before a fire dying in a downpour. Where possible, they slept under the protection of the forest, hastily constructing lean-to shelters to keep off the worst of the rain and wind. The summer nights had vanished and the smell of frost was in the air. It was only a matter of time before they would experience their first snowy night along the banks of the St. Lawrence River. But, for the most part they had made good time when the roads were dry and easily passable.

The horses were strong and healthy and had been allowed sufficient rest and grazing during the particularly wet days. The families had remained miraculously healthy with not even so much as a cold to their detriment. Matthew was fairly blooming. Molly had insisted that everyone should walk as far as possible every day. They all took turns carrying baby Michael, cocooned in a knapsack on their backs. The steady rhythm of their walking kept him peacefully lulled and he would stare, as if in a trance at the trees meeting the sky until his baby eyes succumbed once again to sleep.

One of the joys of their journey was the constant

sighting of the majestic moose and his family. A bull was often seen grazing alone, lazily lifting his giant, antlered head, only long enough to observe the passers-by. The cow and her youngster would pointedly ignore them, knowing protection was close at hand. No one breathed a word, least they disturb this king of the wilderness and his family. It was like trespassing on sacred ground.

When they reached the mighty St. Lawrence River, they were relieved to find villages where they were able to clean and dry their clothing and bedding. The sun shone, the wind blew and the clothes fluttered in the breeze, competing with the red, yellow and orange leaves of the maple trees lining the river. The colours were lively and brilliant and helped to lift the spirits of the road-weary travellers.

Villages sprinkled the landscape along the river's edge. Ships were traversing the river by the dozens. Sailboats much like the *Looshtank*, lay at anchor along its shores. Many were obviously filled with travellers while others lay in deathly silence. The closer they came to Québec City, the busier became the scene before them. As they looked toward the far shore of the river they noted groups of people, some washing clothes, some constructing makeshift shelters and others, just huddled around fires in an attempt to keep warm. Many were in rags and shoeless. Others draped themselves in ragged blankets and shawls. Nearer to the city their numbers increased to hundreds. A shanty-town was constructed right on the very shores of the St. Lawrence

The reports that had come to Dr. Langley, could not describe the numbing sight that greeted Molly and her family on their arrival that October morning in 1847.

"My God," Molly breathed. "The season is supposed to be nearly over. What in God's name must it have been like here all year? These people are starving and will soon be freezing. What chance do they have?"

"For that matter, what desire can they have? God has definitely forsaken these people." Liam added, surveying the dreadful scene before him.

After safely transporting the wagon, animals and families across the river, John suggested, "we must find a temporary place to settle ourselves for the night and get our bearings. We have no idea what's happening on the river. I suggest we carry on and make camp outside of the city until we can all figure out where we'll be going next. I know Québec City was our destination for now, but I don't want to invite harm into this family. We have too many lives to consider."

They quietly nodded agreement and proceeded silently on their way. Scene upon scene of despair would capture their gazes. Barely a child was seen to be clad with shoes or boots. Some had rags, no longer fit to wear, wrapped and bound with twine around their feet, but the majority were barefoot. A woman sat listlessly, feeding a babe at her sunken breast. Every muscle in her emaciated body sagged feebly. She looked to be a hundred years old. A man crouched on his haunches before a dying fire, lethargically poking a stick into the ashes in an attempt to capture some hidden warmth beneath. They passed others returning from the river with pans filled with water, while others were heading out on the very same mission. But through it all, could still be heard the sound of a melodeon, a voice raised in song, and the magical sound of youngsters laughing at their play. The human spirit was undeniably alive and in some cases, very strong.

Chapter 5

Québec City/Grosse Isle, P.Q. – 1847-1851

Life in Québec City was not at all what the O'Connors or the Dermitts had expected. The Irish immigration was deeply imbedded in the lives of all the city's residents. Thousands of people could not pass through any port annually and not have a permanent effect on its population. And this particular year there had reportedly been over 100,000 migrants pass through the port of Québec City alone. The potato famine had reached its peak in 1847 and the majority of immigrants arriving from Irish shores were starving, malnourished and extremely poor. No wonder the dreaded typhoid fever ravaged the passengers on the often poorly-equipped ships that transported them to Canada. In that same year nearly four hundred and fifty ships registered in Québec City and of those, nearly four hundred were inspected at Grosse Isle. They would remain quarantined from one to three weeks and in that time would lay at anchor between Québec City and Grosse Isle some thirty miles downstream from the city.

The situation was desperate at Grosse Isle, a small island only three miles long and less than one mile wide. It had been a quarantine station since before 1830 when European immigrants had fled epidemics that were raging across Europe and Great Britain. A cholera pandemic hit England in 1831 and the disease was carried to Canada by migrants that were, for the greater part, Irish. Thus, Grosse Isle was founded to accommodate the 30,000 plus, yearly immigrants wanting to settle in Canada. Immigration was constant for the most part over the years leading up to the explosive Irish exodus in 1847. That year alone Grosse Isle processed roughly nine thousand patients with typhoid fever, of which close to six thousand were believed to have died. The island became a massive graveyard. Thousands more were to die elsewhere in Canada.

Finding decent living arrangements was the first obstacle facing the city's newest residents. Although many of the permanent residents were themselves of Irish background, it was virtually impossible to find decent, clean accommodations that would accept Irish tenants. The slums and outskirts were filled with vermin-infested hovels, where disease bred uncontrollably. Finally, as luck would have it, they would eventually find a firm but kindly French Canadian landlord who was willing to put them up, but only with the understanding, that he would be, collecting the weekly rent, in advance, and inspecting the premises himself.

"Any sign of the dirt or the cockroach, and out youse go. Simple as dat!" he adamantly informed them.

Molly smiled and assured him, he definitely didn't have to be concerned. "We are only travel weary and dusty, Mr. Lavoie. We'll all soon be right as rain. A hot, soapy tub, will transform us before your eyes, rest assured."

It wasn't the house in the glen, but once again, a few feminine touches would brighten the place considerably. Fuel must be found for the stove and fireplace, clean mattresses purchased and some articles of furniture provided. Many pieces had arrived safely on the wagon but others had naturally been left behind when space could not be found to transport them to their new home. Some linens and clothing had begun to mildew after the rains, there being little opportunity to properly dry and air them. But now the two women set to work washing, drying and sorting, cleaning, hanging, and generally settling in.

Molly's mind's eye continually crept back to the sight of the poor wretches they had passed on the waterfront and throughout the city. She was desperate to get out among them to lend her hand and try to make their lives more bearable. Typhoid she knew spread like wild fire when left unattended and she had already recognised many signs of the disease among those ignored in their misery. Shivering, congested faces and bloodshot eyes were apparent in most, but some even had the drunken appearance of those close to delirium. The starvation, dirt and overcrowded conditions would only exacerbate the situation.

Many had escaped the crowding of the city to venture into the outlying countryside, only to take the scourge with them. They would have no medical attention, resulting in only the strongest surviving. The rest would be scattered over the landscape in poorly or unmarked graves, a sad testimony to their struggle to find a safe haven in a new land.

While the women scrubbed, the men ventured out to explore the city and bring back a supply of stove and lamp fuel. Mattresses were purchased for the second floor bedrooms where they could lay directing on the floor without fear of moisture and damage. In the common room, where John, Colin, and Patrick would sleep, wooden bed frames were quickly constructed to keep the mattresses off the cold, damp, main-level floor. Liam and Sean's young families would be able to maintain some sense of privacy in the two bedrooms above. By the evening on the day following their arrival at 15 Rue Montagne, they sat before a warm fire, sipping Irish Whiskey and reliving the past month as they travelled the forests of New Brunswick and the shores of the St. Lawrence River. That behind them, they could now plan for the future, look for employment and save towards their proposed homestead in Upper Canada's Ottawa Valley.

*   *   *

The week following their arrival brought blessedly mild, sunny weather. The evenings carried a bite in the air. Just a gentle warning of mother nature's intent. The men were up and out early in the mornings to comb the city and surrounding areas in search of work. Liam accompanied Molly in search of the offices of the chief medical officers. It was apparent, the current immigration season had worn them down and most responded lethargically and showed little interest. They viewed the situation as hopeless and she was to learn that the station at Grosse Isle was to be shut down very soon as the season was coming to an end. Merciful as that was, it did not take into consideration the swarms of people living in the open air on the water's edge or secreted in hidden passages and alleys throughout the city.

Before the station was closed for the season on November 3rd, 1847, Molly and Liam were privileged to meet Dr. George Douglas, a kind, compassionate human being who just happened to be the administrator of Grosse Isle. He was the same Dr. Douglas to whom Dr. Langley had so kindly introduced her in a letter of reference. He took them to Grosse Isle as it was being prepared for shut down ending a particularly horrendous season. The station had been expanded that season to allow for the excessive amount of migrants to pass through its doors. The original, shed-like hospital was able to house two-hundred patients with some comfort. The three mile long, island was inhabited with clusters of sheds, shanties and tents, augmenting the completely overrun hospital facilities. They visited two fever sheds, a building to house the staff and a bakery. Two small chapels had also been erected for patient and staff use. Other small buildings dotted the landscape. Some 10,000 infected emigrants and staff had already inhabited these meagre accommodations over the past six months. If the patients were able to walk, they were sent on to Montreal or Québec City to make room for others. Only the most desperate were kept on, with the result that over half of the roughly nine thousand processed at Grosse Isle hospital would remain on the island forever. The number of burial sites was staggering, the worst being the unmarked mass graves.

Molly choked back her misery. Liam enfolded her in his arms as they silently surveyed the remains of the battlefield before them. "I just can't believe all these poor souls have travelled so far to escape death, only to end up rotting on strange shores. What have our people ever done to deserve this? How many more will die just like this before it ends? Damn the potato! Damn the landlords! Damn the greedy ship owners! Damn them all to bloody hell!" Her body shook uncontrollably as the frustrations of the past year came to the fore. She wept for all those who had died. She wept for those who still lived, but faced a grim future, without those they left behind. But mostly she wept for Ireland.

As the month of October drew to a close, so too did the arrival of migrant ships. On November 3rd, the doors closed to new patients and the station shut down for the winter season. Many people still wandered the streets, dangerously ill. Those who still suffered the effects of typhoid often succumbed to pneumonia in their weakened state. Often the local residents disregarded the needs of these hapless strangers in their city. It seemed easier to turn a blind eye than to offer decent shelter, food, and medical care. Often through desperation and just sheer driving hunger, some of the squatters would become reckless and violent in their attempts to find food and secure a dry, warm shelter. Fights would break out between the long-time residents and the marauding gangs of desperadoes. The very worst of their nature manifested itself as they fought for survival.

*   *   *

Winter was closing in as even the days were taking on a bite, even under the bright sunlight. Frost filled the nights, and the odd drifting flake of snow landed on the frozen earth. The men combed the city for jobs that were scarce or only temporary. But with everyone contributing they were able to eat and keep comfortably warm. Saving for their trip to the Ottawa Valley was not a concern now until the end of the winter, when they hoped they would all be able to secure permanent employment.

It was agreed among the family members that Liam should stay with Molly and accompany her in her endeavours to help the remaining migrants in the city. From early morning until dusk they combed the shanty towns, giving what relief they could. Dr. Douglas supplied them with medications, dressings, and bandages in the hope that they would be able to comfort at least a few poor souls in their misery. Their maladies ranged from stomach cramps to haemorrhaging, from chest cold to full-blown typhoid fever. Child mortality was high, their already-weakened bodies unable to cope with most fever and infection. Newborns were sapping the life from their diseased mothers. The watery milk from their sunken breasts caused diarrhoea in the infants, resulting dehydration, starvation, and eventually merciful death.

Liam hired a hand cart, which they would take daily to the local soup kitchen, load up with supplies of beef tea, biscuits, potatoes, oatmeal, and molasses and deliver to those unable to make their way and stand in line for their daily nourishment.

In some cases, women were left to survive on their own with starving children clinging to their skirts, their husbands off hunting for employment or more often drinking and brawling with cronies. Molly found one such mother with four children under the age of five, all in advanced stages of starvation, hanging listlessly from her body, the only meagre comfort they could find. Their shelter was made with segments of fencing, covered with canvas sail material. Rags littering the dirt floor, served as their bed. Their only belongings appeared to be a battered pot for cooking, a chipped enamel basin for washing, a few stained bowls, mugs and a handful of tarnished cutlery. The serviceable clothes they owned all seemed to be on their backs. Hanging on the wall was a single kerosene lamp, it's globe blackened with use. It was only used for emergencies as the fuel was hard to find and extremely expensive. The only touch of luxury to be seen was a single, brass-framed picture of the Blessed Virgin that hung conspicuously above the chaos. The brass was polished to a brilliant sheen and the glass covering the Virgin's picture, displayed not a hint of dust. A hand crafted quilt, somewhat worse for wear, featuring the likeness of the green hills of Ireland, was draped near the open front of the shanty.

Molly ventured closer to the despondent woman, offering what scant sustenance the city could still provide. Even the shivering waifs that clung desperately to her side were scarce able to show any interest in the food being offered. The rags in the hovel behind them erupted suddenly and a growl came forth. "Wha the hell you be wantin now? Can't ya leave a poor bugger alone? Get ta hell away with ya." The growl retreated back into the stinking rags, leaving Molly and Liam staring in disbelief.

"It's only the drink, Miss," the listless woman offered. "He can't be finding work, but there's always a bottle at hand. God provides," she shrugged, staring at the frozen ground.

Knowing the woman was too weak and tired to prepare nourishment for her youngsters, they left bread and beef tea, promising to return with better fare in the evening. She was just one of many who had, or would some day succumb to starvation, leaving behind her small, helpless family to the sanctuary of the church orphanages. Others may be taken into service, while a few, possibly more fortunate, would be adopted into Canadian families.

"You're very quiet, darlin," Liam noted as they headed back home with their empty cart.

"I'm just having a hard time believing God has forsaken so many of our people. They've only escaped one horror to be confronted with another. Only it's worse here because nothing is familiar to them. At least starving and dying on Irish soil, meant they would at least be buried on Irish soil. But here there is nothing for them, absolutely nothing." Tears filled her eyes as Liam pulled her close and she comforted herself in his warm strength.

Winter settled in around them, a blanket of white covering everything in sight. Gone were the dreary, dark days of rain so common on the Irish winter landscape. The cold was biting and seemingly never ending, but the air was crisp and clean. Even invigorating in its severity. As the winter months marched on, the men of the O'Connor and Dermitt families continued to find work in one form or another. The Irish where known to be hard working and fast learners. Those who stayed away from the demon drink could easily secure and maintain jobs. The mighty river became frozen solid, virtually putting the shipping traffic on hold until the spring thaw. The men were able to find work supplying fuel, black-smithing, offering repair and delivery services.

Molly convinced John and Patrick to keep their work close to home until the harsh winter months subsided. The cold, indeed aggravated Patrick's arthritis and many times kept him bed ridden. Yet he refused to complain and continued to count his blessings, although often consumed with sadness over the loss, the previous year, of his beloved Colleen. John saw to the family's daily needs, while still taking periodic jobs close to home. All in all, their first winter in Québec City was comfortable and rather uneventful.

Molly's eldest brother Colin had taken a bartending job at a local public house. After some weeks, he announced to his family, "I've met a wonderful little lass. Her name's Lisette. A French Canadian girl. Pretty as a picture. Her hair's long and raven like our ma had. I want you all to meet her."

Clapping her hands in delight, Molly laughed. "Well, finally our Colin has fallen," she sang. "I've never known our Colin to be in love. Finally the mighty has fallen," she winked at him and danced away laughing.

"Oh, Lord, what have I created?" Colin grimaced in jest. "The likes of you will scare her away to be sure. I haven't a chance now."

"Don't try getting out of this one, big brother," Sean smirked. "You nearly drove Kathleen screaming down the hills of Creggan with your practical jokes, so be prepared. It's time to pay for the sins of the past. Ha, ha." Sean smacked his brother hard on the back, nearly sending him sprawling.

"Sweet Jesus, what have I done?" Colin lamented, falling on his knees in supplication to an unseen Deity. "If this harridan gets her hands on Lisette, I may never see her again."

"Get up you silly fool and go get your Lisette. Corned beef and cabbage for dinner this evening. I hope she likes ...," and off went Molly, muttering preparations to herself, a smile of anticipation lighting up her face. Lisette would be their first formal guest since their arrival in Québec.

Lisette proved to be the very centre of Colin's reason for being. Molly watched with amusement as this once, rough edged brother of hers, fairly doted on the new miss in his life. He couldn't seem to lavish enough attention upon her as she responded with a sweet, shy smile. French was her mother language, but she managed to speak enough to be understood. Molly was astounded at the resemblance to her own dead mother. John gazed at her in disbelief. They all promptly fell under her spell.

*   *   *

Winter edged into spring, the snow retreated and the breaking ice floes in the river roared incessantly as they fought their way downstream towards the Atlantic Ocean. The sweet smell of cherry and apple blossoms permeated the air. The maple trees formed their buds and covered the city with pollen dust, Mother Nature's bounty. It was amid this setting of life's renewal that Colin and Lisette took their marriage vows.

When having first met Lisette, John had wondered about the religious obstacle that confronted his eldest son and his new love. Lisette was French Canadian and

Roman Catholic. The O'Connors were Irish and Protestant. "Have you considered the possibility of future problems that may arise from this union lad? The lass is, and has been, Roman Catholic all her life. I know your religious convictions are not the strongest, but you still must consider what lies ahead for the both of you."

Sitting before his father, the man he most respected and loved in the world, Colin volunteered his decision. Raising his head from his cupped hands he spoke softly but firmly. "Da, I've never loved anyone so desperately in my whole life. I've always been so guarded in that respect. Now I've found Lisette and she means the world to me. We can't let anything get in our way. No matter what, we still believe in the same God and that must account for something." He spread his huge hands in question. "I've agreed to take instruction in the church and with that I will promise to raise our children in the Roman Catholic faith. This is Canada dad, not Ireland. The church doesn't run this country. What we do with our lives should be our concern and in all truthfulness I find nothing wrong with what we plan to do." Looking back down at his hands he waited for his father's reply.

It came slowly. "Colin, you're my eldest child. You've never taken the matter of 'love' lightly. I've often wondered if you would ever find the right lass and settle down. But it's quite obvious to me, you love Lisette with all your heart. As long as you know what you are facing and are willing to meet it together, you will always have my blessing. This family is strong, and it takes strong individuals to make it work. So just remember, we'll always be here for one another. Lisette will soon be the newest member of our family and we'll love her as our own. Congratulations son." Clasping his son in his arms, he quipped, "get on with it now lad. Make us proud."

Springtime in Québec was beautiful and a better time could not be found for the wedding of Lisette Boudreau and Colin O'Connor. Preparations consumed the household as they attempted to have Colin and Lisette married before the new season of immigration was upon them. Laughter and excitement filled their hearts. The gentle weather prevailed and soon they were all gathered under a grove of lush green maple and giant oaks, to unite a shy, delicate Lisette to a nervously beaming Colin. Their vows exchanged, celebrations duly attended, and congratulations accepted, they hastily excused themselves, and headed off to begin their new life.

*   *   *

Rumours had it that this year's first emigrant ships would be arriving up river very soon. Once this began, Molly and Liam would be spending considerable time between Grosse Isle and Québec City. Having witnessed their hard, driving work during the past winter, tending to the sick and starving squatters throughout the city, Dr. Douglas had confirmed his decision to have them work with his patients on the quarantine island. It was not expected that such massive amounts of people would be settling on these shores as had the previous year, but many would still be arriving, and of those who survived the Atlantic crossing, many would be starving and ill. Many of last years Grosse Island staff had succumbed to the typhoid themselves. Long hours and dangerously infectious conditions had eventually resulted in loss of life for dozens of the tired, hard-working staff. Grosse Isle had become known as the Coffin Island.

Life carried on, much as usual in the O'Connor/ Dermitt household. Kathleen cared for the children and the house, while still finding time to tutor some of the neighbourhood children to read and write. Patrick agreed to remain at home while the others worked at whatever they could find. Molly and Liam often spent days at a time away from home, working at the station. As was predicted, the number of immigrants had greatly decreased from the year before, but so also had the staff. They worked feverishly hard, but the mental anguish was the most difficult obstacle to overcome. Returning home in the evenings, they related the stories from their homeland and counted their blessings they were all safe here in Canada.

Stories began to spread that an Irish rebel faction were becoming a force to be reckoned with, even in Canada, thousands of miles away from Irish shores. Gangs of marauders had continued to comb the city streets at night, harassing its citizens in search of food, money and support. These rebels were feeding off the desperation of the homeless emigrants. Fights would break out for seemingly no reason, but for the attention it caused. Recruiting was swift, and loyalty to Ireland and the cause was their only criteria for membership.

Each family member, had at one time or another been approached by members of these bands. The Irish families who refused to follow their lead were often shunned or badgered into submission. As it was common knowledge that Molly Dermitt tended the sick, it was not uncommon for her to arrive home, to find a wounded marauder waiting on their doorstep expecting to be treated, no questions asked. After some months of her freely given attention to these troublemakers, she gradually began to refuse her services and would send them off to the local hospital clinic for treatment. The actions of these brawlers troubled her, and it worried her that they were in her home and around the children. Eventually, no one from the bands came to their door.

The season carried on through the sultry, hot summer months. By day's end, the heat and hard, driving work would sap the strength from those on the station. By evening Molly and Liam welcomed the steamer trip back home. This excursion, allowed them a much needed respite from the world around them and time to enjoy one another. The scenery on the north shore of the St. Lawrence River was pristine. Pretty little villages with shining white homes, colourful gardens and neat little chapels, dotted the forest-backed shoreline. Molly lay back in the protection of her husband's arms as they admired the scenes before them. "They're such a world apart from our world, Liam. Do you think they care, or even know, what lies on that little island back there? Look at that church spire. It's reaching right through the cloud. Maybe it's connecting them to God. Why do I feel our people have lost their connection to God, Liam? Why do you think God has forsaken Ireland?"

Hugging his wife, Liam attempted to lighten the mood by responding, "and why, my darlin', do you pose such complicated questions to this uncomplicated man?"

Laughing, they hugged and lay back once again to enjoy the peace before them.

*   *   *

The house was in an uproar when they arrived home in the early evening. Kathleen was at wits end because she hadn't seen hide nor hair of Matthew since the dinner hour. He played with the neighbouring children after lessons were finished, but it was out of character for him to be gone for more than an hour or so without pestering Kathleen for snacks for himself and friends. He had not been seen for over six hours and none of the neighbouring children seemed to know where he had gone. The men that had returned from work were all out combing the city. Someone had to have seen a little boy on his own in the streets.

Shortly after Molly and Liam's arrival home, a ragged looking youth of fourteen or fifteen came to their door bearing a message. He waited for no response, but fled off down the street as if attempting to outrun the devil. Ripping it open, Liam read, 'Molly Dermitt— Come to 100 rue Royale immediate. Man shot. No constabulary! We have the boy. Tell no one.' In stunned disbelief, Liam dropped the paper. "The dirty bastards. They have Matthew."

"What Liam, what in God's name are you saying?" Molly screamed. Picking up the paper she read the message for herself. "My God. Who are they? Let's go Liam. Now!" Grabbing her satchel, she headed for the door.

"They said, 'no constabulary'. They must be dangerous." Breathing hard, he ordered Kathleen, "tell no one where we've gone. Tell da and the rest that we've found Matthew but you don't know where we've gone. We can't have anyone running off half-cocked after this bunch, whoever they are." Kathleen nodded her agreement, her cupped hands to her mouth, holding back the sobs.

Asking directions to rue Royale, they quickly combed the streets of the city. At the end of rue Royale lay a shanty town of wooden shacks and lean-tos. The shanty town was 100 rue Royale. "Where do we begin?" Molly sobbed.

Standing in the middle of the jumble of shacks, wondering where to search next, Liam felt a hard rap on his shoulder. Spinning around, he was jabbed with the end of a shillelagh to his chest. A burly, unkempt Irishman demanded, "what's the likes of him doin here?" His question was directed to Molly, but his black eyes never left Liam's.

"He's my husband. His name is Liam Dermitt. We told no one. Now where's our son?" She was nervous, but her voice was forceful.

"Don't get yer knickers in a knot, m'lady," the giant offered sarcastically. "We have to make sure no one be followin' ya. Come on then."

Cautiously they followed, wanting to know where their son was, but not wanting to anger the rogue who was hopefully leading them to Matthew. Eventually, the giant approached one of the shacks and announced their arrival. A burlap sack, covering the doorway was drawn back by a slatternly looking female occupant. Her hair hung in greasy strings around an emaciated face. Her eyes were black holes, devoid of any expression. Without a word, she beckoned them inside. The interior was black with no windows to offer light. As their eyes were attempting to adjust to the darkness, their ears heard moans from the rear portion of the shack. A man lay on his back in the dimness with just the rays of light from the sack-covered doorway reaching his supine form.

"Bring me my son before I look at this man." She ordered the woman at the door. "If my son is not alive, I have no reason to keep you alive," she snarled at the man on the cot. "You could have sent someone to my home for me, without resorting to kidnapping my son. What kind of man are you?"

"Shut up, woman," he growled. "You refused to help my men before. What makes you think I should trust you to come to me? This way I knew you'd not deny me. I'm not a stupid man."

"That's debatable now I'm sure." She spun around as she heard the woman return and grabbed Matthew as he ran into her arms. Soothing her young son, she ran her fingertips over his tear-stained cheeks and down his trembling frame. "It's all right my darling, you're safe now. Be a good lad and go with your da and wait for me outside. I shan't be long. There's my brave little lad." Handing him over to Liam, she said, "I'll be fine. It's best you wait outside with Matthew. Go now." Reluctantly, Liam turned to go, carrying their young son out into the sunlight.

"Now then, let's get on with it, shall we?" She faced the man before her, who was now at her mercy. She wasted no sympathy as she got on with the job of removing a bullet, lodged deeply in the man's hip. The woman lit a lantern and poured white whiskey from a half-empty bottle, into a battered mug. The man gulped it greedily, preparing for what he knew was in store for him. Molly, none too gently, prepared the wounded area, cleaning it with carbolic acid from her satchel. "What's your first name?" she inquired of the still conscious man.

"Sean," he whispered hoarsely.

"Well, Sean, I won't let you die, but I can't say I shan't let you suffer," she breathed into his tortured face. "But then, no amount of pain will compare to the torture you yourself has just put Matthew's father and myself through. Now, are you ready for your sentence?" With those cryptic words, she laid open the wound at his hip, rendering her patient helpless. The bullet had lodged in the bone with barely enough protruding to attach her forceps. Her work was swift and sure as she quickly staunched the fresh flow of blood.

The whiskey had barely deadened the excruciating torture Molly was inflicting on her helpless victim. "God, you're one cruel bitch," he croaked, as sweat raced down his brow to soak the pillow beneath his head.

"Be thankful you're still alive. Bleeding to death could be an option." She dressed the wound quickly and rose to leave. "My brother's name is Sean. It disgusts me to think of the likes of you with such a noble name."

As she headed for the door and the blessed freshness of the outside world she heard him whisper, "Molly, I'm sorry for the pain I put ye through. You have a fine lad there."

In a short time, they were home once again. As the evening's events were related to the rest of the family and Matthew fell asleep in his fathers arms, Molly retreated to their second-floor room where she wept and prayed undisturbed until her body succumbed to exhaustion and she retreated into a deep sleep.

Chapter 6

Québec City/Grosse Isle, P.Q. – 1850-1851

Three years had passed since the *Looshtank* brought Molly and her family from Liverpool to the shores of Canada. They were to learn, that in 1847 the *Looshtank* again returned to Canada with yet another load of Irish immigrants but under the direction of another captain. Sickness had forced her captain to put in at Chatham, New Brunswick. Some hundred and seventeen of her four-hundred and sixty passengers had died during the seven-week voyage across the Atlantic. Forty more had died on Middle Island where they were housed in old fish sheds, victims to the elements. The survivors were taken on to Grosse Isle where there were over twenty-five-hundred patients, many sharing beds. Waiting to be cared for, others lay on the beaches and throughout the grassy hills of the island.

The spring and summer months of 1848 and 1849 found the numbers of emigrants drop by about one third as news of the tragedy of 1847 reached England and Ireland. In these two years, the Port of Québec accepted roughly 65,000 new emigrants. Of those, only fifteen hundred were transported to Grosse Isle and three-hundred and twenty died. So although the work at the station was difficult, it was bearable both physically and mentally. Dr. Douglas eventually became ill with typhoid but recovered to carry on his miraculous work.

In the summer of 1850 Colin and Lisette were blessed with a baby boy they named John Pierre. Although his birth was relatively uncomplicated, in the months to follow, Lisette's fragile health got progressively more tenuous. John Pierre was a healthy, demanding baby who continually sapped her already frail form. An epidemic of Influenza struck the city that autumn attacking even the strongest of its citizens. Lisette in her weakened condition, contracted the disease and was dead within two weeks of its onset. John Pierre was taken home with Kathleen to care for him, but Colin refused to leave the only home he and his beloved wife had known. He sunk into despondency, lost his job, and eventually took every penny they had saved for the future and turned to drink. Thomas and Sean dragged him home from the waterfront pubs, cleaned him up, and coerced him into sleeping off his drugged condition. Upon arising he spoke to no one, but dressed and left to repeat the cycle. He showed no interest in his young son despite Kathleen's pleadings. His life was taking a down hill spiral and he had no desire to stop its progress.

Molly's heart broke to see her handsome brother's life deteriorate into a shambles. By September she was well advanced into her second pregnancy. Confused by the rather excelerated growth of the child she carried she requested that Dr. Douglas offer his opinion on her condition. Shortly into the examination he smiled and exclaimed, "well, Molly lass, you are going to be the mother of twins! By your calculations they should be with us sometime before Christmas. Congratulations! From now on, get off your feet as often as possible and get in touch with me at any sign of trouble. I'll check on you each week." Smiling, he left them to digest the latest news.

"Soon, we'll be having more children than adults in this household," laughed Kathleen as her sister-in-law stared mutely at her own distended belly.

"I think it's time we made one of the bedrooms into

a nursery. Now with John Pierre and these two to come, there'll be babies all over the place. We'll need more cribs. Either that, or we need to find a larger home. What will Liam say?" Molly rambled on.

"He'll say, 'two for the price of one'," Liam laughed as he entered the room. He had met Dr. Douglas on his way up the street and just received the astonishing news. He was just so relieved his Molly was healthy, the news of the extra baby they would soon have was secondary in his mind. "Come on lass, don't you be worrying now. We'll do just fine. By the time the babies are big enough, we'll be on our way to Upper Canada. Just you mind yourself now, and no dancin' jigs or doing head stands up the rue," he teased her. "Come here, give us a hug, while I can still get me arms around you. I love you, babies and all."

Memories of Creggan returned, the evenings once again filled with the round-table discussions of plans for moving on towards the Ottawa Valley. Many reasons were building up to feed their desire to move on. They all felt Colin would be better off away from the continuous reminder of Lisette and their life together. John Pierre would still be a factor in his life but it was hoped it would be easier for him to accept his son if they moved away from Québec. With five children, their families were growing rapidly and it was time to consider settling down and homesteading. The dream was still to build the family lumber business into a thriving venture

On one such evening while the families discussed travelling plans and the best time of the year to begin their trek into the wilderness, Thomas entered the house in a great state of agitation. "John, I need to talk with you right away. Can we go outside for a moment?"

Nodding, John rose and the rest looked to one

another questioningly.

Outside, Thomas quickly explained to John that Colin was in grave danger. After getting very drunk he found himself in the middle of a donnybrook in a public house known for its nightly brawls between the orange and the green Irish factions. In those environments, one was usually as drunk as the next, but in this particular case Colin had stopped the end of a knife several times in his gut. As if by a miracle, Thomas had left his work on the docks late and was wending his way home. He heard the scuffle and shouts in the pub and stopped to investigate only to find his brother-in-law lying in the middle of the floor, his lower body bathed in blood. Patrons scurried out the door in their attempt to flee the scene. Thomas was able to get help and transported Colin in a pony cart to the hospital where he was now holding onto life by a hair. Thomas had not wanted Molly, in her state, to become alarmed, so had called John from the house.

Re-entering the house, John called to Sean, "there's been an accident on the docks. We need your help." Sean jumped to his father's command.

Liam rose to leave with them, but John put up his hand to detain him. "It's alright lad. You stay here with the women. We'll be back directly. This shouldn't take long. We'll explain later." His choppy speech revealed his agitation but warned Liam to ask no questions as they left.

As the evening wore on, the stressful wait for Molly was probably no less difficult than had she known of Colin's predicament. She was thankful Liam was at home with them, but his continuous pacing and opening and closing the front door nearly drove them to distraction. Shortly after he was about to leave the house in search of his brother and the others, they returned home.

They had not noticed that Thomas was covered in blood when he had come to collect John and Sean. As he entered the house Molly cried in horror as she observed the dried, caked blood covering his shirt and arms. "My God, Thomas, what's happened to ye?"

"He's alright Molly. Sit you down while we explain what's happened." John steered her to a chair at the table. "It's our Colin. He's in the hospital. He was in a fight in a waterfront pub and suffered multiple knife wounds to the stomach. They've performed surgery on him and he's recovering as we speak. The doctor said he's still in grave danger, but a day or two will tell the story."

Molly rose to gather her cloak. "Take me to him," she whispered. "No, don't look at me that way. He's my brother and I want to be with him, now. You either get the cart and take me, or I walk."

Not wanting to agitate her further, they helped her to the cart. She remained dry-eyed until she sat by the bed of her unconscious brother. The tears flowed as she mopped his brow with a damp cloth and whispered encouragement to his unresponsive form lying so deathly still on the hospital bed. She talked to him through the night. She talked of Ireland when they were children. She talked of the many practical jokes he had always played on herself and Sean. She talked of Lisette and baby John Pierre. She talked of their plans to leave for Upper Canada in the new year. She poured out her soul to her eldest brother and she begged him to muster the will to live.

She finally dozed, her head in his outstretched hand. Some hours into the new day a weak voice came to her like an angel. "God help me, will this harridan not let a man die in peace. It seems no matter what I do, she's right there to badger me." Colin smiled weakly at his sleepy-eyed sister.

"If you don't remember every word I've said Colin O'Connor, I shall be right here to repeat it to you word for word." Tears filled her eyes as she kissed his hand and held it again her soaked cheek. "Don't ever do this again. I can't lose my big brother. We have so many things to do yet."

Once Colin regained consciousness, John left to join Sean, Liam, and Thomas to trace the whereabouts of Colin's assailant. Questioning the owner of the drinking house, they found out that Colin was not caught in the middle of a political melee of the Orange and the Green, but was a victim of his own confrontation with a French Canadian patron who had challenged him on his marriage to Lisette. The Frenchman had made many unfound accusations with the influence of the drink egging him on. Colin, although in no condition to retaliate, had responded. The Frenchman had nearly fatally stabbed an unarmed man but was no where to be found. They learned shortly thereafter that he had fled into the northern reaches of Québec. They knew it was highly unlikely he would be found, but armed with his name and description they planned to publish his likeness on every police billboard they could find. With determination, they would eventually bring this man to justice.

Molly returned daily to redress his wounds. She always brought his favourite meals to assure he would eat and quickly gain back his strength. In a very short time he was released to go home under her care. "If I was a true Catholic, I'd be sure I was heading for purgatory," he moaned playfully as Molly fussed over him. "I'm definitely paying for my sins to be sure."

Over the following weeks of convalescence Colin grew closer to his tiny son. It was hard, not to look into his eyes and see the woman he grieved for so desperately. But holding his young son in his arms, he soon realised this helpless child, who would never know his mother, could not lose his father as well. "I've been such a selfish, foolish man, John Pierre. I'll not leave you again, sweet boy."

By November, Molly was barely able to stand her pregnant condition. Her ankles and feet swelled until the skin was taut and purple, forcing her to spend much of her time propped in bed with her legs elevated. Her position in bed caused the babies to press up against her lungs and stomach, causing great discomfort. Dr. Douglas suggested she should try to hold out for as long as possible in her last month of the pregnancy, but if the worst came to the worst he would perform a caesarean section. Molly was determined to suffer out the remaining month unless her life or the babies' were in danger. Her normal sweet nature turned decidedly worse because of her immobility. She was the one being cared for and she wanted none of it.

"Darlin' there'll soon be four babies in this household and you and Kathleen will have your hands full and all. Rest while you can now." Liam's attempts to console his wife seemed to infuriate her more.

"Quit mollycoddling me man! I'm sick to death of listening to the likes of you all telling me what I should be feeling. Get to work, the lot of you, and leave us women alone. We can do just fine without you all hanging around, thank you." Waving them off with her hands, they all quickly retreated out the door. Even poor Patrick headed off up the street to the bakery, where he could enjoy the aromas and the heat blasting from the bread ovens.

In two more weeks Molly was suffering from false labours, seemingly brought on the by the pressures of the two babies growing rapidly in her body. Dr. Douglas had attempted to convince her to complete her last few days in the hospital, but to no avail. She remained where she thought she should be and where her babies should be born. One particularly stormy night in December 1850, two baby boys announced their arrival to the world. Sean, born first, was there before Dr. Douglas could make his appearance. Erin took his sweet time and heralded his arrival in the lustiest fashion. Though both were relatively small they were healthy and strong. Sean was quiet, and content to rest at his mother's breast, while Erin squalled and kicked at his wrappings until his little body lay free to the open air. Now he was satisfied to search out and nuzzle his mother.

With four babies and Matthew, Christmas was a time to behold. Neighbours came in droves with gifts for all the children and baked goods for the adults. Molly and Liam's hard work had paid off over the past three years and friends and neighbours knew how to show their appreciation. The family was respected and recognised by all as hard working and honest. They had suffered many setbacks this past year but their strength had prevailed. The births of Sean and Erin had been a much needed catharsis. Colin was on the mend and his baby son was the focus of his life. Life was good, as 1850 drew to a close.

Chapter 7

Québec City/Upper Canada -1852

As the new year rolled into spring, plans to move to Upper Canada were near to completion. Once again a travel route had been mapped and provisions stockpiled in preparation. This time they would travel without livestock. The animals they had brought from New Brunswick to Québec City they had sold off when they settled in their Québec home. Matthew had grieved for weeks after that transaction and it was decided by all that it would be best not to purchase more until they were able to settle in Upper Canada. What food they needed could be purchased or hunted along the way. Their wagon this time would be equipped with a canvas cover to protect them from any inclement weather. Having so many babies to care for on this journey, the men equipped the wagon for comfort and convenience as best they could. Once again, they purchased two sturdy horses to transport them into the Canadian wilderness.

In the earlier part of the nineteenth century a good percentage of the surviving emigrants from Ireland eventually settled in Upper Canada. Many worked in the lumber trade or farmed the fertile Ottawa Valley. Work was plentiful and although life in the back woods was difficult and often near impossible, the O'Connor/Dermitt family were blessed with their numbers of healthy, hardworking adults. They knew what they were facing and they welcomed the challenge. Their goals were high but far from unrealistic. They certainly didn't lack manpower, with the addition of five young sons to carry on the family tradition. God willing, they would all be allowed to survive into manhood.

Now that Matthew was approaching age nine, he spent much of his time in the company of the men. He learned to care for the horses, collect wood and build a cooking fire. He was eager to be a man, and begged to help where he could. On occasion, much to his nine-year-old chagrin, Aunt Kathleen or his mother would ask him to watch that five-year-old Michael did not wander off away from the campsite while they cleaned and prepared meals. "It's time there was some girls brought into this family. My God, we're overrun with boys."

They laughed together in spite of the drudgery. "I suppose you're thinking it's my turn now?" Kathleen rolled her eyes in mock horror.

"Well, Michael is five years old now. I should think he'd love a little sister or two." Molly joked, dodging as Kathleen batted a urine-soaked napkin in her direction.

"Well let's just wait now 'til we get these three scallywags out of nappies. I've never seen so many wet bottoms in all m'life." But Kathleen's eyes shone as she picked up John Pierre and cuddled him to her bosom. "He's such a beautiful boy. I love him as if he were my own." Her mood changing, she asked. "Molly? Do you think Colin will ever marry again? He's suffered so much since Lisette's death."

"I can't say, Kat. He's so terribly quiet," Molly mused. "I worry so much about him. Liam thinks this trip will do him good. He'll be busy day and night, and eventually Sean will break through that barrier he's built around himself. He won't push him though. Sean knows his brother better than anyone. If anyone is able to reach him, Sean will." Molly watched her sister-in-law hug John Pierre to her and kiss his tousled little head. "Don't worry your head Kathleen. John Pierre will be with you a very long time I'm sure. You know that Colin wants to work with Liam and da to build the lumber mill when we homestead. He's a very sad man, but his son is very important to him and he wants him to grow up with love. He knows how good you are for John Pierre."

Kathleen smiled, reassured. "It's so good to have you for my sister. I love Sean but sometimes I just need another woman's point of view to help keep my sanity."

"Likewise!" Molly agreed.

They laughed together and went on with the preparation of the evening meal. In a few minutes they would be barraged with seven starving men, all expecting a hearty meal. At nine years old, they placed Matthew into the adult category because his appetite would often exceed that of any full-grown man. He was often asked, "where do you put it lad? You must have a hollow leg!" much to Matthews delight. He would then carry on eating with great gusto.

*   *   *

For some time their route followed the north shore of the St. Lawrence. In places, the banks of the river rose hundreds of feet above the churning river. The scenes were breathtakingly beautiful and the land around and below them seemed to be endless. Once they left the course of the river, they headed deep into untamed wilderness. The road they followed often traversed creek beds and was rutted and almost impassable at times. There was varying opinions from passers-by of the best route to follow on towards the Ottawa River. Many preferred the longer but more inhabited river route, while others suggested what could be a faster, cross country trek. The condition of the roads of course was dependent on the weather. Having begun their journey in the hotter, drier season, it was decided when they reached the village of Trois Rivieres, North East of the City of Montreal, they would make their way into the Québec wilderness and head west into the Ottawa Valley.

Small outposts dotted the highway where they could replenish provisions, repair spare wheels and harnesses and on occasion enjoy the luxury of a hot bath. Along the road they met new settlers, many of them pushing on into Northern Québec, others returning from the far reaches of the province, on business or gathering provisions for the coming winter. The greatest majority were Irish or French Canadian and those who were not farmers generally worked in the lumber industry or were suppliers to the lumber mills. This enabled the family to gather valuable information and opinions about the lumber industry and where the best prospects might lie.

Since their departure from Ireland, Kathleen had kept a personal journal. It was filled with their adventures, mishaps and celebrations of the past four years. Now, as they made their way through the wilderness, the journal was filling rapidly with the descriptions of the fascinating characters they encountered daily. One of the strangest creatures they came across on the narrow roadway was Lafayette, a merchant. If the truth be known, Lafayette, would be renowned as one of the biggest hustlers in the Québec forests. His black hair hung loosely to his waist. Two long braids, interwoven with leather thongs, framed each side of his face. His massive head was crowned with a twisted band of leather, a single eagle feather covered what should have been his left ear. Matthew stared, his mouth hanging open in disbelief at this mammoth creature now talking to his father.

They had set up camp for the night under a grove of giant oak. The wagon heading towards their campsite seemed twice as high as it was wide. Everything imaginable was suspended from the sides and piled upon the roof. The wagon swayed precariously along the rutted road. Lafayette reined in his two road weary horses and blithely jumped down from his perch. He called out a cheery greeting to his newly found acquaintances as he lumbered his huge frame across the clearing towards the campsite. He introduced himself to each and every member of the family, nodding approval at each hand shake. Each child was duly admired. "Ah, now you meet my wife." He waved towards the wagon. "Sweet Water. Come. Bring gifts for the children."

A shy, beautiful girl of perhaps twenty years old emerged from the wagon. Her dress of soft brown deerskin hung to her ankles where it met with colourfully beaded, skin moccasins. She was enormously huge with child, but none-the-less, carried a large basket filled with delights for any youngster. While Lafayette was busy with the men, showing them his wagon of goods, Sweet Water told Molly of her desire to have her baby on her reservation some miles to the north. She was a full-blooded Algonquin and desperately wanted to be with her mother and sisters at the birth of her first child. The reservation was currently plagued by an influenza epidemic and many of her people were dying. Lafayette was taking her to Québec City where he felt she would safely have their child and at the same time he could replenish his supplies before heading back into the northern woods. Sweet Water was desperately unhappy, yet she knew the importance of having her baby away from the diseased reservation. Molly did her very best to ease Sweet Water's troubled mind. She told her all about the hospital in Québec City.

"I will write a letter to introduce you to Dr. Douglas. He is a wonderful man and he will have them take good care of you and your baby. I know you will miss your mother and sisters but don't be frightened, you will be well cared for." Molly quietly attempted to ease the fear in her new friend. Most new mothers were fearful but she couldn't image the feeling of alienation this poor girl would experience her first time in a white man's hospital.

Early the next morning, after spending an entertaining evening in the company of the backwoods hustler and his enchanting wife, they bid their farewells and headed off in their respective directions. The men felt they had struck some good bargains with Lafayette and Sweet Water left clutching her letter of introduction to her bosom as she waved goodbye.

John had purchased a good hunting rifle and under Lafayette's tutelage had acquired some knowledge as to where the best hunting could be found and what signs to watch for. He had explained to them about the taste of wild game such a bear and venison and when it was best to kill so as to get the best flavoured meat. When the black bear was feeding on fish his meat would take on a distinctive fishy flavour. Venison if hunted in rutting season would taste strong and 'gamey'. They were learning valuable lessons about the wilderness.

At most settlements they were to find a trading post to restock fresh produce, flour, sugar and tea. They learned it was best not to carry a large stock of these goods because they may often be ruined with dampness or bugs. The extra weight they generated could make it nearly impossible to transverse the often impassable roads. So they learned to keep the weight down to a minimum in order to save time and energy.

The larger settlements offered the services of a bank, an inn, medical post, church, general store, and trading post. A bath could be found for a price and entertaining ladies for the road weary man. Molly and Kathleen, learned to reluctantly hold their tongues as Thomas and Colin would head off to explore the town and its offerings. More concerned about her big brother returning to the drink, Molly was eventually assured by Colin's continuous sobriety that she had little to fear. He was still not the happy-go-lucky brother of her youth, but he was slowly recovering from his loss of Lisette, and that she could be thankful for.

Sweet Water had told them of the epidemic of influenza ravaging her tribe. This particular tribe was many miles into the woods of Northern Québec but they were to learn of other closer encampments that were experiencing the same deadly scourge. Infection was quickly spreading from one camp to another as visiting tribes congregated with relatives and friends. Eventually the infection worked its way into the outposts and villages.

After leaving the St. Lawrence at Trois Rivieres and heading west towards the Ottawa River and the western border of Québec, travelling became slower and more laborious. The road was often badly rutted or even washed out in areas. Not wanting to tire the horses they moved on at a relatively slow, comfortable pace. On good days they could average twenty miles, whereas on days when the weather didn't co-operate or the terrain was particularly difficult only five to ten. The land had become very hilly and particularly thick growth lined the road. Summer rains arrived with a vengeance, converting the furrowed roadway to rushing streams of mud. At these times it was best to make camp, take time to hunt, wash clothes, and bake.

Matthew surprised Molly at his insistence to be taken along when the men went out to hunt for wild game. He had always been so tender-hearted when it came to animals, but he was rapidly growing into manhood and recognised the necessity of the hunt and the need for fresh meat. He learned that rainy weather was the best time in which to hunt as the sound of the falling rain would muffle their sounds and lessen the strange scent of the men in the bush. While accompanying his father and Uncle Sean on their first hunting trips, Matthew carried supplies and watched his father carefully as they made their way through the thick, tangled overgrowth. Over the weeks, Liam had allowed Matthew to practise holding and aiming the low-calibre rifle, when they found a clearing in which to rest and wait for sign of deer, rabbit, or even bear. This day Liam decided, if opportunity allowed, Matthew would have his first attempt at bagging a small animal.

The campsite exploded with youthful exuberance as Liam and Matthew headed in from their day of hunting. "Ma, ma, I did it ma," he shouted, walking towards his mother with a huge jackrabbit suspended from the end of the rifle slung over his shoulder. He was itching to run towards the camp with his trophy, but he knew, as his father had taught him, never to run while carrying his rifle.

Molly clapped her hands in delight as her young son so proudly displayed his prize. "Well now, we'll never lack for meat with such an accomplished hunter in our midst." She admired the hare and winking at Liam, said to her son, "now, as you know, every good hunter must know how to clean and cook his catch. So, now's as good a time as any I would say. It's rabbit stew for supper, everyone!" she called out, as everyone cheered.

Days later, as the weary troupe headed into a small town called St Luke, the only thing on their minds was the prospect of a hot bath and tasty meal in a somewhat civilised surrounding. The inn was crowded with trappers, peddlers, and traders all appearing to be negotiating deals over drinks and meals. The innkeeper, seeing the travel worn family, took them in hand. "Bridget," he called to his buxom wife. "Work yer wonders with these fine people lass. After a good bath, they'll be right as rain. A good venison stew will put the spark in their eyes again." Turning to the ladies, his eyes danced, "I'll clear this lot out for you, sure as shootin'. My Bridget will take care of you. She makes the best venison stew this side of the Atlantic, to be sure." He bowed and turned back to his rowdy customers.

Myles was right! After a delightful meal of venison stew, fresh baked bread, and blackberry and rhubarb pie, they all agreed that Bridget was the best cook west of Ireland.

"Myles, you're one lucky bloke," Thomas offered as he loosened his belt to allow for more steaming coffee.

"Well, he didn't marry me for me girlish figure, I assure you." Bridget raised her eyebrows and laughed, bustling off with an armload of dishes.

As Molly and Kathleen rose to help their hostess, a silence fell on the rest of the customers. All turned and stared at the man standing in the open doorway. Molly thought he was the most beautifully sculptured creature she had ever seen. His tall frame had barely cleared the opening, obviously built to accommodate the shorter European patron. He wore skin leggings and moccasins with a fringed skirt circumventing his hips. No other clothing adorned his body. A massive beaded necklace hugged his throat and cascaded down the centre of his chest. A single feather suspended from a headband trailed down to the tip of his shoulder length hair. A rifle was slung over his shoulder and a knife at his belt suggesting he was part of a hunting party.

Several of the patrons nodded their greetings, while others turned back to their conversations. Myles, making his way around the bar, hurried to greet his new guest.

Clasping his arm in a brotherly fashion, his greeting was that of a long lost friend. "Come, come, you know most of these other vagabonds," he waved towards his other patrons. "Now, I want you to meet a most interesting family. Dancing Eagle, the O'Connors and Dermitts."

Dancing Eagle welcomed the men with a firm European handshake and nodded politely at the women.

"Dancing Eagle is chief of an Algonquin tribe, some fifty miles north of here," he exclaimed. "What brings you down here my friend?" he asked the chief.

"My people are sick and dying. The shaman and medicine woman are of no help. I look for white man doctor to come to my village. My people do not want white doctor because they say he will make them worse. They remember how the white man brought sickness when they were still babies, but someone must help. Many are dying now and more are getting sick every day." His huge frame seemed to slump as he told his story.

Without so much as a thought, Molly whispered, "Dancing Eagle, my name is Molly Dermitt. This is my husband Liam and my family. I have been a medicine woman for many years among my people. If you can tell me how your people suffer, I may be able to help you."

The big chief looked from one member of the family to the other and then slowly looked into Molly's eyes. When she didn't drop her gaze he began. "My son lies helpless, his eyes clouded, his skin burning. He spews foulness from his body and becomes weaker as the days pass. He eats nothing and we must force water upon him or he would take nothing. He cries in his sleep and speaks nonsense the few times he wakes. The shaman says he will die. He is my only son."

Molly looked helplessly at her husband whom she could see was deep in thought. "It would take us days to reach the village. How far did you say, Myles?" he asked their host.

"Fifty or so miles through some pretty rough territory," he offered. "You're only option is horseback."

"My God, you could count on one hand, the number of times I've been on horseback," Molly winced. "But if that's the only way to go, what can we do?"

"I have brought a scout. He leads two extra mounts. We leave before dawn. The medicine woman and her husband will come with us." The decision was made as simply as his words were spoken.

Liam looked at the others and shrugged. "I suppose that be it! The pitfalls of being married to a medicine woman."

Molly apologised to Kathleen for deserting her and the children. "That's all right love, I'll just enlist a bit of manly help to change a few nappies. Just you take care of yourself. I suppose we'll be following on in the wagon and will see you in a few days." She hugged her sister-in-law and only female companion. "I'll miss you."

The evening was filled with plans for the following day. Myles was able to assure them, there would be little chance of getting lost between St. Luke and Dancing Eagle's village. The trip with the wagon would be difficult but the road was passable and if they took their time, few problems should arise.

Before dawn broke, the chief, his scout, Molly and Liam were on their way. Fortunately for Molly, the horse on which she rode was used to a European saddle, thus making the journey much more bearable. They bid goodbye to Matthew and the babies. Although Sean and Erin had been taken from the breast at six months, Molly found it difficult to tear herself away, berating herself as she did. Finally, on the road with her three companions, she began to enjoy the beauty of the early morning venture into the wilderness.

*   *   *

Their arrival at Dancing Eagle's camp was a somewhat subdued affair. The scout had preceded them to warn of their coming. Although the chief was greeted with some enthusiasm and much warmth, Molly and Liam were ignored. Though the chief had brought them into the encampment, it was obvious they were not trusted. Molly dismounted from her horse with every bit of dignity she could muster. She thought her legs would collapse beneath her and every bone in her body screamed. She thanked God for the sweeping dress that covered her wobbling legs.

"You will look at my son and then you will rest," Dancing Eagle ordered. He led them into a longhouse, bending at the low doorframe to allow himself inside. It was dark and smoky within, reminding Molly of the bowels of the *Looshtank*. Bed ledges, covered with cedar bows and animal furs lined the walls. A communal cooking fire-pit claimed the centre of the open room. Weapons lined the walls above the ledges and the supporting beams were hung with herbs, cooking utensils, and tools.

Molly followed Dancing Eagle to the side of his son's bed. "His name is Little Beaver and this is his mother, Skylark." Molly smiled at Skylark, but she lowered her eyes and looked at her son. "This medicine woman has come to help our son. You will do as she bids." Dancing Eagle commanded his wife. Her eyes flashed in his direction but she kept silent.

In a very short time Molly confirmed her suspicions. When the chief had described his son's symptoms back in St. Luke, she had suspected influenza. She was now certain of it. Little Beaver was in an advanced stage of the disease with spiking fever, laboured breathing, coughing, and diarrhoea. "Your son is extremely ill. I can only do my best, but I can't guarantee his recovery. You must do everything I say." Looking towards the mother, she saw the pool of tears forming in her weary eyes. "Please help me Skylark. We don't have much time."

From the saddle bag, Liam brought a large bag of medicinal leaves and barks. While on the Atlantic Coast they had gathered the bark and berries of barberry. Its medicinal properties were useful in cases of diarrhoea and fever along with the white bark of the willow tree. She would use red root to ease the coughing, congestion and sore throat.

"He needs to continuously breath in moist, warm air but the smoke in the lodge is not doing him any good," she explained to Dancing Eagle and Skylark.

"Then we will put him in the sweat lodge." He called to his men in Algonquian to have them prepare the sweat lodge for Little Beaver. In the mean time Molly prepared a poultice made from the bark of slippery-elm, and boiling the inner bark, steeped a tea to soothe the cough.

The sweat lodge was unbearably hot, but Molly sat by the boy through the night. After applying the poultice and having him drink the tea of barberry, red root and slippery elm, she instructed the mother to bathe his limbs in tepid water until his fever subsided. The steamy heat of the lodge, caused her to doze off periodically but she refused to leave until she saw a change in her young patient.

Little Beaver's laboured breathing began to subside almost immediately. By dawn his fever was greatly reduced and he smiled feebly at his mother. Molly applied a new poultice and forced the reluctant young man agreement and smiling, spoke to Molly. "Go, rest now, medicine woman. Thank you."

Molly rose to meet Dancing Eagle at the low entrance of the sweat lodge. "Your son is out of danger, but care must be taken for the next few days. Keep him isolated until he is strong again." With these words, she stumbled into his arms.

Picking her up, he took her to his lodge and her waiting husband. "She needs rest. She has watched my son through the night and needs to sleep." Placing her in Liam's arms, he turned and left.

Following a much-needed sleep, Molly continued her care for the sick in the village. The shaman, and his medicine woman remained wary of the newcomer and continued to practise their traditional form of magic on the tribe. Some of the elderly were still dying, but the children were improving one by one as Molly administered to them. More mothers came to the chief's lodge, begging to be helped. At Molly's insistence, Dancing Eagle had more sweat lodges erected allowing her to treat and monitor the care to her charges. After removal from the sweat lodges, the patients were taken to the chief's own lodge, the largest in the camp. Sweet cedar bows and fresh fur pelts were laid for new beds. The shaman was horrified that the chief's own lodging was to be contaminated by the sick, but Dancing Eagle ignored his pleas and insisted his home be used as the communal healing house Molly requested. All family members spent much of their time tending to sick relatives and followed Molly's lead with the required care.

In just short of a week the O'Connor/Dermitt clan made their way into the encampment. Dancing Eagle had sent a scout back to meet and lead them to his village. They made camp in a sheltered glen a few hundred feet from the entrance to the village. It was best for the children not to mingle with the tribe until the influenza was eradicated. Within the village a temporary shelter had been built for Molly where she and Liam could rest, wash, and change their clothes. Upon the news of the family's arrival, they both quickly washed and changed before heading to the campsite.

Running to meet his mother and father, Matthew threw himself into their arms. "God love you. Not even a week and I swear you've grown!" Molly danced her son in circles. But what caught her eye was the head band and feather adorning his once boyish shock of auburn hair. "Now, what could this be?" she asked, stroking the feather.

Mother and father smiled indulgently as he related his story in great detail. On the second day out, while the wagon was being prepared for camp, Matthew, Uncle Colin and the scout, Three Feathers, prepared to take a short trek into the woodlands in search of small game for their evening meal. Three Feathers was on his knee showing them crushed leaves and broken twigs, sure signs of wildlife. Raising his head, Matthew spotted a lone male deer emerging from the perimeter of thick undergrowth onto the pasture. His white tale stood to attention and his ears flicked as if sensing danger. Matthew knew, with a low-calibre weapon, he must hit the animal straight between the eyes. Allowing him the first shot, Colin and Three Feathers aimed in preparation. Matthew's shot was true and the beast slowly fell to its knees in bewilderment. Making sure their prey did not suffer, Colin and the scout adjusted their aims to take the creature out of its misery. Matthew of course was given full credit for the kill, and that evening Three Feathers fashioned a headband, attaching a small eagle feather to denote the boy's first major hunting achievement. Three Feathers performed a solemn ceremony of thanksgiving before they proceeded with the delicious feast. Their son was too quickly approaching manhood.

Spending time with the Algonquin people over the following weeks served to prepare them for the rigors of the Canadian wilderness. More native villages were suffering the ravages of influenza that year and the word spread rapidly among them of the white medicine woman and her magic. As the days began to grow shorter and the nights cooler, they realised that heading into unknown territory as the colder weather approached would be folly. They were welcome to stay in all villages but Dancing Eagle had suggested, if they should stay in his camp, they would be comfortable and provided for over the winter months. He would have a large house erected for the entire family and they would learn the ways of the land. Learning how to survive by the best of teachers was both appealing and necessary at this point. Meanwhile, in exchange for the generosity of the people, Molly would help them learn the white man's medicine and how to protect themselves from spreading epidemics.

Canadian winters can be notoriously cold which the family had learned over the past years. But nothing would compare to the experience of winter in a native encampment. Their sole concern was to remain warm and fed. The house in Québec City was a palace compared to the lodge on Dancing Eagle's reserve. The lodges were equipped with many furs to cut the draft seeping between the moss-chinked poles that formed the walls. The hole at the centre of the roof allowed for the smoke from the cooking fire to escape. Unfortunately, much of the dense smoke remained in the lodge, blackening the interior walls. In the cold of winter, the only other opening was the entrance that would normally be kept closed to prevent precious heat from escaping.

Molly's concern with her family's exposure to the continuous smoky air eventually spawned the decision to find some sort of cook-stove that would accommodate their needs and allow them to live in a more healthy atmosphere. Before the heavy snowfalls were upon them, Thomas and Colin returned to St. Luke in search of a stove.

Two weeks later, the pair returned with their much coveted prize. The stove had been disassembled and loaded aboard the packhorse they had taken along to carry supplies. The poor beast hung its head in exhaustion as they made their way into camp. Dancing Eagle's people surrounded the men as they unburdened the horse and laid out the wrapped pieces of stove and pipe. The women giggled and the men pondered the pieces of metal as they were laid out before them. Molly and Kathleen stopped dead in the middle of their greetings to the men.

"What in God's name do you have there?" Kathleen asked.

"It's called a pot-bellied stove," Colin offered proudly.

"Looks like a piece of junk to my eye. What's the good of it?" Molly winced.

"We found it in an abandoned prospector's shack not far from St. Luke." Thomas added excitedly.

"Should have left it there, in my opinion." Kathleen stifled a laugh.

"Come on now. Just you wait and see. We tried it out before we took it down and it worked like Billy be damned," Thomas smiled, noting the scepticism.

"That's what happens when you send boys to do a man's job!" Liam laughed, shaking his head.

Within the hour, Thomas and Colin had proved their point. The stove fairly jumped as the dry wood crackled and spat in its round little belly. The lodge hummed with warmth and throughout the afternoon it welcomed visitors from throughout the village. As a form of apology the women cooked a huge pot of rabbit stew to welcome their heroes.

With no more hole in the roof and virtually no smoke to clog their lungs, the lodge became a relatively comfortable winter home. The little stove almost took on a personality as they coaxed it into firing up in the chilled mornings and fed its insatiable appetite through the day. It became the butt of many jokes in the village, but it did its job and the family prized it.

Molly was happy to be with her babies again and spent her free time wrapping them in her love. When she was called to another village to tend to the sick, she missed them terribly, but Dancing Eagle had assigned a young maiden to help Kathleen with the children when Molly was away from them. Liam always accompanied his wife to the other encampments and was becoming an accomplished assistant. He found it fascinating how his wife could incorporate her treatment with that of the traditional native medicine and still work her wonders. She was lauded throughout the Algonquin nations in Québec and was instantly recognised in her emerald cloak whereever she went. She became known to them as 'Little Sister of the Pines', as they envisioned her cloaked arms enfolding them like the trees of the forest.

The men learned to hunt, indian fashion. They were amazed at the expert weaponry displayed by the native hunters. They learned how to effectively use every part of the kill. Although it was the woman's responsibility, to cure the animal pelts and sew the garments, Matthew was eager to learn, despite the sniggers of the other boys. By the end of winter, he had prepared the soft deer skin and sewn moccasins for himself and Michael. Idolising his older cousin, Michael wore them day and night.

Winter brought the usual maladies, but by following Molly's suggestions to isolate the sick and to utilise the sweat lodges to purge them of their illnesses, the Algonquin villages remained epidemic-free for at least that winter.

*   *   *

As the winter progressed towards spring, the lakes thawed and the weather took on a less aggressive nature, and Dancing Eagle invited them to take part in a ceremony of renewal. Before the event began, two women of the chief's lodge came to collect Molly and prepare her for the ceremony. Back in Dancing Eagle's lodge, he waited to present her with an elaborately-beaded dress of soft white deerskin. "My women will now prepare you for presentation to our people." As he made no move to leave, but lowered himself to rest on his haunches, Molly responded indignantly.

"I'll not disrobe in front of you! Get out with you, now," she admonished the Algonquin leader.

"Ssh, ssh. It is our chief's right to inspect all women of his tribe," Dancing Eagle's young wife chided.

"But, I am not a woman of his tribe. He can not 'inspect' me as you say. It is our tradition that no man but a woman's husband may inspect her." Molly cried as her knees began to weaken.

Dancing Eagle's steely eyes met hers as he explained. "You will become a member of my tribe tonight at the Ceremony of Renewal. I could take you as my wife, but out of respect for your 'tradition' as you put it, I will not. You will truly become 'Little Sister of the Pines' and will carry the Algonquin name to your grave. My people and I have decided. Now prepare."

Without further hesitation, Dancing Eagle's wives undressed Molly, oiled her body and slipped the ankle length dress over her shoulders. All the while her eyes never left his and she knew in her heart she had done what was right. As he rose to leave, a faint smile escaped from his eyes, telling her she had passed his inspection.

The ceremony applauded the anticipated arrival of spring. Dancers emulated the hunt, new growth, and the power of the sun, wind, and rain. Molly and Liam were given prominent seats on either side of the chief. The leader's family and tribal elders formed a protective circle around them. Molly had no idea what was in store for her, but she knew she felt personal pride in the fact that these people were accepting her into their tribe. Only the very respected were given this honour. Once the dancing and singing ended the chief's two wives escorted Molly to stand before the whole tribe, resplendent in her new gown, her skin shining in the firelight. Her hair had been woven into one long thick braid that trailed to her waist. The shaman and medicine woman approached, carrying an amulet of bear teeth and feathers. With great reverence they placed the heavy amulet around her neck uttering Algonquin words in high nasal tones. The chief then came forward and placed a beaded headband on her head. The right side of her face was framed with a single grey and white feather that trailed to her shoulder. In Algonquian he sang his welcome to her before speaking in her native tongue so that she might understand what was being said. "I welcome you. My people welcome you. You will be welcomed by all peoples of the Algonquin nation and you will be known by all as 'Little Sister of the Pines'. Your name will become legendary among our people and you will be protected by our Spirit Gods. As chief to this tribe, I take you as my sister. Welcome, Molly Dermitt, Little Sister of the Pines.

A cheer rose from the many onlookers as they formed a line to greet her and show their approval. They touched her dress, her feather, her hair, and her face. Gifts of jewelry, clothing, food, and utensils were piled before her. She felt as if she had just been anointed Queen of England. There were no words to express her appreciation but her happiness was evident to all.

The dancing and singing carried on well into the night. Children fell asleep in their parent's arms or where-ever they chose to lay their heads. Matthew was in awe of his mother and pride swelled in his young heart as he watched her every move.

Chapter 8

Ottawa Valley – Upper Canada – 1852

The urge to move on deepened as the weather warmed and the days grew longer. Energy oozed from the children as they ran naked around the encampment with their friends. It would be difficult pulling up roots and leaving now that they had bonded with the children of the tribe. Quite often Matthew and Michael were not seen from dawn to dusk as they played and explored with their friends. John Pierre was two years old. Being an extremely sociable child, he attached himself to any woman who would mother him and every man who would play with him. He was a child of the tribe. At a year and a half, Erin and Sean's personalities began to bloom. They were as different as night and day, but both delightful children in their own special ways.

The day they boarded the wagon in preparation to leave was a sad day for all. They were loaded down with gifts including new travelling clothes and moccasins for each member of the family. The farewells had been difficult despite their eagerness to be on the road again. There was absolutely no regrets at the length of their stay in Dancing Eagle's village. They had come to learn so much about the life in the Canadian backwoods. The knowledge they acquired would serve them well and safe passage was assured where ever they travelled in Algonquin territory.

Dancing Eagle assigned two of his best scouts to accompany the travellers to the Ottawa River, the boundary between upper and lower Canada. The two had become great friends with Colin and Thomas over the long winter months and were pleased to have been chosen to accompany them through the mountains and on into the Ottawa Valley. They were an entertaining lot as they played practical jokes on one another, gambled and gossiped together about the young women they left behind. When the tales became too ribald, Kathleen and Molly warned them of their behaviour around the children.

"Matthew need not hear about your escapades now. He's growing up far too fast for my liking. You just teach him to hunt and fish, and leave the lasses to me." Molly warned them good-heartedly.

"Ah, Molly girl, sure we're not in Ireland now. Life is different here. Life is hard, but we're free to make what we will of it." Colin had turned serious but the will to live was in his eyes once again and Molly could not dispute that.

Spring rains made the going slow. The wagon swayed to and fro on the furrowed road. At times the constant rolling motion caused Molly to retch as her stomach churned. "Are you all right lass? It's not like you to be bothered with the wagon motion." Liam asked, concerned at his wife's paleness and retching. Feeling it was just the excessive motion of the wagon, she told him not to be concerned. By the afternoon she would feel much improved and ride more comfortably. The problem did not subside but became progressively worse as the weeks rolled by.

"Kathleen, I'm going to have a baby," she confided one day.

"I know, lass. I was wondering when you'd tell me." Kathleen smiled.

"But there's something wrong. I can't quite tell what it is, but I know there's something wrong. All pregnan-

cies are different, but I just feel this one was not meant
to be. If I tell Liam now, he'll insist we make camp until
I'm well. That would be a waste of good weather and I
know it's not the travelling that's causing the problems.
What can I do? I can't hide it forever, and Liam is already suspicious." Dissolving into her friends arms, she
cried the tears of an already-bereaved mother.

Within the week Molly had lost what would have
been her fourth child. Attempting to dismount from the
wagon she had tumbled out onto the ground in a dead
faint. Before the night was through she had miscarried
and began to haemorrhage excessively. The excruciating
pain she experienced while aborting the foetus led her to
realise she would never be able to save this baby. She
now understood the reason for her feeling of uneasiness
over the past weeks. Once her miscarriage began and
Liam realised the distress his wife was having, he
ordered permanent camp to be made until she regained
her strength and was ready for travel again. She continued to haemorrhage well into the night. She instructed
Kathleen to prepare tincture of ergot to stop the bleeding
and a few drops of laudanum to dull the pain. Kathleen
rolled linen bandages to staunch the flow of blood and
kept close watch on Molly's progress. As the night
edged towards dawn, her fever spiked, sweat rolled from
her body and she shivered uncontrollably. The bleeding
had stopped but she was weak and barely conscious.
Liam sponged her body with cool spring water until the
fever gradually fell and she seemed to rest peacefully.
After repeating the tincture of ergot and drops of laudanum she eventually fell into a tranquil sleep.

Before they had even set up camp, one of the scouts
had set out to the nearest settlement in search of a doctor.
Riding through the night, he was able to make contact
soon after dawn and by suppertime the next day had

returned with a backwoods doctor. The man unfortunately was as incompetent as he was dirty. His last patient had obviously resided in a pig trough and his breath smelled like yesterday's slop. Liam refused to let him touch Molly, but the doctor did confirm they had done all the right things and now they would just have to wait a couple of days and allow her to rest. They paid him handsomely, filled him with food and whiskey, and early the next morning he was on his way.

Two days later the men rigged the wagon up so that Molly could lie comfortably as they proceeded on. Other than being somewhat weak and tired, she was ready to travel. The sorrow at losing her baby left her melancholy for some days, but she quickly recovered as her other children commanded her time and attention.

*   *   *

By the time they reached Tremblay, their last sojourn in the Québec mountains they had repaired a broken axle, replaced shattered wheel spokes, and mended frayed reins. The wagon was showing the worse for wear, the horses needed new shoes, and everyone began to feel the journey would never end. Needing to build up their faltering optimism and take care of some much needed repairs, they decided to spend some time in Tremblay. Being the largest settlement after many miles of rugged territory it provided a blacksmith shop where horses could be reshoed and any repairs required for worn wagon parts could be obtained. The men had been able to make satisfactory repairs to keep them on the road but the wagon was close to being on its last legs.

The blacksmith was a burly man of German descent. He gruffly surveyed the sagging axle and missing or cracked wheel spokes. "Big job," he snorted. "I'm busy man. Take one, two week maybe." Pursing his lips, he frowned and grunted at the men.

"He must be head of the social committee here," Sean stated under his breath.

"Well, I suppose the women should have a rest and this be as good a place as any," John proposed. "The horses need shoeing. Can you take care of that too?" he asked turning once again to the blacksmith. When the German nodded his affirmation, John replied, "Fine, where should we be unloading the wagon?"

After brusque directions and another grunt from the smithy they made their way to the shores of a beautiful lake only a few hundred yards from the settlement. The weather had remained good despite the chilly mountain nights and setting up camp on the shores of the lake seemed a pleasant alternative to the local lodging house. From what they had seen, the boarders coming and going from the ramshackle house were a pretty seasoned looking lot.

The landlady lounged upon the front stoop, her booted feet propped up on the porch railing. Removing her battered hat from a head of bright red, untamed curls, she waved her greetings to the passing travellers. "Stop by for a cup of tea ladies," she cackled. "Bring those fine looking lads along and I'll give them a drop of my finest." She laughed uproariously at her own offhanded comment.

Molly slapped Thomas as he raised his eyebrows and grinned back at the shrew. "Don't be getting any bright ideas now. Lord only knows what you'd be coming out of there with, " Molly cautioned. Thomas laughed as he warded off her blows.

After unloading the wagon, the men returned to the blacksmith with Molly's admonishing words assaulting their ears. Following warning looks from their wives,

Liam and Sean relented to stay and help set up camp.

Much to his chagrin, Matthew was assigned the care of the children while the adults settled in and prepared meals. The blacksmith shop had fascinated him and he wanted to see it once again.

"We'll be here for a while, young lad. You'll be seeing plenty of the blacksmith shop. Now get on with the youngsters," his father ordered.

It was a difficult age to be. He felt he was no longer a child, but not yet an adult. He didn't seem to fit in anywhere.

Seeing his young friend's trouble, the Algonquin scout Little Bear, approached his unhappy companion. In his tribe, watching the children was not the responsibility of a young man and he could sympathise with his friend. But noting the situation and the lack of female members of this band, he approached Matthew with his offer to help while he fashioned fishing spears. "When the children sleep, we go fishing," he proposed with a wink. Matthew grinned, and their plan was formed.

The week was just what was needed to rejuvenate the whole family. The women spent their time cooking, washing, and mending, all in leisurely time. They played by the water with the babies and pretended they were at a lakeside resort as they basked in the summer sun. The men fished, hunted, and also enjoyed the relaxed atmosphere. Thomas and Colin even managed to explore the village under the guise of checking out the work in progress at the blacksmith's shop.

But they also returned with valued information on the Ottawa Valley lumber industry and where they could find the best area to cross the Ottawa River. Knowing the Ottawa River was well within their reach they were now willing to formulate plans for homesteading.

Chapter 9

Ottawa Valley – Cherry Creek – 1852

They had arrived unbelievably intact with the loss of only three lives since the onset of their journey some six years ago. These three lives had been replaced with the birth of four healthy little boys.

Matthew, having been born before the departure from Ireland, was old enough to remember his experiences crossing the Atlantic, life near the quarantine stations, the miseries of Québec City and life in the Algonquin encampment. In his young mind, the trek across the mountains of Québec was just another adventure in his still short life. He was sad to leave his companion Little Bear at the Ottawa River crossing but he promised that when he was fully grown, he would return to Dancing Eagle's village to visit his friends.

The Ottawa River was a major tributary to the St. Lawrence. The lumber industry was massive along its shores and barges continuously transported raw logs and lumber downstream to the St. Lawrence River. From the ports of Montreal and Québec City they would be shipped to other Canadian ports, Europe, and the United States.

The men could hardly contain their excitement as they watched barge upon barge pass them on the river, laden down with the precious cargo. Of course they had heard the stories about the bountiful forests of Upper Canada, but now they were seeing with their own eyes what could be accomplished in and beyond the valley.

Making enquiries along the way, John had been

advised , once across the river, to head for Bytown, and seek out the Lands Claims Office. There, they would be shown what tracks of land were still available and where they could stake their claim. Free land was a thing of the past, but large areas could still be purchased for relatively low prices. The monies set aside for homesteading and claim staking were still left untouched and they were anxious to reach Bytown and secure their future in land. The journey down the Ottawa Valley was less arduous than the travels through the wilderness of Québec. The population had increased dramatically and everyone seemed happy to offer an opinion. New settlers were welcomed and everyone was rich with dreams. They were advised by many to find their land and settle quickly before the winter set in.

Bytown was a thriving centre, situated on the banks of the Ottawa River. The citizens were primarily of Irish decent, from the banker, doctor, public house owner on down to the dockhands and labourers. Having settled the family as close to the business section of town as they dared, John and Liam entered the first bank they reached. Neither man had ever set foot in a bank in his life, let alone enter to make a transaction. Both men attempted to appear as business-like as possible despite their long hair and unshaved appearance. When a clerk finally deemed to offer his services, they opened an account and deposited their entire wealth before venturing to the Land Claims Office. The bank manager, Clarence Larkin, himself an emigrant of some twelve years, recognised the determination in John and Liam and readily offered his advice. After discussing their long term plans, he invited himself to accompany them to the Land Claims Office. After spending the afternoon, pouring over maps of the Ottawa Valley and beyond, they settled on two tracks of land they intended to inspect. A down-payment was applied to assure their claim would be kept open until the purchase was finalised. They returned to the rest of the family to make plans. All agreed, that John, Liam, Colin, and Matthew would go to investigate the chosen areas. Thomas, Sean, and Patrick would remain with the women and children and take care of the wagon and horses, now lodged with the blacksmith. Matthew had raised such a commotion about being allowed to accompany them, the men finally conceded it would be in his best interest.

"After all," John stated: "There is plenty to learn about the lumber industry and we're going to need young blood. He may as well start at the beginning."

Michael's pleas to stay with his hero, fell on deaf ears. Sean came to the sad little boy's rescue and he soon forgot the reason for his misery.

Trail horses and a guide were hired and provisions purchased to take the men deeper into the forested regions of Upper Canada. The trip was more than one hundred miles there and back again, so it was expected they would be gone for two to three weeks, depending on how quickly they could make their decision on a purchase. The guide was Algonquin and French and knew the region like the back of his hands. He had spent his life exploring and guiding, and many new settlers could thank him for finding them the very best land to settle. He was also a wealth of information on the flora and fauna of the area, and in the evening by firelight, Liam eagerly wrote down everything Francois related. The varieties of timber and for what they were best used was overwhelming. In Québec they had watched their Algonquin friends build birch-bark canoes and wondered at their weight and durability. Cedar, pine, spruce, fir, and maple were all readily used for building and export. The forest was a goldmine waiting to be harvested. John could see that a well-managed operation had endless possibilities. Their family business could be stable for many generations to come.

Along the way they visited other operations, some thriving, others faltering. They listened and perused each situation, often discovering the reasons for failure or success. Realising the most successful were generally family operations with sound financial backing and competent hard-working members, they knew success was in their future. They knew not to overstep their boundaries, to grow slowly and surely into a thriving business. Many businesses were sinking, not because of the lack of desire and hard work, but because everything they held was owned by the bank. Everyone knew, if you were owned by the bank, the devil had your soul.

Technology was another thing to consider. Until quite recently, sawmills were operated by waterpower and a single sash-saw. This slow, labour intensive system was gradually giving way to the new steam-powered operation with the larger, more powerful circular saw. So, although the expenses of starting the Cherry Creek mill would be much higher than anticipated, it was imperative they keep up with the new technology in order not to face immediate failure.

When they reached the shores of Cherry Creek, a tributary to the Madawaska River, they reined in their horses to survey the land before them. John immediately envisioned two or three neat little farm houses nestled on its shores, framed by the dark green forests behind. "I certainly hope this be the place. If our women should see this and its not ours to claim, they'll likely never forgive us."

All agreed, it was a perfect location for settling. Clear sweet water rushing by their doorstep. Enough land to comfortably farm, and acre upon acre of woodland to harvest. On further inspection, they decided the mill could be situated farther downstream to protect the homestead from the noise and dust of the saws. The logs could be floated and the lumber rafted down to the Madawaska, and out onto the Ottawa River, where it would then be barged to Bytown, Montreal, Québec City, and on to Europe and the world.

"Why do you think, this hasn't been bargained for Francois?" Liam asked of their guide.

"I should think, although it is a prime location, the expense of barging down the Ottawa is much more than if you were closer to Bytown. There is still available land farther south towards the St. Lawrence, where the lumber can be taken directly upstream to the Great Lake's settlements or straight on to Montreal. But of course, most of the choice land closer to the major waterways is already claimed. This is probably the best you're going to find and at a reasonable price, at that.

Carefully surveying the area they decided to claim the land bordering Cherry Creek for as far upstream as was plausible. In the future they would be able to spread farther back from the river while still controlling the land at its shores. The banker had suggested they divide their land under two families. So Liam, Thomas, Patrick, and Molly would claim one tract along the southern bank; John, Colin, Sean, and Kathleen the northern shore. Within three weeks the O'Connor/Dermitt clan would own approximately two-hundred acres of choice land, a good percentage of it forest, bordering on the Ottawa Valley.

* * *

Once again they found themselves being barged up the Ottawa River, on up the Madawaska and towards their new home. Much of the journey was treacherous as many parts of the Madawaska were negotiable only by canoe. The horses followed an Algonquin hunting trail along the river and were their only form of transport for some time. The wagon had been unloaded and stripped as they left the Ottawa and they foraged their way by canoe and packhorse the remaining distance. They came in relays, people, and provisions. Even the little pot-bellied stove found it's way on the back of a sure-footed pony. Within a month, by September 1852, the family and all their possessions rested on the shores of Cherry Creek. But the feeling of elation was short lived as they all realised the cold winter weather would soon be upon them.

They began working from dawn until dusk, cutting and preparing logs for their first winter home. Not having to clear an area to build on was a bonus and saved them much time. Anyone old enough to hold an axe spent his time peeling and cleaning the freshly cut logs. Kathleen and Molly took turns cooking and caring for the children and helping the men with the house. Every possible hand was needed if they were to be safe and warm by the time the snows came. They also needed to bring in enough provisions to last the winter, as at times they would be unable to leave in the stormy season. Each man took his turn with a pack-horse, travelling to the nearest settlement to purchase whatever was needed for their survival.

During the stay in the Algonquin village, they had learned to cure and tan pelts. The larger animal furs such as the bear were used for bedding and to line draughty walls. Now, when the men were able to bring down larger game, Kathleen and Molly took time out from house building to prepare the meat and hides for the winter.

The days, rain or shine, were long and exhausting for all. They were on a head-long race with Mother Nature. By mid October the nights were growing cold and the temporary shelter of canvas was not able to keep the dampness from penetrating their beds and clothing. Every sunny day, Molly would remove the bedding and hang it to air and dry. Hurriedly she would roll a warmed hide to trap the coveted heat within its folds. Immediately on retiring, the hide would be unrolled, its warmth soothing the aching brought on by the day's labour.

By October's end a lodge similar to that of Dancing Eagle's was ready for occupancy. Dancing Eagle's lodge had seen them through one winter, and until a permanent house was constructed, this lodge would serve them well. The only thing they lacked was privacy and that would have to be a luxury to be anticipated. Once they were safely settled within, beds and rough hewn bits of furniture were constructed. The pot-bellied stove took its place of honour in the middle of the lodge once again. Its cheery presence and the flicker of tallow candles accompanied them through many, cold, blustering nights that first winter on the Cherry Creek homestead.

Shortly after their arrival at Cherry Creek, Kathleen announced that she and Sean were expecting their second child. Molly kept close watch on her dear friend and sister for fear the exhausting work of home building and caring for the family would take its toll on her. Kathleen carried out a normal healthy pregnancy and delivered the first baby girl to the family on a cold March day in 1853. When Michael finally saw his baby sister, he was so enthralled with her delicate baby hands and feet, he stayed by her side for hours on end, looking back and forth from her to his mother. Kathleen smiled and tousled his head of curls. "She's your baby sister, Michael. Would you like to name her?"

Without hesitation, he whispered, "Sarah. I think she's a Sarah."

Laughing, Sean picked up his little son and swinging him in the air, said, "Well my young lad, how about you and I leave Sarah and your ma to rest awhile. You can come see her again soon." Kissing his wife he dressed Michael in his warmest coat and hat and ushered him out the door. Michael was no longer a baby and the harsh life of the homesteader required a child to mature into adulthood rapidly. New lessons were about to be learned as the strings to mother's apron were cut and he bonded with his father.

Through the winter, as the weather prevented much action other than survival, many hours were spent planning the first permanent home as well as perfecting designs for a new saw-mill. When the weather allowed, Liam being the expert lumberman, would head back into Bytown to order and purchase the machinery needed to start their first small operation. It had been decided by all, that once the savings were depleted, John and Liam would approach the bank as the prime borrowers. Colin, Sean, and Thomas would gradually be brought into the fold as the business grew and prospered.

Patrick preferred to remain in the background, helping where he could with the mill, but mostly with the homestead. He had aged dramatically since Colleen's passing and preferred to spend the time with his grandson and young Michael. "I'm no businessman, and the youngsters need a man about. There's plenty to be done, and the women can use some help, I'm sure," he explained. Knowing the pain he suffered with his arthritis, the family was happy he was able to find peace in his decision to remain at the homestead.

As the snow melted and the creek's banks began to overflow, it became apparent the homestead must be constructed on higher ground. A few hundred feet from the river's edge the land formed a plateau large enough to accommodate a house and garden before reaching the thickly-wooded area. The water supply would be near at hand, yet the home would not be threatened by the rushing waters of the meltoff.

While Liam journeyed to Bytown the others staked out and prepared the sight for the new mill and house, both to be completed before the end of 1853.

Matthew had begged to be allowed to go with his father. Molly, with some trepidation, eventually conceded defeat, and allowed her eldest son his freedom. "My God, I remember the day he was born, like it was yesterday! And here he is now, canoeing down a river in the wilderness, without a second thought. Am I getting soft in me old age girl?" she asked, turning to Kathleen.

Looking at her bewildered friend she offered, "You're neither old nor soft, my girl. Just being a good mother and allowing her eldest son to leave the nest, so to speak. I don't think I've ever seen him so happy as you've made him today. Cheer up, lass, you've two more left to break your heart!" With that, they both laughed and returned to the demands of the four remaining babies in their care.

While waiting for Liam's return, the men began falling and preparing logs for the construction of the new home. Now that the snow was mostly gone, they were able to lay out the foundation of the floor, and collect boulders from the river for the new fireplace and hearth.

As soon as the frost had left the ground the women busied themselves preparing a garden plot. The trail horses provided the much needed manure, which they mixed with rotted layers of leaves and needles that covered the forest floor. The ground was hard and the digging was back breaking. The children, under the coaching of Michael, ran back and forth, removing rocks and sticks from the freshly dug area.

Molly missed Liam and Matthew terribly in the two weeks they were gone. At night she would take her two babies into her bed and in her weariness cry herself to sleep. She knew Liam would allow nothing to happen to their young son, but she also knew the rivers were swollen and treacherous at this time of year and she prayed constantly for their safe return.

They had made it downstream in a few short days, but the return trip with the loaded canoes was more than a challenge for the two. At the mouth of the Madawaska they happened upon an Algonquin hunting party camped on its shores. After some finagling, Liam was able to hire one of the hunters and his canoe to accompany them upstream to Cherry Creek. Battling the current was becoming too much for Matthew's young body and they needed to lighten the load in order to make it home with all they had purchased. Liam had at first considered hiding the larger items off shore but meeting the hunting party had allowed them to carry on with the full load.

Their arrival was heralded by Michael as he helped gather boulders at the river's edge. The adults and children came running down the embankment to greet the voyageurs. Molly threw herself into Liam's arms and hugged Matthew close, crying and laughing at once. "Ah, you both are a sight for sore eyes, my darlin's. I've been worried half to death. You look so weary," she said running her fingers over Liam's bearded face. "Let's get a good meal into your bellies and clean you both up." She began to lead them away towards the lodge.

"Wait, wait darlin' I've something to show you first!" Liam added excitedly. As tired as he was, he refused to go before showing his wife what they had brought all the way up three rivers and many gruelling miles.

All three canoes were laden down with goods and equipment for the mill and home. The Algonquin hunter was emptying his canoe in preparation to leave when Liam invited him to stay to eat and rest before his return to his fellow hunters.

"No, thank you, I return to my brothers before they move camp."

Thanking his friend, Liam paid him and bid him farewell.

Helping the others to unload the remaining canoes, he soon uncovered the prized bounty that lay hidden under piles of other provisions and the tarpaulin. Before leaving two weeks ago, Liam had discussed with the other men, the need to provide some comfort for the women and to a somewhat lesser degree, themselves. They had agreed unanimously on this special purchase and vowed to keep it's secret from the women. When the prize was unveiled, the women shrieked in delight. Four clawed, metal feet held the most beautiful copper bath-tub they had ever envisioned. The men delighted in the girlish joy their women displayed.

"I suppose now they'll be insisting we take a bath at least once a week," Colin snorted gruffly.

"Yes, brother, to be sure. As soon as my two men are taken care of, you're next on the list." Molly wrinkled her nose at her big brother.

While Liam and Matthew were gone, a shelter was built to protect the goods they would return with from Bytown. The lodge was naturally too small for storing tools and machinery and the rains would rust them if not protected, so a rainproof shed was quickly erected. They now unloaded the canoes of a variety of saws, axes, blades, gears, belts, and other paraphernalia required to build the lumber-mill. Some items such as the motor needed to run the mill's saws were on special order and would arrive by barge from Montreal within the month.

Precious seeds for the garden and a few young chickens and two goats were housed in cages and had survived the rough journey. But the most coveted bit of cargo, by young and old alike, was a golden puppy Matthew gently lifted from its resting place in the canoe. He had wrapped it in his jacket as it slept, until now, oblivious to the excitement on shore. It shivered pitifully as the children all vied for its attention and cried to hold its chubby body. But warming up to their attention, it was soon stumbling and rolling around them in typical puppy fashion as they laughed at its antics.

Molly and Liam took this time of distraction to wander off by themselves to properly greet one another after the long separation. She had yearned for her man like never before and was anxious to have him to herself, away from the children and the hustle and bustle their return created. "I have a sneaky feeling the dog was your idea, Mr. Dermitt," Molly teased. Winking at his wife in reply, he kissed her soundly and led her off to their solitude.

*   *   *

During the early summer months Liam and Colin headed to a village on the mouth of the Madawaska River where the river barge was to deliver the motors required to run the machinery in the lumber mill. With the installation of the motors the mill would be ready for production. They had all worked particularly hard over the past months and their excitement was justified as they prepared to turn on the engines and run the first log through the giant saw blade. Before they made the test-run, the entire family gathered to witness the miracle.

Molly and Kathleen gathered the children around them and covered the ears of the babies. Molly ordered Matthew and Michael to cover theirs and Matthew retorted, "Oh, ma, I'm no sissy. When I'm working here I can't cover my ears!"

"Me neither," Michael chimed in, folding his little arms defiantly across his chest.

"Well, I'll be—I think the two of you are getting too big for your britches. You're not too big for me to turn over my knee yet, you know." Molly attempted to catch the two little boys as they fled to the sides of their fathers.

Within seconds the engines jumped into action and the log edged its way towards the giant saw-blade. The whine of the saw working its teeth into the log, sent the boys scurrying away, hands over ears in mock terror. To the adults of the family, that sound heralded in the beginning of a new and exciting period in their lives.

Once the mill was in full production, the house could be completed. The walls and roof were built with the first lumber cut and planed in the Cherry Creek Lumber Mill. Logs had been stockpiled over the spring months and everyone was anxious to see the completion of their home.

The initial homestead was a four-room log house. For the first winter, the house was very basic and functional. The first priority was to keep it warm and dry within. The stone fireplace was completed and the little pot-bellied stove took its place in the kitchen until a proper cook-stove would replace it. Windows were framed and open to the warmth of the sun. The first winter, they would be covered with animal skins and only opened on the brighter days to freshen the interior. It wasn't perfect, but it was definitely an improvement on the lodge.

*   *   *

Very early one fall morning the entire family was awakened by McGinty's barking. Deer and other small game often came to the river to drink and McGinty would attempt to warn them away from his territory. But this particular morning his bark had an urgent, fearful sound. Rising, sleepy-eyed from his bed, Matthew went to investigate his friends cause for alarm. As he pulled back the bearskin flap to call out to McGinty, he was surprised to see three men sitting astride their horses, quietly starring at the lodge. Nothing moved but the grazing heads of the horses. Replacing the skin he moved towards his father's bed. "Da, wake up, da. There's three strangers on horses waiting outside," he whispered to his father, not wanting to alarm the rest of the family. Immediately awake, Liam rose to quickly dress and secure his rifle from the wall. Cautioning his son to stay within, he exited the lodge to greet the newcomers. Dressed only in deerskin britches with rifle cartridge belts spanning their bare chests, he immediately recognised them as an Algonquin hunting party. They looked much the same as the men they met with at the mouth of the Madawaska on the trip back from Bytown.

"Welcome," Liam nodded to the three men. "Can I be of help to you?" he asked warily. Not knowing these men, and having heard tales of renegade Indian bands, he approached them with caution.

The older man in the centre and of obvious higher rank, moved his mount slightly forward. "We look for the medicine woman, Little Sister of the Pines. We know of her from our brothers to the east and need her services. Our village is north, across the Ottawa, some two days ride." He stopped, waiting for Liam's reply.

"Wait here, I will speak to my wife," Liam replied,

turning to enter the lodge.

By the time he entered, Molly was dressed and met him with questions. "Who are they, and what do they want?"

"They are from a tribe across the river and have come in search for you. I don't know what the problem is, but they learned about you from another tribe and want your help." Liam explained quietly.

"Let's find out what their trouble is before we make any decisions." Molly made to leave the lodge but Liam opened the flap, bidding her to follow him.

"My wife will listen to your trouble. Please dismount so we can talk." He motioned for them to leave their horses to graze and follow himself and Molly to a comfortable sitting area near the garden and away from the lodge. "Take McGinty into the lodge son, so we can talk in peace." He ordered his son.

"This is my wife, Molly Dermitt, 'Little Sister of the Pines'. Liam offered as introduction.

"My name is Crooked Tooth, elder of the Black River tribe. These are my sons, Raven and White Cloud. Our chief, Black Owl has been injured in a fall from his horse while hunting. The horse was startled by a small animal, darting across its path. Our chief suffered a broken shoulder, that was also pierced by a branch. Streaks of red run down his arm and his skin burns. He becomes unconscious and talks nonsense while he sleeps. Our shaman has done nothing. Our chief only worsens. We have been told this medicine woman might help us." He looked questioningly at Molly.

"It sounds like your chief has poison in his blood. And, yes, if we reach him soon enough, I may be able to help him." As Molly rose to leave, Liam bid them wait.

Within the hour they were packed and prepared to leave. When they showed their concern at leaving the family with no horse, Crooked Tooth offered to have two horses brought back to the homestead immediately. It would be considered as partial payment for the treatment of their chief.

Molly had become an avid horsewoman and she now welcomed the adventure taking them back into unknown territory. They followed the Algonquin hunting trails for two days, crossed numerous streams and mountains and drank in the beauty of the changing landscape. Fall was in the air and the leaves were changing from their summer shades of green to the brilliant yellows, oranges and reds of autumn. Some were already carpeting the trail before them.

By early evening of the second day, they entered the village of Black Owl. They were greeted with quiet regard as Molly and Liam dismounted and were ushered to Black Owl's lodge. They had heard of this woman in the emerald cloak, but their chief was in grave danger and they chose to withhold opinion until his fate was established. His wife met them and motioned Molly to enter. She held her hand up to stop Liam. Molly nodded to him to wait.

Within minutes of seeing Black Owl, she had confirmed her suspicions that the inflammation in his injured shoulder and the possibility of blood poisoning was the cause of his high fever and delirium. The wound had been cleaned and packed with moss but had evidently festered and become badly inflamed. If she didn't lance the wound and remove the poison that was seeping into his bloodstream, he would surely die. She carefully explained to his wife what she was about to do, as the sight of the lancet would most likely frighten her if she didn't understand its purpose. She asked that the two sons of Crooked Tooth be brought in to hold down her patient as she operated. Black Owl could periodically regain consciousness, at least enough to feel the pain of the knife in his shoulder. She couldn't have him lashing out as she worked. The laudanum she administered would help somewhat, but not enough to totally dull the pain.

After she lanced and drained the puncture, she applied a poultice of hair-cap moss to draw out the infection, then wrapped his shoulder in clean dressings to hold the poultice in place. As the infection cleared, so to would the fever. His wife bathed him down with cool water and once he regained consciousness Molly had him drink a tea of liverwort. As he looked at her with fevered eyes, she explained who she was. He then closed his eyes and fell back into a more restful, laudanum-induced sleep

By morning the fever had broken, but he remained weak and drowsy. Molly took the opportunity to request a resting place. The elder, Crooked Tooth took her and Liam to his lodge and told his wife to make the medicine woman and her man comfortable. After a light meal they both fell into an exhausted sleep.

After arising in the afternoon, Molly checked on Black Owl. Her arrival was greeted by the obsidian eyes of the tribal shaman as he knelt over his chief. His distrust flowed from them like molten lava. Molly knew that to thwart the powers of the ancient medicine man was to tempt folly. "Greetings, shaman," she bowed reverently. "You must be a powerful healer. Without your great wisdom, Black Owl would not have lived to see another sunrise. This unworthy medicine woman has much to learn about spirit healing."

As he spoke, his eyes softened ever so slightly. "You are a healer of the body, medicine woman. You must learn, the body will die without the spirit, but the spirit will not die without the body."

"Yes," Molly whispered. "I have so much to learn." She had seen the spirit of so many of her countrymen die on these strange shores. It was little wonder so many had succumbed to the physical diseases that ravaged their bodies. This Indian shaman was truly a great healer.

Finding Black Owl resting comfortably, she rose to leave the lodge. She sought out Crooked Tooth and asked him if there might be any other problems she could help with before her return home. She treated some children with cuts and abrasions, checked on a very frightened, first-time mother-to-be, lanced a boil on a scrawny old elder's backside, and eased an infected ingrown toenail. She found these people to be surprisingly healthy. Their contact with the outside world was probably the only great threat to their survival.

By the time Black Owl was well enough for Molly to feel comfortable about leaving him, he had ordered many gifts of pelts, tools, jewelry, and two more pack-horses to accompany them home. On the journey back to Cherry Creek, Raven and White Cloud shot a mule deer and presented it to the family on their arrival at the homestead. What Molly had done for their chief, commanded respect and gratitude from the tribe, and they were willing to offer whatever they could to show their appreciation.

*   *   *

While Molly and Liam were gone, the rest of the family had pulled together in an attempt to have the new home ready for their return. Although a bearskin hung at the entrance, the interior had been made quite comfortable. Memories of the past twenty years had been hung on the walls, right down to the portrait of Molly's dead mother, Bridget. Colourful quilts brightened the rooms.

A bearskin rug lay before the fireplace and copper cooking pots hung to either side. The pot-bellied stove hummed merrily in the corner, topped with a simmering rabbit stew.

"Oh, Kat, this is so wonderful!" Molly said, hugging her sister-in-law. "The past few miles have been agony. All I could imagine was my own bed and a glorious bath. Now you've gone and done this," she waved her arm around, surveying the room. "We've only been gone a week. How did you manage all this?" she asked in wonder.

"Well, I cracked the whip, so to speak. Thomas and Colin, whipped up the beds as soon as the lumber was dry; complaining the whole time I might add. John and Patrick installed the stove, and I must admit, I spent a good deal of my time covering the children's ears, as the air was fairly blue around here much of the time." They laughed, both collapsing on the nearest bed. Matthew arrived with the twins. He quietly hugged his mother, welcoming her home, as the two three-years-olds clambered over her, pinning her to the bed. They were old enough to have missed her terribly and their excitement bubbled over.

"Without this young man, none of this would have been possible," Kathleen said, smiling at Matthew. "It was his idea to have the house ready for your return and he is responsible for nearly all of the decorating."

Molly looked at her eldest son in wonder. Taking him by the hands, she looked up at him from where she sat on the bedstead. "I can't believe I have such a grown son. It seems just like yesterday, you were a wee babe in my arms, and now look at you. Thank you so much Matthew, for being such a wonderful son." She hugged him to her as tears rolled down her face. "What more could I ask for? I have it all."

Tousling the heads of her three beautiful children, she chided. "Besides, I couldn't handle any more than these three young scallywags." Laughing, they all headed outside to see where the rest of the family might be.

Chapter 10

Cherry Creek – Upper Canada – 1853-1855

Settlers were flooding into the Ottawa Valley, with new townships cropping up everywhere. As the years rolled by, the influx of people created the demand for lumber. With the Cherry Creek operation it started with new neighbours settling on the Madawaska, clearing their land and bringing the logs to the mill to be cut into lumber. Most lumber remained rough-hewn as the process of planing was laborious and time consuming. Eventually, as the mill expanded in size and production, all family members were required in its operation. Seasoned lumberjacks had to be hired to keep up with the demand for lumber. These men not only fell and cleaned the trees, but also cleared and built the roads to accommodate the oxen hauling the logs from the bush to the mill. Lumber was generally moved by rafts on the smaller rivers and barge on the larger until suitable roads were built into the mills from the local townships.

Sheds were built to house the workers and meals had to be prepared for all. Much of Molly's time was spent setting broken bones, and treating lacerations and sprains. Many times she was called to other sites to treat an injured worker. She often found deplorable living conditions where they lived in unweathered shacks, often in subzero weather. Conditions were filthy and provided perfect breeding grounds for infectious disease. Her complaints to the mill owners, usually fell on deaf ears or they would likely plead poverty or ignorance. It disgusted her that most of these so-called businessmen were her countrymen and most of the men they hired, as

216

barely slave labour, were generally also of Irish background. Rough bushmen or not, no one should be expected to live in such conditions. So she waged war against those she referred to as 'unscrupulous lumber barons'. Many of these same companies were in production long before the Cherry Creek Lumber Mill was ever formed. Rivalry among them had been evident for years. But, now they had a common thorn in their sides, in the local medicine woman. Doctors were few and far between in the backwoods and her services were much in demand. The sight of her riding into camp, emerald cloak flying, could send the most hardened lumberman heading for the hills. Her advice to them was always the same. "You can clean up your act, or, listen to me harping on you every time I enter your camp." She formed her own system of grading the living and safety conditions of each camp, and felt no compunction at letting the workers know where the best operations existed. The woodsmen thought she was an angel and it was well known that if any harm should befall her, full-scale war would break out.

In 1854 Liam and Molly welcomed their last child into the world. Baby Kathleen was born in the deep of winter after Molly slipped and fell down the embankment leading to the river. It had been a particularly bright, crisp day and Molly had insisted on going to the river for water. Each day as the weather allowed, she would venture out to get as much fresh air and exercise as possible. Only her sister-in-law and the children remained at home as the mill was currently in full production in preparation for the demand for lumber in the early spring.

After her fall, McGinty ran back and forth from the river to the house again and again until he was able to alarm those inside. Realising something was amiss,

Kathleen headed out in search for Molly. Within an hour of their return to the house, she went into labour and gave birth, one month prematurely, to Kathleen Meagan Dermitt. The delicate little girl was completely adored. No more than five pounds at birth with the face of a Dresden doll, she captured the hearts of all. Four months earlier, Sean and Kathleen had welcomed the birth of Seamus, to be their third and final child. Young Sarah, was now an active toddler. Once again their home was filled with three tiny children.

Prior to the births of Seamus and Kathleen, it was decided that the children should be receiving some formal education. Kathleen was more than happy to take up her old profession of schoolteacher and welcomed the change in routine. With Molly periodically gone and their families increasing in size it was resolved there was need to hire someone to help with the children and housekeeping. When the weather finally warmed Sean suggested he would take Kathleen to Bytown to search out a suitable lass for their needs. Having not been away from the homestead in nearly three years since their arrival, Kathleen was excited at the prospect of the trip. Once in Bytown, she would buy muslin and calico material for the children's summer clothing and new dresses for herself and Molly. The previous year, John and Colin had returned from buying provisions needed for the winter months with a wonderful surprise. At first glance neither woman had an idea of what it was. Colin explained it was the latest invention for stitching and was called a sewing machine. It was operated by a foot peddle called a treadle and a threaded needle worked its way up and down, through the material, sewing it as securely as if done by hand. For weeks the ladies were like children with a new toy and proceeded to restitch everything in sight. Now they could have new clothes, curtains, and bed linens, and the men definitely needed new work clothes.

Listening to their excited chatter, Sean finally said, "I think we'll be needing two canoes or we'll be beached before we get halfway home. Or might be we'll just hire a barge to bring us up the Madawaska." Everyone laughed at Sean's pretended chagrin. The truth was, he was pleased to see his wife so excited about their upcoming excursion. Molly too, was warmed by the enthusiasm of her sister-in-law. She had always, without complaint, cared for the children in Molly's absences, and if anyone deserved this shift in her day by day routine, it was Kathleen.

While they were in Bytown, Sean would be visiting the banker, and discussing the plans for expansion of the mill. New technology was constantly flooding the market and in order to keep up with the demands, they needed to incorporate the new machines and conveyance systems into the operation. The family had never jumped blindly into any situation, and with the information Sean supplied, they were better able to make plans for the future of the mill.

As the years passed, the mill grew steadily in response to the ever-increasing population. As the townships grew, so did the demand for their lumber. They were known as an honest, hard-working family operation and this reflected on the business passed their way. Many of the small mills, not being able to keep up with the new technology, were closing down. At every opportunity, the O'Connor/Dermitt clan purchased new tracts of land, increasing their supply and wealth. They logged wisely, nurturing the saplings left behind. They utilised every part of the timber they harvested and considered future growth in all areas.

The year following the births of Seamus and Kathleen, a much-needed second house was built. Space had been added to the original homestead, but with nine adults and eight children it became ridiculously crowded. In the warmer weather, Thomas, Colin and Patrick slept in the lodge but only as a temporary measure.

To add to the crowded conditions, Kathleen and Sean had returned from Bytown with a shy young girl of Indian/French background. Having lost her family, she had been forced into service to survive. Town life had not agreed with her nature and she became melancholy. After meeting Colette, Kathleen knew in her heart, she was doing the right thing by taking her back to the homestead.

In the weeks following her welcome into the family, the children grew to love her like a sister. She loved the children in return, but better still, she loved the solitude of the homestead. There was always lots of activity of course with sixteen other people living close at hand, but the lifestyle was completely different than town life and she felt at peace.

When the new home was completed, Sean, Kathleen, their three children, and John Pierre, along with John and Colin moved on. Molly, Liam, their four children, Thomas and Patrick remained in the original homestead. Having built the second house larger, and on two floors, Colette was able to have her own room tucked in the loft and away from the family.

The children quickly bonded with their new family member. Though, only eighteen years old, Colette loved children. She was more than a willing worker and spent many hours with the children. For some reason she was drawn to John Pierre, whether it was his French heritage or only that he seemed to be a rather lonely little boy. Some evenings, before she would put him to bed, the two of them could be found sitting in a field by the river, making daisy chains or watching butterflies. She was someone he could talk to about his mother, someone he could disclose his sadness too. Some time later Colin was seen joining his son and Colette on one of their evening walks. It eventually became a fairly frequent occurrence. Speculation began to bud in his big sister's mind.

"Don't you dare breathe a word to either one of them," Liam warned under his breath one evening as they watched the three wander off towards the river.

"Why, Liam Dermitt, what do you take me for now?" Molly sniffed in mock indignation.

"I'm just warning you, my little matchmaker, a single word could break the spell. How would you be feelin' then? I've never seen Colin look seriously at another woman since Lisette. So, let's act as if nothing's going on and maybe you'll be planning a wedding very soon." Liam winked and lifting her chin, kissed her squarely on the lips.

"Go away with you," she slapped at him. "You've been thinking the same as I have all along." Becoming more serious she continued, "really though, wouldn't it be grand for John Pierre to have his own mother. He adores her, and she him." Arms entwined, they turned back to the house and their own brood. Life was so good.

Chapter 11

Cherry Creek, Upper Canada – 1860

"I really wish Matthew wouldn't stay out so long on these hunting trips of his." Molly commented one evening over supper. "He's been gone over a week now. What could take him so far away from home?" A worried frown gathered as she spoke.

"You know his love for hunting, lass'," Liam attempted to soothe his wife's fears but he knew once she had something on her mind he had little chance of altering her train of thought. "He's a growing boy and he needs adventure. His Algonquin friends give him that freedom."

"But he's only eighteen. He's still a child." Molly pleaded.

"No lass, he's a man. Living in the backwoods he's been forced to grow up quickly. He's seen and done things no child back in Ireland would ever dream of. He'll be home soon lass, so don't go fretting yourself."

At eighteen Matthew was the chief hunter in the family. The mill demanded the time of his father and uncles and the truth known, he much preferred it that way. He felt a part of the forest and his Algonquin friends welcomed him into their hunting circle.

But the usual four to five days allotted for the normal hunting expedition had come and gone. Matthew was always prompt to send word if for some reason he was to be late arriving back home. He knew his mother worried for his safety.

By the end of the second week, Molly became frantic, working herself into a fearful state as she continued to watch for her eldest son's return.

"I know there's something wrong Liam, and all you're patronising isn't going to stop this feeling I have. Something's wrong with our son and I want you to take one of the boys out and look for him. You know its not like Matthew to be gone for so long without letting us know. Man or no man, he's our son and I want you to go out after him. Please Liam," Molly pleaded. "You know I wouldn't ask you unless I felt there was a problem."

"All right darlin'," Liam said, kissing her forehead. "I must admit, the young devil's been gone too long for my liking too. I'll fetch Thomas. Pack up some food and we'll be on our way in short order. And don't worry lass, we'll bring him home safe and sound."

In his heart, Liam had a foreboding feeling that their son would not return with him, but shrugging it aside as only a father's natural worry for his son, he set out in search of Thomas and to prepare their mounts.

Michael begged to be taken along, but not knowing where their search would take them or what they might find, he was left behind. At fourteen, he too was becoming a man. Matthew was his idol and he wanted desperately to be in on the search. So it was decided for the time being, he and his father would take daily excursions down the river and along the Madawaska to make inquires of any hunting parties or other settlers in the area.

After four days Liam and Thomas returned without a trace of Matthew. Many of those they met on the trail had seen him at some time or other but the closest clue they had to his whereabouts came from some hunters in a village close to the Ottawa River. They claimed he had camped with them two weeks earlier and was heading north, deeper into wilderness area. Being his friend, they had agreed to set out on a search themselves, allowing Liam and Thomas to return home to their families. At this point, Liam was loath to give up the search, but Thomas convinced him they must return home as they promised. If Matthew was to be found, his friends, born to the life of the forest and experienced hunters would bring him home.

Arriving home without his son was probably the hardest thing Liam had ever done. Molly had dissolved into his arms, overcome with dread.

"Listen to me love," Liam soothed his wife, kissing her tear filled eyes. "His friends are all searching for him. Messages will be sent from village to village until he's found."

"But what if he's not found Liam? What if he's not found?" she sobbed uncontrollably.

"He'll be found darlin'," he said with a forced conviction. "Matthew's a crafty lad and not at all foolhardy. Whatever trouble he's facing, he'll overcome."

Another week dragged by as the whole family waited and prayed for Matthew's safe return. Late one evening as plans were being made to once again set out in search for some answers to his whereabouts, a lone scout made his way onto the homestead. After a perfunctory greeting from Liam the rider dismounted and presented him with a leather headband and eagle's feather. Molly seeing the band, groaned in dismay as she recognised the woven headband worn by her son on his hunting trips.

"I am Wind Walker of the Algonquin nation. I bring the message that your son lies in a Chippewa village north of the Ottawa," the runner began. "He was found near death by one of their hunting party after being attacked by a bear. His face is badly scarred, but he lives. He could not talk for many days so the Chippewa did not know where he came from. We met with some hunters and they told us where he was taken. He will be brought to you within ten days. He asked that you wait for him here."

Molly collapsed at their feet, the headband clasped to her face. "Dear God, thank You for keeping our boy alive," she offered simply.

Lifting his wife to her feet Liam turned to Wind Walker to offer him food and rest. "Thank you for this news. And thank you for finding our son. We are indebted to you and your people."

"There is no debt owing. Little Sister is of our people and so is her son. We do for her what we would for any of our people." He smiled at Molly and turned to lead his horse to the river.

Wind Walker left, and good to his word, returned ten days later with the rest of his hunting party and Matthew strapped to a traverse behind the lead horse. He was cocooned in wrappings to his neck to limit any jarring movements and sedated enough to allow the constant movement to lull him to sleep.

Running to his side as the hunters approached the homestead, Molly whimpered in dismay as she looked at the barely recognisable face of her son. Strapped to the right side of his face, covering one eye, an ear and on down to his neck was a poultice of moss held secure with strips of soft deer skin. His left eye was open and at seeing his mother, filled with tears. The poultice prevented him from speaking but all he need say, flowed from his one sighted eye.

While Liam and Molly gently released their son from the traverse and carried him into the house and his awaiting bed, the other men helped the hunters feed and water their horses. They insisted the men should stay the night, using the original lodge if they so wished. In order that Matthew could have some solitude with his mother and father, the men built a fire-pit near the lodge and prepared to cook a pig in honour of Matthew's rescuers.

Matthew's wounds were massive, from the hairline above his right eye, which remained swollen shut, through to his jawbone. But his most startling and invasive injury was the almost complete loss of his right ear. Molly was not prepared for what she saw as she carefully removed the poultice covering his face. Her gasp was barely audible but the look on Liam's face cautioned her to restrain her reaction to her son's plight. Instead she commented, "Your Chippewa friends have tended you well, Matthew. They have good medicine and have saved your life. We'll always be indebted to them. Thank God you're home with us again, son." She bent and kissed his forehead. "You've had a hard journey. I want you to take this laudanum while I dress your wound. It will help dull the pain, and you must sleep to gain your strength back."

After applying healing ointment and bandaging the gapping hollow where his ear had once been, they prepared to leave him to rest. Bending down, his father kissed him, "welcome back lad." As he drew away he spotted one large tear escape the corner of his son's closed eye. He uttered not a word.

In the adjoining room, Liam clung to his wife and wept like a baby. "Oh, God this brings back so many memories. I know exactly how our son feels. The physical pain fades in no time but the other is much worse. Back then, when you looked at me with such pity, I remember feeling so much shame. I thought I'd never walk again and it was so painful to have this pretty lass looking at every scar on my body. I felt so ugly and useless and I thought no lass would ever love me."

"I suppose that just shows, how wrong you can be, Liam Dermitt," she whispered into his ear. "Because this lass loves you like no other. You're a good father and you'll make Matthew realise he can't give up on life just yet. We're strong, and we'll make it through this just fine." One last hug and they were out to join the others.

The children begged to see Matthew. For weeks, Michael had been at wits' end with the disappearance of his cousin. He knew it was unlike Matthew to not report home or at least send word after a few days and he wanted more than anything to set out in search for him. Now he sat outside the bedroom door until he was allowed to see for himself that Matthew was safe and sound. Because of their closeness, Molly consented to allow Michael to visit her son before he was fully coherent.

"He's not himself yet love, but you mustn't worry yourself. A few weeks and he'll be right as rain. You just wait and see." Molly forced her most cheery smile.

"It's all right Aunt Molly, I know what's wrong with him. I heard you all talking last night. I just want him to know I'm here and I don't care he doesn't have an ear. I don't care what he looks like. He's the bravest friend I could ever have and I just want him to know that." Tears welled in his fourteen-year-old eyes as he looked at her pleadingly.

"Oh, love," she said, taking him in her arms. "Our boy couldn't want for a better friend than you. Dry those eyes now and go in there and tell him how you feel. Let him cry and then make him laugh. That's the very best medicine you know."

Opening the door to Matthew's room, Molly announced, "there's someone here wants to see you in the worst way. He's been sitting at your door for hours now and just won't let me be. Do you think you can take him off my hands for a while?" Ushering Michael into the room, she gently closed the door, leaving them together.

In the weeks of his son's convalescence, Liam spent many hours fishing, talking and discussing the future plans for the mill with him. In many ways they both enjoyed their time together but the malaise in his son's eyes concerned him.

"If nothing else good comes from all this," Matthew quipped almost bitterly, "you finally learned how to fish, da."

After a few moments silence Liam asked his son, "do you want to talk about it, lad? Will you tell me what happened?"

"I got careless, that's all," Matthew volunteered quietly.

"I can't believe that, son. I've never known you to be careless in the bush. You know the dangers far too well. What happened?"

"I left my friends at the Ottawa. They offered to ride with me back to the homestead, but they had been out a long time and I knew they wanted to get home to their women and families. That night I started to make camp on the edge of a small stream. As I unpacked the horse I looked up to see a young bear cub on the opposite shore. The only other thing I can remember was the horse bolting and something huge ramming me to the ground. I regained consciousness in the Chippewa village with the worst pain imaginable screaming in my head. I wanted to die, it hurt so much." Matthew paused, looking at his father. "So you see da, I was careless. I should never have travelled alone on those trails. Like you said, I know the dangers of the forest and I know I shouldn't have been alone."

"We're all entitled to make mistakes, son. We're only human. Don't blame yourself, but learn from this mistake. Don't ever take this land for granted. She's beautiful but she can be very cruel. I suppose that's what makes it so exciting to live here. You never know what the next day will bring. In Ireland every day was the same. We trudged down the hill to the mine. Spent twelve hours a day on our hands and knees in stinking sludge. Ate our lunches in a black, cold tomb, oblivious to the sunshine or rainfall up top. Then, backs and knees aching, trudged back up the hill to prepare for the trudge back down the next day. So you see, maybe my accident in the mine was for a good reason. I couldn't see it at the time, but now it seems so clear. So, as cruel as it may seem at this moment, son, learn from this and it will make you a much stronger man."

Slapping Matthew on the knee as he rose to leave, he said, "now, we best get back or your mother will be sending out a search party for us. She does tend to get her dander up if she's not in control of the show." They laughed together, and headed back to the homestead, and the smell of fresh home made bread and rabbit stew to welcome them home.

In the weeks to follow, many of Matthew's Algonquin brothers would take time out from their hunting expeditions to visit and encourage him through his recovery. As the years had progressed he had learned to speak Algonquian fluently and his family marvelled at the comfort and ease he displayed while in the Algonquins' company. Molly harboured mixed blessings at the sight of her eldest sons rising spirits while in the company of his friends. She was of course, relieved at the exhubrance he displayed while in their company but confused at his sadness and the solitude he sought while with his family. Liam had suggested that he felt more at ease with those closer to his own age and interests, but Molly felt there was much more to it than that. When she approached her son with her concerns, his answer was simple.

"My friends are Algonquin ma. They look at me differently. When you and da and the family look at me I see pity and sadness. When my Algonquin brothers look at me I see pride and respect. They even invite me to meet their sisters."

"Oh, God help me, son. I'm sorry if we've made you unhappy. We just want to see you well and back to your old self." Molly wept.

"But you don't understand ma, I'll never be 'my old self' again. I'm changed. I'm grown." Pointing at his face he whispered. "This, what you see now, is me. This face has changed forever," and moving his hand to his chest, "this soul has changed forever."

Beginning that very year, their ties with the Algonquin nation became even stronger. They attended a tribal gathering and festival of thanks, where Molly spoke of her healing methods to the gathered tribes. Over the years she has learned to incorporate the healing rites of the shaman with modern medicine. She has learned the importance of the spirit as well as the physical being and tells how she has combined the two methods to enhance the healing process. The shaman she has worked along side over the years, nod their agreement and ask her to share the European methods with all of the gathered healers. Many were wary, but soon realize she had not come to usurp their authority. She addressed them cautiously. "In my culture diseases such as influenza, small pox, thyphoid, and diptheria are referred to as communicable diseases. This simply means that the seed that causes the illness is passed from person to person when in close contact. Those who may be weaker in body such as the very young or very old will find it hard to fight off the disease. We have learned that one way of helping to prevent the spread of the disease is to separate the ill from the healthy. Cleanliness while dealing with the ill is also very important, to clean away the seeds of disease."

After she finished speaking, many of the shaman asked questions of her. Some showed skepticism, but for the most part they seemed eager to learn and welcomed her comments.

Chapter 12

Cherry Creek – Upper Canada – 1860-1865

"That son-of-a-bitch," Colin seethed. "The next time the bastard comes into camp I'll ram his flaming teeth down his throat. Who the hell does he think he is?"

Thomas hauled in the reins as they approached the mill with the final load of logs for that day. "Settle yourself man, before we reach the mill. If Liam hears what they're saying about our Molly, there'll be war for sure. Cooper's an ignorant sod and he's not the only one. I've heard bits here and there through the settlements about Molly and about you and Colette. So what if we're called 'Indian lovers'. What does it mean? I'd rather be an 'indian lover' than be known to associate with the likes of Cooper and his bunch."

"Look. One of these days, that bastard will come face to face with Molly or Colette. God only knows what he'll say to them. I've heard too many stories about what scum like that do to half-breed women." Colin looked steely eyed at Thomas. "Just so you know, if anything happens to Colette, there'll be murder. I'd have nothing to lose anyway, if anything happened to her." The whip cracked and they lurched onward towards the mill.

Thomas, having often visited the local settlements had heard more than he cared to share. In fact, he had frequently engaged in rather hot discussions on the subject. Many of the settlers considered the Indian population as savage and untrustworthy. They were fearful of Indian ways and wanted nothing to do with them. They felt that those who did associate with the enemy, so to

232

speak, became the enemy. Consequently, the demand for lumber from the surrounding areas gradually slowed to a trickle. John and Liam were puzzled with the turn of events but surmised that the competing lumber mills were outbidding them and winning more contracts. It was just what they needed to convince them that the outside markets should be approached. The European market was bottomless and it was time to take advantage of the situation. John, Sean and fifteen-year-old Michael travelled to Montreal in search of overseas contracts as well as newly-upgraded machinery and supplies. It was time for change.

*   *   *

One summer night as the homestead lay in darkness and all within its houses were deep in slumber, Matthew bolted from his bed. His injuries from the bear attack had resulted in the heightening of his senses. Somewhere off in the barnyard, the animals were sounding an alarm. McGinty was barking furiously. At first he wondered at the possiblility of a fox or some other predator visiting the coops but then he realised there was more to it than that. Pulling his pants and moccasins on he quietly left the house. Before he was fully out of the door he smelled the smoke and saw the flickering lights within the larger barn that housed the horses and oxen. Shouting an alarm, he ran full tilt for the barn, hoping all the while he wouldn't be too late to save the animals inside. Others came quickly behind him as the flames started to spew out the open loft door. Throwing the bars on the double doors, they hauled the doors wide and called to the terrified animals within. Three of the beasts were in secured stalls and the only way they would be able to escape, was if someone went in and released them.

Colin screamed for a soaked blanket to be brought. A horse blanket was doused in a nearby rain barrel. Thomas threw it over his own head and made his way into the smoke-filled barn. By this time water was being relayed in buckets in order to squelch the fire burning in the lower part of the barn. They could see it wasn't possible to save the building. All they could hope for, was to buy time for Thomas to release the oxen, and escape himself before the building collapsed. Thomas could be heard screaming at the frightened beasts to herd them out into the yard. He emerged directly behind them, face blackened and coughing the smoke from his seared lungs.

"Get away. Everyone get away. It's going to collapse," John cried at the top of his lungs. Get Thomas, Liam. Take him out of the smoke."

Liam dropped his bucket and ran to his brother. "Come on," he yelled. "Let's get you out of here. You got them all out. They'll be fine." Grabbing Thomas by the shoulders, they ran stumbling towards the house where Molly had returned to retrieve her medical case. Thomas's hair was singed, ears and nose seared with the heat of the flames and his hands blistered and blackened from hauling on the stall gates.

Leaving him in Molly's hands Liam headed back to the barn and the stampeding animals. The barn was now engulfed in flames with the tremendous heat reaching out to the rest of the buildings and beyond. The older boys were corralling the horses and oxen and attempting to calm them. The men were, for the most part, standing dumb-founded, watching the barn slowly disintegrate into a heap of smoldering ashes. The time of panic had passed. Now they could only stand in disbelief, wondering how on earth this could have happened.

"It had to have started in the loft," Colin offered after

a lengthy silence. "Which means, it had to be set," he stated emphatically.

"Come on lad," John pleaded, looking in disbelief at his son. "You don't know that. Don't go borrowing trouble now."

"All right da, you tell me how a fire could start up in a hayloft. Maybe one of the lads was up there sparkin'," he offered sarcastically.

"Look, it's time to calm down now," John said quietly, knowing his son was aggitated and worried. "After we know this mess is settled down, we'll head back in and talk rationally."

After checking the area for any runaway fire, and assuring the animals were calmed and secure, they made their way back to the house. Matthew had silently gone to retrieve his hunting rifle and cartridge and headed back to the smaller barn and corral where he continued to tend to the livestock. He too, believed there was more than just a simple explanation to this fire. Nothing could have inadvertently started a fire in the loft. There was something very discomforting about the whole situation and Matthew was not about to treat it lightly. He knew there were more vicious creatures, than the wild animals, that called the wilderness their home, and he felt no qualms in protecting his family from their likes.

As light began to dawn and the livestock were fed and watered, Matthew headed out to search the outskirts of the homestead. Within minutes he discovered signs of shod-horse tracks and booted foot prints, telling him they were made by settlers and not Indian renegades. The area of pathway was badly chewed up indicating there was definitely more that one animal and rider. It was in direct line with the open loft door and a flame could easily have been propelled straight into the piles of hay. Judging by the surrounding signs in the disturbed folliage and a pile of fresh horse dung, Matthew estimated the visitors had been there within the last few hours.

By the time he finished his investigation and entered the house, the discussion was in full swing at the breakfast table. Colin still was insisting the fire was deliberately set while John and the rest continued to speculate on other possible reasons.

Hanging his rifle on the rack above the fireplace, Matthew turned to his grandfather and the others saying, "I know you don't want to think ill of anyone grandda but I've found signs out by the woodlot that tell a different story. I think we're lucky the barn was the only thing to go. McGinty's ruckus likely saved the whole lot."

Only Colin spoke up as they all waited for Matthew to continue, "What did you find, lad?"

Matthews years of hunting with the Algonquins had perfected his talent for tracking and he was able to read signs like any of his indian friends.

"We had visitors last night. There's fresh horse tracks and signs of men walking. The horse dung is only a few hours old and the ground is well trampled. The entrance to the trail is in direct line with the front of the barn and well within shooting distance."

"Then how do you think the fire was started?' John asked of his grandson.

"I would say it was done by flaming arrow, as there was sign of charred grass by the prints. The horses were shod and the men's feet booted, so it had to be settlers or outlaws. My guess though, would be settlers. The manure was filled with corn and hay and I would think most outlaws would graze their horses mostly." Matthew offered, pouring himself fresh coffee.

"Looks perfectly clear to me," Colin rose slamming his chair towards the table. "Do you think that son-of-a-bitch Cooper isn't behind this now, da?

"All right lad, I must agree, it's all very suspicious," John nodded. "But we still don't know for sure who's responsible. Now, we can't go off half-cocked chasing after Devin Cooper and his crew. We have to keep our eyes and ears open for the next while and let whoever did this, eventually hang himself. People who do things like this are generally big-mouthed and you can guarantee they'll be shooting it off in the settlements."

"Right, da," Colin agreed, "but one thing we should do for a while is post a watch around the homestead. Who knows what the bastards will do next. The next visit we have, I for one, want to be prepared."

Everyone agreed with this approach and scheduled watch times over the next few days. For the time being, they also agreed there should always be a male family member left at the homestead even during the daylight hours. The children were to be kept together under the watchful eyes of the women while not attending Kathleen's classes. Whoever remained behind to watch the homestead could busy themselves with repairs and stockpiling firewood for the winter months. There was always plenty to do in preparation for the cold months so it was a workable plan.

Over the weeks, whoever went into the settlements for supplies kept their ears alert for any information. Good whisky usually opened the flood gates to gossip so of course it had to be a wise decision to visit the local drinking house. There was no shortage of volunteers for this important fact finding mission but often by the time the chosen informer found his way home, the fire was the farthest thing from his mind.

"I think it's time we put a stop to this nonsense once and for all," Molly faced the men one night at the kitchen table. "It seems your fact-finding forays are a waste of time to my thinking. You've not brought back a whit of information that's worthwhile, so I would say it's time to revamp your plans." Hands placed firmly on her hips, she paced back and forth eyeing them reproachfully.

Not long after, a settler from some miles up the Madawaska River came riding into the homestead with news that a seemingly destructive illness was attacking many of the villagers and local farmers. Many were afflicted with a throat infection that had worsened in some and eventually had taken the lives of an elderly couple. Most were children whose parents thought them to have common throat infections. Unfortunately the infections were not clearing up as would normally happen, but getting worse and spreading rapidly among the local population, young and old.

Molly quickly prepared for the journey up river with Matthew and the message bearer. She was not about to speculate on the nature of the outbreak but was reminded of a recent article she had read of a disease called diptheria, spreading out from the region of the State of New York. A relatively new illness in the Americas, it was reported to be spreading rapidly as it appeared to be transported through the air by the acts of coughing, and sneezing. The diptheria germ was reported to be very tenacious, resulting in all articles belonging to the victim needing extensive cleaning and the patient, if possible, being segregated from the rest of their family.

Molly's first two patients were twin girls. At first sight, any normal parent would have suspected croupe or tonsilitis, but on inspection, both children were found to have a thick grey membrane firmly adhered to the throat. The tissues in their throats had become swollen and both laboured with their breathing. One of the little girls discharged slightly bloody mucus from her nose. Both were restless and their voices husky and hoarse. From what Molly had read about diptheria, the membrane that originated in the throat often spread into the larynx and could even result in death. The hoarseness was a sign that the membrane was spreading and there was no time to be wasted.

"Do you have any idea how many more people are suffering the same symptoms?" she asked of the twins parents.

"The schoolhouse has been closed temporarily these past few days. So many children are sick, there was little sense in keeping it going," the farmer offered. "What do you think it is, Miss?" he asked worriedly.

"I'm not sure as yet. I must see more cases before I'll know. In the meantime I want you to isolate these children from the rest of the family. Whoever works in the sickroom must always wash with carbolic acid before leaving. Keep the linens as fresh as possible. Wipe down everything the girls and yourselves have been in contact with, with carbolic acid. In fact, everything that comes into your home should be cleaned first. It's most important that you do this. Now, after I find out how many are ill, I might want them all brought to the school house. There, they will be cared for but most importantly others won't be in contact with the disease and it will be less likely to spread so rapidly."

Within the next two days, Molly had inspected most of the sick and arranged to have the one-room school house supplied with beds and linens from the local residents. Having already been through the horrors of quarantine upon their arrival in Canada, no one wanted to have a repeat of that experience and consequently, most were co-operative and helpful.

Meanwhile, Matthew on his rounds of the countryside in search of other victims, came across a newly emigrated family from the northernmost regions of the United States. Two of their children had come down with sickness during their journey, one of which had died. They had thought it to be influenza and although grieving, had given the disease no further thought. The second child had survived and none of the remaining family had symptoms of any illness.

Molly read and reread the article on the diptheria outbreak and finally assured herself this was what she was seeing now. She solicited help at the schoolhouse and then called a meeting of all local residents which she ordered to be held outside in the fresh air. She apprised the residents of the situation facing them, offered her suggestions to minimise the spread of the disease and asked that anyone found to be ill, be brought to the schoolhouse immediately.

During her treatment of the ill, she ordered that clear soups, beef tea, and other light foods be supplied. Alcohol in the form or brandy and whiskey was administered to all patients, even the very young. While she busied herself syringing throats to remove spreading membranes, and administering antiseptic sprays and medications, the others fed, bathed, and changed the patients.

A few days along, a familiar figure entered the schoolhouse, a child in obvious distress folded in his arms. Hearing the coughing child, Molly turned from her task to look into the eyes of Devin Cooper. Molly showed no expression until Cooper lowered his eyes and stated, "This is my son, Myles. We need your help, Mrs. Dermitt."

"Well, Mr. Cooper, are you very certain that you want these hands that have touched so many filthy savages, as you once so elegantly put it, touch your precious son?" Her eyes never left his face as he shifted from side to side. The burden of her gaze bore down on him. His lower lip began to twitch as he looked down at his son.

"What do you want woman? He whispered hoarsely at her. "If it's an apology your wanting, then you have it."

"Not unless you mean it Mr. Cooper," her eyes flashed at him. "Not unless you mean it!" As he nodded curtly she continued. "Will you apologise for trying to bring harm to my family and for spreading ugly rumours about myself and my son and my brother?"

He looked at her with shock, knowing she was referring to the attack on their homestead and the burning of the barn. So much time had passed and he had not thought he was under any suspicion. "Yes," he sighed resignedly. "Yes, I apologise and I will promise you never to malign you or your family again."

"Thank you," Molly stated curtly. "Now bring your boy here and leave before I regret my decision. Go home and have your quarters disinfected and aired as well as possible. If anyone else shows symptoms, bring them in immediately." As he turned to leave, she closed her eyes and released a long deep sigh. Her head pounded and she craved sleep, but there was too much still to be done.

When Matthew arrived that evening she told him of Cooper and what had transpired between them. Smiling at his mother, he shook his head in mock horror as he said, "Ma, no one of us could have had the effect on him that you would. I can just see him trying to squirm his way out of that one. I'm sorry I missed it. Ma, you're a gem to be sure. If Colin or Thomas or even myself had found him, we would have gone off screaming like banshees, making all sorts of accusations about barn burning and the likes and he could have denied them flat. But you mother, are very cagey. You had the little worm right where you wanted him. I can just see him squirming at every word." Thinking of the sight of Cooper in his discomfort, Matthew laughed with gratification.

"Alright mister, to sleep with you," Molly giggled. "I have plenty planned for you tomorrow, guaranteed!"

Over the following two weeks, three of the twenty-nine to come down with the disease could not be saved. Diptheria had become known as one of the most fatal as well as one of the common children's diseases. Those that had succumbed to the ailment had previously been of a weak disposition and treatment had not come to them quickly enough. But for the most part, the recovery rate had been much higher than Molly had hoped for. She was saddened at their loss but confident the threat had passed. After two weeks Matthew and his mother headed home exhausted but thankful.

Chapter 13

Cherry Creek, Upper Canada – 1867

The diptheria epidemic of the sixty's had rapidly spread and many thousand died from the scourge. Between the times she spent caring for and nursing the ill, and tending to her family and the homestead, Molly, with the help of her sister-in-law Kathleen, wrote letters to the government voicing their concern on the lack of medical facilities in the rural areas.

Molly was growing tired of being put off by politicians sending polite but dismissive letters thanking her for her concern. She was harbouring the idea of approaching the legislature in person with her proposals, when one day a very harried looking gentleman, obviously of city stock, visited the homestead. He had journeyed by boat up the Ottawa River, then by stagecoach on a recently-constructed road along the Madawaska and on horseback the remaining miles to the homestead. His bowler hat perched precariously atop his head of white hair. His once shiny shoes and white spats were splattered with mud and his city suit wrinkled and smudged. He was accompanied by an equally disheveled man of rather ponderous girth. Watching them enter the yard, Kathleen, suppressing a chuckle, called to her sister.

"Top of the mornin' to you, ladies," the first gentleman greeted, tipping his hat to them both. Smiling, Molly and Kathleen returned his greeting.

Alighting from his mount, he offered, "My name is Patrick Flannigan and this be Mr. Robert Stoddard I have with me," indicating the still mounted rider.

"Good morning, gentlemen," Molly smiled. "How can we be of service to you?"

"Well madam, if you or your companion be Molly Dermitt, then it's, how I can be of service to you, " he flourished his hat and bowed.

"Well then, I am Molly Dermitt and this is my sister-in-law Kathleen Dermitt. My nephew," beaconing Michael from the barn, "will see to your horses and we shall talk."

Noting the large gentleman was making no attempt to dismount she asked Michael to lead him to the mounting step where he could more easily maneuver his huge frame and descend safely to the ground. The horse appeared to visibly sigh as the weight was lifted from its sagging back. Once down, she invited them into the house for refreshments.

"Well now," Mr. Bowler Hat volunteered flamboyantly. "I've told you our names but not our reason for travelling these many miles to visit you Mrs. Dermitt."

"Well now, Mr. Flannigan, feel free to elaborate." She responded almost ruefully.

"Yes, yes, well, Mr. Stoddard here is your government representative for the Upper Canada region and I am the rather newly-appointed Government Indian Agent," he said, peaking Molly's interest. "You must feel after all this time, your correspondence has been ignored, but I assure you that is definitely not the case. I have wanted to meet you for quite some time, so when I was appointed as Indian Agent I decided to make it one of my first priorities. We're very impressed with your work, and myself in particular with what you have done among the Indian tribes of Ontario and Québec."

"The Government is prepared to issue funding to set up medical centres in these areas but we need some good constructive advice with regards to the size and locale of each centre," Robert Stoddard wheezed.

Molly could understand now, listening to Mr. Stoddard's laboured breathing, why Patrick Flannigan was the spokesman.

"You are very well known within the area we are discussing and we have taken the liberty of contacting some of the renouned physicians you have worked side by side with since your arrival in Canada," Patrick Flannigan continued. "Those we were able to contact recommended you highly, for what we have come to personally request of you."

"And what might that be gentlemen?" Molly asked, looking from one to the other.

"We would like you to help us decide where the medical facilities are most needed and what exactly will be required to supply them and run them. We will be required to staff them with competent people and of course there must be an administrator. Someone must oversee the operation of these clinics." Mr. Stoddard stopped, his breath coming in short, laboured gasps.

"Mr. Stoddard, please, you seem in distress!" Molly exclaimed as she watched the poor man redden and sweat profusely as he laboured to breathe. "Before we go on I want you to relax while I prepare a remedy. It will ease your breathing and make you more comfortable."

Returning from her medical supply room where she kept most treatments and remedies at the ready, she continued, "I've found many people in Canada suffer from asthma. I truly believe, the endless amounts of flora in this country causes many distressing symptoms. I've noticed that during the spring season when all the trees are budding and flowering, and the pollen is flying in the air, many people suffer with respiratory problems. Of course they're generally not life-threatening but none-the-less uncomfortable," she chattered as she prepared her potion.

She had taken the fluid extract of skunk cabbage, lobelia, blood root, and ginger, combined with water and alcohol, and placed it into a corked bottle. "Now, as dreadful as it tastes, I want you to take two to three teaspoonsful, twice a day until you find considerable relief. Each time you feel an attack coming on, repeat."

"Well," the corpulent man heaved, "I think I shall be returning home from this trip with much more than I expected. Thank you so much, Mrs. Dermitt."

"Now, where were we gentlemen?" Molly sat down expectantly.

Taking a map, they had outlined the area into population grids. Mr. Flannigan had noted all the native reservations and villages and the approximate population of each. Next, the emigrant villages and settled areas were added to the map. "Now we must decide where the greatest needs lie," the Indian Agent looked to Molly. "You and your family know more about these areas than either one of us and unfortunately I have little to draw from where my predecessor was concerned." Molly found making these decisions very difficult but exhilarating. Realising how important her suggestions would be and how many lives they would affect, she became very cautious.

"I believe it would be best if our son Matthew was here to advise us. He knows the countryside like the back of his hand, and he spends a good deal of time with many of the Algonquin people."

"Wonderful, Mrs. Dermitt. The more expert opinions we have the better, don't you think?" Flannigan looked towards the government representative as he nodded.

"Fine then gentlemen. Make yourselves at home while I prepare dinner. Our men will be arriving shortly and you can discuss your aims with Matthew and the rest over your meal." Turning to Mr. Stoddard she continued, "and you sir, should be taking more of the remedy along with a good rest. I'll show you to your room." Obediently he followed.

Patrick Flannigan smiled to himself. He had never seen the opulent Mr. Stoddard as an acquiescent individual. But now he followed their hostess meekly, hat in hand. 'What a magnificent woman' he thought admiringly.

Two hours later, the same magnificent woman, served up the best venison roast, fresh potatoes and yams, either gentleman had every enjoyed. In respect for the two important visitors, they had brought the two households together for what would normally be Sunday dinner. Many years ago, both families had decided that Sunday would be kept as family day and eating together was part of that tradition. Even Matthew very rarely missed Sundays although his hunting forays often took him far afield. Everyone contributed to the preparing and cleaning up of dinner and the big house fairly bounced with activity. After dinner, the whole family would gather around John as he read to them from the bible. Although not a fervently religious family, they all recognized the importance of this time together. The rest of the time could be spent fishing, playing cards, chatting, or just relaxing.

After introductions and dinner, Mr. Flannigan was asked to outline the government plans for the new medical centres and everyone was encouraged to contribute any suggestions they might have.

The first question came from Matthew. "Has anyone spoken to the tribal chiefs and asked their opinions?"

"Very little I'm afraid," Flannigan began. "We need a good interpreter. Someone who knows indian customs and lifestyle."

"You realise, I'm sure, that most of the tribes are very hesitant to trust your government, and for good reason," Colin added.

"Oh, yes, that is our main stumbling block," Flannigan agreed. "I'm very new to this particular job, so I've had very little contact with the chiefs as yet."

"Why don't you let Matthew help you out there, if he will?" Liam looked toward his son for his endorsement. "He probably knows more about the Algonquin than any other settler in this area. They trust him and know he wants what's best for them."

"What you must understand, Mr. Flannigan, is that you can't come down on them full bore, telling them you're going to change their lives for the good. Because they don't live as we do, doesn't mean their lives are not good," Molly explained. "In fact, we have learned more from the Algonquin than from any other faction in this country. So they must be approached with respect. We must recognise strengths and improve on weaknesses, but only where they want us to help. Matthew and I will do the best we can to convince them of the advantages of combining modern medicine with their own traditional medicine. Many already realise that and many of their shaman agree with that approach, but some are still very wary and refuse to change."

"Thank you so much Mrs. Dermitt for your insight'" said Mr. Stoddard, wiping his brow. "I think we have plenty to take back with us to put before the committees. You have helped us infinitely. We will spend the next few months compiling all of this information and then we'll be in contact with you. You have been a very gracious hostess and I've enjoyed this time with you immensely." Rising from his chair, he smiled and continued, "now, I think I shall take my elixir and retire."

The following day, after the agents had departed with Matthew as escort to the Madawaska, the family was abuzz with all that had transpired. Molly could finally relax and release all her contained excitement. "I can't believe this is happening. The next few months are going to be an eternity. Lord only knows what the governments decision will be after all of this. I mustn't get my hopes up or I could be in for a terrible disappointment. All the letters Kathleen and I have written ..."

"Come on love, settle down now." Liam folded his great arms around his wife, smiling down and kissing her nose. "Let's you an I have a good cup of mash before I head off to work. You just take yourself off into that bedroom and I'll bring us in a nice hot cup. Go on with you now." Patting her on the rump he steered her off in the direction of their bedroom.

He lowered the steaming cup onto her lap where she sat propped on the pillows. Draping his free arm around his wife, he said, "now lass, you know you've done all you can. Whatever happens, happens. For now you must put this out of your mind or otherwise drive yourself to distraction. Worrying and speculating won't make it happen any sooner. Remember, if these two men hadn't come here you'd be back to square one, so you've accomplished a great deal these two days."

Looking up at her husband, she murmured, "how do you always know how to take the bumps out of things, Mr. Dermitt?"

"Well one of us has to have a level head in the family," he chided laughingly.

"Oh, go on with you! Get to work or there won't be any level head where dinner's concerned, Your Lordship." Laughing, she pushed him from the bed and sat, arms folded, smirking back at him.

*   *   *

Summer passed and the autumn months brought with them the usual maladies. Molly was kept busy with small outbreaks of influenza, along with the usual cases of broken bones, burns, allergies, and childbirth.

Matthew brought back reports that the Indian agent, Mr. Flannigan, was very busy visiting various Indian settlements and reservations. He had met with Matthew once in his travels and had reported favourable response from many of the chiefs.

By the time the winter of '67 approached there was no word from either Mr. Stoddard or Mr. Flannigan. Molly's hopes began to fade, but she stoically refused to give up hope. The winter storms were some of the worst in the history of the area and the reports of influenza poured in unceasingly. Whenever the weather allowed, Molly and Matthew would find themselves visiting local settlements to care for those afflicted. Many times they would be stranded away from home for days on end. The results of not eating properly and going for days without sufficient sleep began to wear on her own health, eventually sending her to her bed. She lay for days, in and out of delirium. Young Kathleen, now thirteen years old, tended her mother night and day. She changed her sweat-soaked bedding and night clothes, bathed her, fed her and administered her medication. For years she had listened and watched and learned well the ways of her healer mother. Now she was prepared to care for her mother as she lay in her sickbed.

One particularly blustery morning Matthew made his way back from the nearest settlement where he had been sent to replenish some dwindling supplies. Throwing his coat and hat off at the door, he made for his mother's room, announcing he had some mail for her from a government office.

"Wait," Liam called to him. "Don't be in such a hurry. We don't know what it says yet, and if it's not good news it will do her no good."

"But da, she's got to know," Matthew paused in this tracks. "She's been waiting for this for months. What if it's good news? It may be just what she needs. You know yourself what she's always saying about the spirit and how important it is in healing."

"I know son," Liam agreed, "but what if the news is bad. It may set her back for weeks. Let's not jump the gun."

"Then why don't we just open it and find out. Surely that's the best thing to do," Matthew suggested, handing the letter to his father.

Taking little time to contemplate his decision, Liam proceeded to open up the official looking envelope, all the while looking up at his son. As he read, his mouth hung open, speechless.

"Well, da, let us have it! What's it say?" Matthew excited by the look on his fathers face, couldn't contain his curiousity.

"No, lad," Liam said, folding the letter, neatly back into its envelope. "Go and bring everyone back to the house here as quickly as possible. Tell them nothing. We'll gather in mother's room." With that he went to sit at his wife's sick bed until she awakened.

"What in heaven's name is going on here?" Molly smiled weakly up at her assembled family.

"Absolutely nothing, m'darlin'," Liam began, "but as matriarch of this family we wanted to give you something and that's why we are all here now. But first, if you like, we'll sit you up a little here," he patted the pillows. "And just so you're comfortable, I have your emerald cloak to put around your shoulders."

The stage set, Liam proceeded to ceremoniously remove the brown envelope from his shirt pocket. Opening the letter he proceeded to read:

Dear Mrs Dermitt;

I regret this delay in my correspondence to you, but Mr. Flannigan and I have been extremely busy working on the execution of our plans you so diligently worked on with us when we visited you last summer. First and foremost, I must inform you that my attacks of asthma have subsided greatly and if they do appear, your remedy makes them much more easy to bear. My gratitude is endless.

Now, down to business. I am happy to inform you, the government has agreed to release funds enough to build four treatment centres in the Ottawa Valley and outlying areas. The largest of these will be erected close to your landholdings on the Madawaska River. It is also our intention, should you agree to this appointment, to install you as Medical Program Administrator for the Ottawa Valley and Regions, effective, April 1st, 1868. Under this umbrella you will be informed of each and every move made by the government in this respect. Once the centres are erected you will be advised of staffing, supplies and whatever else it takes to run the centres efficiently and effectively. I will not elaborate further at this time but will await your decision. You are a credit to this great country of ours and I sincerely hope you will see yourself clear to accept this very important appointment.

Until I hear from you again, I send my best wishes to you and your wonderful family.

Sincerely,
Robert T. Stoddard,
Member of Parliament,
Ottawa Valley and Regions

A pin could be heard to drop as Molly looked to her husband and then to each member of her family, one by one. Her eyes filled with tears of the joy she felt as she clutched the letter to her heart. "I can't believe this. I just can't believe it.... I never hoped to dream it would finally come to this. And me, an administrator!"

"Oh, sure now, look at the head swelling already." Colin quipped. "Can't live with her now. What's it going to be like when the crown's on the royal head?"

"Alright, out with you now," Liam ordered. "We'll let Her Majesty rest and digest all this for now." One by one they kissed their Molly and filed out to leave her to her thoughts. Only Liam remained, smiling down at this wife. "I always knew one day you'd do it my darlin'. Nobody deserves this more than you. So, you just remember, our children are grown, the business is operating at its peak, so it's time for you to spread those wings. You follow your dream my lady and I'll be right there with you." Kissing her gently on the lips, he turned and left her to her reverie.

Epilogue

Cherry Creek—Upper Canada—1868

The spring of '68 brought many changes to the lives of the families on the Cherry Creek homestead. The overseas lumber market had exploded and the Cherry Creek Lumber Mill was forced to double its size and production to keep up with the demand. The Canadian government had decided to finance a road through the Ottawa Valley and up the Madawaska within miles of Cherry Creek. A site was already being prepared for the construction of the medical centre, which was adjacent to the nearest settlement to the homestead. They had also agreed to help in the construction of a lesser road on into the Cherry Creek Lumber Mill where they would purchase the lumber needed to erect the new building. This road opened up access to the major waterway of the Madawaska cutting out the necessity to roll the processed logs down Cherry Creek to be barged. The men who normally worked on the river, could now transport the logs and lumber by ox-drawn wagons directly to barges on the Madawaska.

Shortly after Molly's recovery from influenza, she wrote a letter, with the help of her articulate sister-in-law, to Mr. Stoddard, accepting the position of Medical Program Administrator for the Ottawa Valley and Regions. For weeks on end, she rolled the title over and over in her mind. When alone at her work, she would find herself repeating the title outloud, hardly able to believe her good fortune. At times the enormity of the position's responsibilities would leave her terrified. But for the most part, she just took it in her stride. Until the Madawaska Medical Centre was constructed and ready for operation, most of her work was done by correspondence. She would be headquartered at the Madawaska clinic and the other centres would be operated under her administration. Two medical doctors would be hired immediately, one to reside at the Madawaska Centre and the second, a circuit doctor for the remainder of the clinics. Eventually each fully staffed clinic would have its own resident doctor.

Colin and Colette were expecting their firstborn in the summer and Molly looked forward to the arrival of a new generation. It would be the first birth in the family in over fourteen years since the arrival of their Kathleen and her brother Sean's son Seamus. But the happiest event for both Molly and Liam was the announcement of Matthew's intention to wed Little Star, daughter of their oldest and dearest friend, Dancing Eagle. The wedding would be celebrated at the end of the summer gathering of the tribes and the entire family would attend. The reunion with Dancing Eagle and his family was anticipated by everyone and the excitement had mounted daily.

For their twin boys Erin and Sean, life has not been quite so arduous as that of their older brother. This year Sean would be leaving to study animal husbandry in Montreal, another dream to be pursued. Erin has followed in Matthew's footsteps as hunter when not working at the mill. The lumber industry is in his blood and he will carry on the family tradition and become his generation's top lumber baron.

Kathleen, their beloved daughter is sprouting into womanhood. Calling to mind, her daughter's tireless care as she herself lay in her sickbed the previous winter, Molly knows in her heart where her daughter's life will lead. Even at this very tender age she would become totally engrossed in the art of healing. Molly, resolved it was time for their daughter to spread her wings and become more involved in the practical side of medicine.

1868 was proving to be life's turning point in so many respects. The years of enduring the hard work, heartache, and uncertainty had finally paid off. Possibly now the love and laughter that had sustained them through the difficult years would become the centerpoint in their daily lives. What once had only been a distant dream was finally to be realised. Persistence had paid off and their lives were taking a complete turn. With her family fully behind her, she could now step into the future, with her dream a reality.

In their darker days, her own sweet husband had put it quite aptly: "Life isn't worth a whit, if all that comes to you is easy."

The End